PUBLIC TRIBUNAL

CLIFF BLAKE

DREAMS & READS PUBLISHING

Printed in the United States of America

First Printing, 2018

eBook ISBN: 978-1-73264-091-7

Print ISBN: 978-1-7326409-0-0

ACKNOWLEDGMENTS

There are a few special people that helped me with this book.

Susan – My best friend, business partner, and wife. You always know where I'm headed and are never afraid to push me back in the right direction.

Vi – I am amazed that you never tired of *one* more edit.

Matt – Thank you! You were my guide through this wilderness they call writing and publishing. There is no way I could do it without you.

Travis – How you converted the mumblings and half directions we gave you into a great book cover is astounding.

Quillan – The web will live in constant change—thanks for helping me get this far.

NOTE FROM THE AUTHOR

As you meet the characters in this story, as you learn what motivates them to react or more accurately sometimes, **NOT** react, keep in mind that they seem to live in an alternate America. And, though it may at first seem a little off, the more you read, the more you understand them, you might find yourself slipping more and more into *their* reality. Who knows, your reality might even start to be shaped by theirs.

CHAPTER 1

"THE TRIBUNAL OF THE AMERICAN PEOPLE IS called to order. The case of the U.S. Congress versus the Constitutional Rights of the American People is ready to proceed."

Daniel Collins turned to his left.

"Judge Matthews, will you read the charges?"

Judge Mathews stood and began to read the charges. "The U.S. Congress has willingly and knowingly violated the Constitutional Rights of the American People and has forsaken their oath of office to obey the Constitution."

While Judge Matthews read the rest of the charges, Daniel looked at the audience and then looked at Professor Ramirez seated on the far side of the auditorium in the first row.

It was hard to believe that this had started as a class project in Constitutional Law less than six weeks ago. Professor Ramirez had approached his senior law students with a challenge. There were ten members of his Senior Constitutional law class. They were a mix of liberal, conservatives, undecided and confused.

Ramirez had called the class together in one of the cafeteria's side rooms. He was known for his unusual choice of classroom settings.

Daniel could still hear him calling the group to order.

"Now, that we are all in a more comfortable setting, I trust everyone has something to drink and are ready to work?" Ramirez paused and looked at each student. The group was quiet, waiting to see what Ramirez had planned.

> "I thought we might try a different approach to our Constitutional law course this semester. Daniel Collins has proposed an idea to hold a mock tribunal trying the U.S. Congress for violations of the Constitution. Mr. Collins, would you like to elaborate?"

Daniel was nervous about the reaction from the class. Most of them had been in other classes together. They all knew each other and were all vocal about their political views.

"I thought we could test the actions of the current Congress in a mock tribunal. Three of us will act as the Tribunal judges. Three of us will act as the defense; three of us will act as the prosecution. One of us will be responsible for oversight, rules, procedures and the general catch-all to make sure the process works according to Hoyle."

I want us to try the U.S. Congress on behalf of the Citizens of the United States, determining if Congress has, in fact, violated the Constitution in the execution of their duties."

"I also think it would be good to broadcast the Tribunal to the school body and let them vote on the verdict."

The group held their response for about thirty seconds then the reactions erupted. Ramirez let their comments and arguments flow for five minutes. Then he tapped his coffee cup with his spoon. The group came to order.

"I think by your reaction that I can assume the class is willing to take on this project? I will expect a one-page summary of which position you feel you are best qualified to fill in this project. I, however, hold the right to assign you to whichever position I think will best suit the project."

"I warn you some of you will not be happy with your roles. My point in doing this is to test your ability to defend the issue from either side of the argument."

Barry Weinstein raised his hand. Ramirez was not surprised. Barry never missed an opportunity to voice his opinion even if it almost always sounded like someone whining. Barry had the unique ability to polarize people's opinions just by opening his mouth and speaking. "If we don't want to participate, can we opt out of this and do something else?"

Ramirez looked up as if he was searching for an answer floating in the air just above Mr. Weinstein's head. "Yes Mr. Weinstein, you do have an option if you choose. It is not too late for you to find another class."

The group was silent waiting for Professor Ramirez to continue. Several of the class looked at Barry and shook their heads. Each of them quietly hoping they would not have to work with Barry as a team member.

Ramirez took a mental poll of the faces of the class "I think that's enough for the day."

It may have been enough for Professor Ramirez that day, but Daniel's life would never be the same and the Tribunal would take over every aspect of his life. Nothing else would get his attention from this point on besides the ins and outs of the Tribunal.

Daniel went home for the weekend to see his family, Daniel's brother, William, an Aide to Senator Liz Tyler had shown up with his fiancé. He was in town for a couple of days to see his fiancé and try to keep their relationship alive.

Shelly and William had gotten engaged right after they graduated college. While William continually professed his love for Shelly, they still were no closer to setting a date for their wedding. He was more in love with his job in D.C. and the hunt for the next deal he could close for the senator. And now the senator's re-election campaign was more important to William than setting a wedding date with Shelly.

Daniel had announced the Tribunal project at dinner. His

brother William had made it clear that he did not want his name associated with this Tribunal project and he would distance himself from anything to do with questioning the Constitution. The arguing continued through dinner. Daniel and Williams's tempers grew hotter than Mom's chili. William and Shelly left before finishing dinner with William making sure that everyone knew where the line in the sand was and no one should cross it.

Daniel was now determined to make his part of the Tribunal an overwhelming success. He would show his brother that he wasn't the only one in the family that could succeed.

CHAPTER 2

Daniel felt his jaw tighten as he thought about William's reaction to the Tribunal. He looked at the audience in the auditorium and wished his brother could see how packed it was.

None of the Tribunal project team had expected the Tribunal to get this much attention. It had begun to grow when several of the on-campus bloggers found out about the Tribunal and wanted to know if they could attend. Professor Ramirez had encouraged them to cover the Tribunal to sharpen their journalistic skills.

And once the school's journalism team learned about the bloggers, it set off a chain reaction like dominos falling into place ending with the student body asking to attend. As the potential audience heard they would be able to vote on the verdict and become the default jury, the social media aspect of the project mushroomed beyond anyone's expectations.

The Tribunal was supposed to have taken place in one of the larger classrooms that seated about a hundred people. As people kept signing up, the venue kept changing till they were using one of the larger auditoriums that seated 2500.

The interest in the Tribunal had continued to spread attracting a couple of national journalist, several internet newsgroups, and finally, several network media groups announced they were sending people.

Then someone suggested they make the Tribunal available via internet, so people could log in from anywhere. Now, this caused a flurry of administrative concerns. And as expected, several self-anointed (or as Ramirez called them self-annoying) staff members protested the event.

After a lot of blustering and heated arguments, the Chancellor had overruled them when a couple of sponsors agreed to fund the expense of the internet broadcast.

Now, the Tribunal Project had become a reality, and here they were trying the U.S. Congress in a mock tribunal.

Judge Matthews had just ended reading the charges. Daniel acting as the Chief Judge of the Tribunal thanked Judge Matthews.

Daniel started to address the Prosecution when a door burst open at the back of the auditorium. The commotion caught everyone's attention as a figure raced down the center aisle, shouting.

> "Your Honors, I would like to present evidence to the Tribunal..." The interloper was dragging a rolling cart with several large briefcases and a large backpack.

Daniel was stunned as he recognized the man interrupting the proceedings.

Daniel looked at Professor Ramirez, asking with his eyes, "What should he do?" Professor Ramirez waved to Daniel to continue.

Daniel cleared his throat. "The tribunal recognizes, Mr. William Collins?"

"Thank you, Judge. I have records that I would like to submit as evidence to the Tribunal of activities, transactions, meetings, and agreements committed by members of Congress against the Constitutional rights of the American people."

William Collins stopped in front of the Tribunal Judges. He was out of breath. "I would like to submit these files as evidence to the Tribunal. I am willing to testify to the validity of the records." He started handing over file after file from his briefcase.

Daniel had gone from being shocked by the interruption, to mad at his brother for interfering with his class project. As

William began handing the records over to the Tribunal, Daniel's emotions now moved to concern as he looked closely at his older brother.

Something was wrong. William was one of the smoothest, composed men Daniel had ever known. William was the guy who always got people to agree. He had begun brokering deals as a kid at school. When anyone got into a disagreement, William just naturally seemed to find the solution that everyone would agree to and think they each had won.

But *this* William was different, and something had changed.

Daniel cleared his throat, gathered up his emotions and shifted back to his role as head of the Tribunal. "Mr. Collins, will you please state your name and position for the record."

"Thank you," began William. "I am William Patrick Collins, senior assistant to the Senator from Texas. My position is to assist the Senator in her duties in the United States Congress."

"I have been in this position for six years. My job includes negotiating, brokering deals and support for the Senator and various other groups and parties. Most of what I have witnessed has violated the Constitutional rights of the American Public. I will explain these violations as I present my documentation."

"For the court's convenience, I have also prepared these files in electronic format. For the audience sake, I have made these available at several FTP sites. If you wish you can access the data files at the addresses on this flash key." William held up a flash key.

Daniel looked at the audio-visual tech standing on the side of the platform and motioned for him. "Can you guys see if you could put this on the screen?"

The tech ran over and grabbed the flash key and trotted back to the projection room.

William continued. "The members of the Tribunal have already been emailed the files and should have them in their various email inboxes as we speak."

The projection system blinked to life, and the locations for the files were exposed for all to see.

As William named the various electronic addresses where the information was available, the clicking of keyboards swept across the auditorium like a plague of locust. The files were being downloaded and spread across the internet. Later some would refer to this as the point of infection that spread across the world. The first Information Pandemic.

The buzz of people whispering into cells phones grew so loud it was hard to hear.

Daniel struck the gavel and called for order. "Please take your conversations outside if you must talk."

The noise lessened but didn't stop.

One of the sound engineers handed William a microphone. The microphone picked up his "Thank you," followed by a high-pitched tone as the sound engineers adjusted the volume of his microphone.

William looked around the auditorium, sighed and began. "I am offering this information as I have recently realized that I have failed the American People. I have been working against them. I have put my ambition and the ambition of others ahead of the American People."

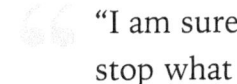 "I am sure that there will be those that will try to stop what I am presenting, so I encourage you to distribute this information quickly."

Professor Ramirez motioned Stanley Wilson to come to him. Stanley was responsible for helping enter evidence and assist the secretary who was acting as a stenographer.

Ramirez whispered to Stanley, "Take the two briefcases and the hard drive William is offering to the court—and quickly get them out of here."

Stanley, nodded and asked, "Where do you want me to take them?"

Ramirez looked around the room. "Take them to Jeffery Tanager's office. He should be in now. Don't give them to anyone else, just him. Tell him I said to bury them until he sees me. And tell him do not come over here."

"Now, get out of here before this thing blows up." Stanley nodded and picked up the hard drive and the briefcases.

As Stanley moved forward to gather the documents, William, kept talking but reached into his backpack and handed Stanley a laptop. He looked at Dr. Ramirez and nodded his thanks.

As William continued laying out the details of over six years of backroom deals and meetings that had never seen the light of day, the audience was growing. Word of what was happening had spread over the campus and through the internet and cell network. People were streaming the information to people all over the cyber world.

The Tribunal members started asking questions as they began operating within their roles. William seemed to relax but still looked like he had picked a fight and lost big time.

At the twenty-three-minute mark of Williams exposing corruption in the swamp known as D.C., another commotion began at the back door. A loud voice burst over William's testimony.

"I am agent Bradley Tillis with Homeland Security. We are closing these proceedings and are seizing all records and computers. Everyone is to remain in their seats until you are told to move by one of our agents."

With that, about ten Homeland Security and FBI agents began spreading out trying to cover the doors.

Seated on the left side of the auditorium, Gator, as he was

known to his friends in the world of protest and let's just demonstrate to show we can, typed a quick text. "FLASH MOB NEEDED AT THE HOUSTON AUDITORIUM. Bring everyone—NOW— follow the sirens."

Gator, who always made sure he had a quick exit plan, stood up and pulled the fire alarm.

Agent Bradley was about halfway down the aisle when the fire alarm sounded. He stopped and looked at the pending stampede and knew the best thing to do when facing a stampede is to try and get out of their way.

> Bradley began to yell to his agents, "Try to hold them outside!"

Daniel looked at Agent Bradley Tillis, then at his brother. His Tribunal was destroyed. A part of him knew William was responsible for this. Daniel watched as Homeland Security lost all control of what was left of the Tribunal to Gator, the fire alarm, and several thousand students leaving the building.

As everyone began to head for the exits, Dr. Ramirez waved at the Tribunal and hollered. "GET OUT! Whales in two hours..."

He turned and merged with the crowd, and exited through the side door.

Daniel was still stunned. He slowly got up and made his way

to the edge of the platform. William gathered up the remains of his backpack and headed towards Daniel.

Daniel sat down on the edge of the platform and William hopped up next to him.

The noise was starting to lessen as the crowd left the auditorium.

Daniel shook his head and reached out to take the backpack from William. He looked exhausted. "So, I assume this means you are changing careers?"

William sighed. "Yeah, I think my political career is over. I think I better lay low for a while. Any good places to hide around here?"

Daniel nodded. "Yeah, I bet. Homeland is going to want to talk to you. But right now, let's head for the tunnel and get out of here."

Daniel guided his brother to the utility tunnel at the back of the stage area. They went down a flight of stairs, and the tunnel led them to another building.

Outside the auditorium, Homeland Security and the FBI were trying to maintain order. They were losing to the sheer number of students flowing into the area and out of the auditorium. Gator had moved off to one side of the crowd preparing to get out of the area, when he saw several of his guys heading towards the same spot.

One thing Gator had learned to do when planning a Flash Mob was to be sure the key people knew where to gather and how to escape. As his guys moved towards him, Gator smiled. Motor, Speed and Tow Truck had shown up wearing the uniform gray hoodie. With every event, they changed street names and colors. After all, if the Secret Service could have unique identity pins for each of their events, why shouldn't the demonstrators follow their lead?

Gator took a quick look around to be sure no one in a suit or badge was paying any attention to them. He lowered his voice, and the four of them knelt down beside the last bench on the left of the auditorium entrance.

Gator smiled and said, "We should be able to keep this stirred up for several days. Circulate and do the usual, shout about injustice and freedom of speech."

"Motor, do you have any smoke?"

Motor, nodded and pulled a smoke bomb from his hoodie pouch, and then slid it back into its nest in his pouch.

"Great, try to drop it right at the bottom of the stairs, that should help the crowd get away."

"We should be out of here in five to ten minutes, and then let's head to the Wok House so we can plan for tomorrow." The group stood up and started off in different directions. Anyone watching would have just seen four gray hoodies mingling in the crowd. Nothing about them was identifiable, just four students wearing the same thing.

Gator climbed the small incline on the left and watched. The crowd was still growing as students came to see what was happening. The fire department was moving through the crowd to silence the fire alarm.

Gator could see a group of Police officers, FBI agents and the Homeland Security agent who had interrupted the meeting gathered at the head of the stairs. Gator chuckled. He knew the questions they were debating, as they tried to figure out who had jurisdiction, who was in charge and how to control the mess surrounding them. Demonstrations and riots could be such fun if you just knew where to watch. And Gator knew where to watch. He was a master of crowd manipulation.

Shortly after, smoke began to blossom from the bottom of the steps as Motor's special effects added to the confusion. Gator smiled as the officials started barking orders and the crowd started pushing past them to get out of the smoke.

One thing Motor was good at was judging which way the wind was moving to get the maximum impact from his special effects.

Gator took a final look at the scenario he had created and left to meet the guys for a little Mongolian beef and strategy.

CHAPTER 3

PROFESSOR RAMIREZ FILED OUT OF THE SIDE DOOR of the auditorium with about a hundred students. The crowd was breaking up as the students scattered and Professor Ramirez moved away from the main group and headed towards Professor Tanager's office in Building 44.

Two students were just leaving as Ramirez caught the door and slipped into building 44. He climbed the stairs and headed down the hall. Most of the rooms were dark as classes were over and the janitorial staff was just beginning to clean the rooms.

Ramirez stopped in front of room 237 and knocked on the door.

"Who is it?" echoed from inside.

"Jeffery it's me. Let me in."

Ramirez heard the shuffle of chairs and then the door unlocked. The door barely opened, and Tanager looked through the crack and asked. "What's the password?"

"Jeffery, let me in before we both get shot..." Ramirez pushed through the door and closed it behind him.

"Better lock it, Patrick. I've been reading through this stuff you sent over." Jeffery returned to his desk and sat down.

> Patrick sat across from him. " Jeffery I suspected it was an angry hornet's nest when Collins was presenting the information to the Tribunal, and Homeland Security and the FBI burst into the meeting.

Jeffery sat up. "Homeland Security and the FBI? What did they want?

Ramirez shook his head. "I suspect they will declare this a national security breach, which means we are holding information that they will be seeking at any cost. And they will want to silence or get rid of anyone who has seen it."

The room grew quiet and filled with questions.

Jeffery drained his coffee cup and started gathering papers. "I think we need to move somewhere a little less conspicuous than our offices."

Ramirez nodded and began helping gather up the evidence. "Any ideas on where we should go?"

Jeffery moved towards the door. "I think we should call Jenny and see if we could use her cabin."

Ramirez paused at the door. "I don't know if we should involve her."

Jeffery, pushed the door closed, locked it and headed down the hall. "Right now, I think we are going to need her help. She has connections in the media that could help. And I am sure she's forgiven you."

Ramirez shook his head, and his voice echoed down the hall. "You're right we will need her, but I don't think forgiveness is going to be on the table, probably a pound or two of flesh."

Jeffery, chuckled, "Patrick, as long as it is your flesh, I am ok with it. Now, I think I should take these files and drive your truck. Take my car just in case they are looking for you. If I get stopped, I'll tell them I borrowed your truck."

"Jeffery are you sure you want in this mess?" Ramirez was trying to grasp just how big a disaster this could be, as doubts were creeping out of the shadows.

Jeffery held out his keys. "I'm parked across the street, green Toyota. Just click the unlock button."

Ramirez handed over his keys and accepted the keys from his accomplice and friend. "I'm behind my office on the lot, red truck, you know it."

"So, what do we tell the girls?"

"Patrick, you know better than that—our wives are way

smarter than we are. We tell them everything. Now, you'd better call Anna quickly. I have a feeling that now that you have the attention of Homeland Security and the FBI, you don't have much time before they show up at your house looking for you."

Ramirez stopped and stuck his cell phone's earpiece in his ear.

He pressed the button on the side of the earpiece and said, "Call Anna, home."

A voice echoed in his ear, "Calling Anna – Home."

"Jeffery, I'll see you at the cabin, I have to make a quick stop to brief my students." Patrick never turned, he just kept walking. Jeffery's voice echoed down the hall. "Better make it quick. They will be looking for you. I'll tell Jill you send your love and ask her to forgive you for dragging me into your sandbox."

CHAPTER 4

As Daniel and William left the utility tunnel and headed up the stairs to the maintenance building, Daniel stopped and reached for Williams' arm.

William stopped, and his usual smile came back. "Before you ask, yes I will need to turn myself in. Everyone will be looking for me, and this is going to be the hardest thing I've ever done."

"I have to face the truth and not the story I typically want people to believe but the real truth. I owe it to Shelly. I promised her I would change."

Daniel's face made it clear he was confused. "What has Shelly to do with what you just did?"

William's face changed. Daniel let go of his arm. The man he saw now had aged dramatically. His face was drawn, he looked smaller more bent like men seem to get when they get old and have seen too much. William's voice cracked, and his eyes filled with tears.

"No one knows but Shelly and her parents. I came home a couple of days ago, and she and I were driving over to that little Italian restaurant she loves. We were trying to talk, but my phone was ringing nonstop. Between calls and texts, we were well on our way to another argument about me working all the time. I just couldn't put the phone down. I was negotiating another deal for the committee. I was just about to close that deal with one of the key senator's aides and took my eyes off the road to look at his text message. I heard Shelly scream "Look out!" and I hit a deer."

William continued, "The Deer's head came through the windshield. One of his antlers caught Shelly in the face."

Daniel was starting to feel sick and looked around for someplace to sit, but all he could do was back up to the wall and listen.

"Is she ok?" Daniel asked.

William lowered his head and nodded. "She's lucky. The deer died instantly, but the tip of his antler struck her face next to her eye. If the deer had been alive and started thrashing it could have blinded her—or even killed her."

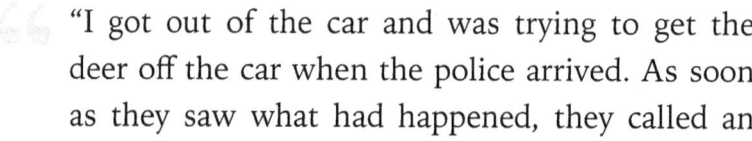

"I got out of the car and was trying to get the deer off the car when the police arrived. As soon as they saw what had happened, they called an ambulance and the fire department. It took them half an hour to untangle her and the deer."

"She is going to have a couple of bad scars on her face," William lamented.

"No one knows I was on the phone, and everyone just assumed the deer came out of nowhere—that it was an accident."

"Shelly and I—and now you—know the truth."

"At the hospital, after they sewed her up, and when we were alone, she told me she was through with me."

"She told me this job had changed me and what I had turned into was not the person she grew up with and loved."

William began to pace back and forth as he did when talking through a deal. The tears began to flow. His voice creaked with the pain of guilt…

"Daniel, I almost killed her trying to make another deal. I was going to ask her to marry me again, but she was furious and was not giving in this time. She was mad and let me have both barrels. She told me if we had been married and had kids, I would probably have killed them. She wanted to know if making one more crooked deal was worth it."

"Shelly has listened to enough of me on the phone to know what I have been doing. She knows I've changed. And she's right."

"I used to like just making deals and see everyone walk away happy with what they got. Now, it's not about doing what's right. It's just about getting my way or making the deal I need to make for my boss and her group."

William continued. "Daniel, everything they say about working in Washington is true. I did go there to make a name and show everyone that I could be different. Instead, I sold out, left my morals outside and stepped right into the Washington pit of lies."

Daniel slowly slipped to the floor while William paced back and forth pumping out his guilt and pain with every word.

"William, we're brothers, what can I do to help?" said Daniel.

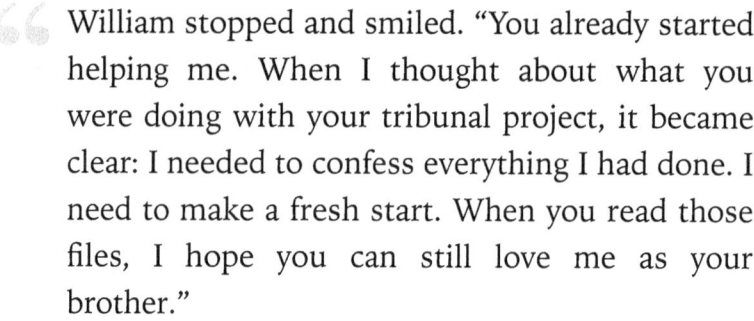 William stopped and smiled. "You already started helping me. When I thought about what you were doing with your tribunal project, it became clear: I needed to confess everything I had done. I need to make a fresh start. When you read those files, I hope you can still love me as your brother."

"Daniel, I have done some things that Mom and Dad will not be proud of hearing about, but I know what I am supposed to do now. Right after the accident and Shelly had torn into me, she got real quiet, and I swear I heard a voice ask me, (*Well, which road are you choosing?*) I looked around the room, and there was no one there but Shelly and me. I shrugged it off as too much stress. But the question just kept coming back. So, I've made a choice."

"Hopefully, you and your Tribunal will be able to at least bring some light to the pit where I've been working. You are not going to believe some of the things we have been doing in the name of the People and the *greater good*."

The sound of a door closing echoed through the tunnel to them, followed by voices.

Daniel got up, and whispered, "We need to get out of here. I know they are looking for you."

William nodded, and they headed out the door of the maintenance building.

"William, I'm parked about a block from here. We probably shouldn't go home right now."

William nodded his head. "Yep, I bet that someone is knocking on mom and dad's door right now looking for me and probably you as well. Any ideas where we can hide out and figure out what's next?"

They were both looking over their shoulders, and trying to stay in the shadows as they headed for Daniel's car.

Daniel continued to whisper, "When the fire alarm went off Professor Ramirez said for us to meet at The Whales. They have a small meeting room in back that we use a lot for class meetings. Let's go there and see who shows up."

William's smile came back as he asked, "Do they still have great burgers?"

Daniel nodded as he opened the car door.

"Yep and the fries are almost as good."

As they drove off, a campus security car was driving through the parking lot looking at license plates.

CHAPTER 5

AGENT TILLIS WAS STANDING AT THE TOP OF THE stairs to the auditorium entrance trying to hear over the crowd. The radio was blaring as the various agents within his detail were trying to round up the suspects, even though they had no idea who was who. The Campus Chief of Security was asking him questions, and the local police had just shown up and were asking how they could help.

The Fire department had turned off the fire alarm, and they were shouting as they ran by Agent Tillis.

Tillis felt old. This was not the way he had planned to spend tonight. He keyed the microphone on his radio and said, "If you don't have William Collins then you have no one to hold. Fall back to the top of the stairs where I am so we can figure this out."

The Chief of Campus Security asked again, "What is going on? Who are you guys looking for and who is William Collins?"

Tillis raised his hand. "Let me tell you what I know..." and was interrupted as his phone rang. Tillis looked at the caller ID, took a deep breath and said to the group gathered around him, "Just a minute, I have to take this call."

As he answered the phone, he turned and moved a couple of steps away trying to shield his conversation.

"Yes, I am on site. No, we did not get to Mr. Collins in time. He had already released the information."

"No, I did not know he had released it through the internet and email.

"No, we do not know where he is at this time."

Tillis stood quietly as the verbal waterboarding began to pour through the phone. Finally, the group heard him say, "Am I to understand that this situation is now declared a National Security incident?" He nodded his head, and those near him became very quiet.

"Yes, I will be waiting here at the auditorium for them. We will use this area as our command post."

"Yes, I understand. I will await their arrival."

Tillis pressed the end button on his phone and felt that his career had also just ended.

As he turned to the little group of police, fire and security officials, the crowd roared back to life. Smoke spread from the bottom of the stairs forcing them to move to get away from the smoke.

A SWAT team officer walked up to the group and asked what they needed to do.

"I understand we are to provide Homeland Security whatever they need," said the officer.

Tillis offered his hand to the SWAT officer and read his name tag.

"Officer Mayland, I am Agent Tillis, Home Land Security. I appreciate your help."

Mayland shook his hand and asked, "What is going on…I just got a call from our chief and was told we were to assist in a National Security investigation and help apprehend a traitor."

At this moment, Bradley Tillis saw his 15-year Law Enforcement career pass before his eyes. "I was just told that someone was on their way to take charge. I am holding down the fort until they arrive."

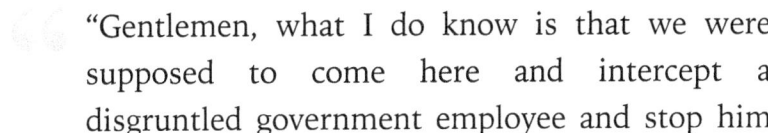

"Gentlemen, what I do know is that we were supposed to come here and intercept a disgruntled government employee and stop him from divulging sensitive government documents and information."

The Campus Security Chief took off his hat and scratched his head. "Are you telling me some spy is passing out Classified Government Secrets?"

Tillis was tired as the words haphazardly tumbled out: "You know how people kid about the guy who knows where all the bodies and secrets are buried."

The group nodded.

"...Everyone has seen some movie or TV show talking about insiders leaking information."

"Well," Tillis continued, "This guy not only knows where all those things that no one wants us to know about got buried, but he also knows what they buried, who buried it, and he just published a map showing all of it."

The group was stunned as each one processed the information and began imaging their own version of how bad this could become.

Tillis continued, "The story we got is a congressional aide was coming to this meeting with the intent of exposing very sensitive information. But before he got here, he copied everything he was carrying and published it to the internet. He also sent a lot of information in emails. We don't have any idea who he sent it to or what he sent."

"That call I just got was from my boss. There are some very

outraged people in D.C. It seems all of this sensitive information is now public domain and the guy who leaked it just moved to the top of almost everyone's wanted list."

Tillis wrapped up with, "Right now our priority is to find William Collins and stop him from distributing any more information. I'll send you photos of him. We are sending agents to his home, his parent's home and any other place he might be. If you find him, call me immediately."

The phone rang, Tillis sighed and answered it.

CHAPTER 6

AGENT PATTERSON RAN OVER TO AGENT TILLIS. "I've got the address for that Professor Ramirez. He's the one in charge of the Tribunal. Let's go over there and see if we can catch up with him."

Tillis looked at the chaos running around outside of the auditorium. Students were running in all directions, smoke was drifting from the stairs, the fire department was trying to respond to the alarm and the local police and campus security were as confused as he was. "Let's go. Maybe Ramirez can fill us in on how this Tribunal thing is tied to Collins."

Patterson and Tillis drove to Professor Ramirez home. It was a quiet street, typical of any small college town. Tillis parked the car and got out. "You really think this guy came home after that mess at the school?"

Tillis shook his head. "No, but we need to let him know we are looking for him."

They walked up to the front door and rang the doorbell. They could hear a dog barking on the inside and the front porch light came on. The door opened slightly and a woman holding a dog looked at them.

Tillis and Patterson held up their credentials. "Mrs. Ramirez, I'm Agent Tillis and this is Agent Patterson. Is your husband home?"

Anna Ramirez held up her hand and abruptly cut them off. "Wait a minute, I need to put the dog up."

The door closed as the dog continued to bark.

The door opened and Anna opened the screen door and stepped on to the porch. "Now, you said you are looking for my husband?"

"Yes, mam. Is he home?" Tillis tried to see into the house.

Anna shook her head. "No, my husband is at school. What is this about?"

Normally, Tillis tried to watch what he said. But he was tired, and immediately regretted the next words he spoke. "Mam we are looking for your husband in connection with a possible national security threat. Your husband may be involved in a conspiracy with a William Collins."

 Anna, reacting almost instinctually to Agent Tillis, slapped him across the right cheek. "How dare you accuse my husband of conspiring with anyone against this country!"

Tillis recoiled from the blow. Patterson stepped between Anna Ramirez and Agent Tillis. "Mam, we didn't mean to accuse Professor Ramirez of anything. We just need to talk to him about this Tribunal thing."

He held out his business card. "When you see him would you please ask him to call us—thank you."

Patterson pushed Tillis back towards the car.

Anna Ramirez was angry, and crushed Patterson's card as she went back in the house and closed the door.

Tillis kept rubbing his face. "Next time you ask the questions."

Patterson started the car. "No way. Next time we talk to her I suggest bringing a SWAT team. Now, let's get back to the school. I think it's safer there."

CHAPTER 7

IN D.C., SENATOR SHERATON HAD JUST HUNG UP from talking to his contact at Home Land Security.

The aide standing at the door of a secure meeting room held out his hand.

Sheraton nodded and handed him his phone.

"Do you have any other electronic devices Senator?" asked the aide.

"No, Thomas, but go ahead and check." The Senator held out his arms and Thomas ran the electronic wand over the Senator, searching for any electronic devices.

"Thank you, Senator. The others are waiting…"

The aide turned and opened the door to the secure conference room.

This room was different than most conference rooms, no electronic devices were allowed in the room. There were no electrical outlets in the room. The walls contained a sheet of lead and a special copper wire mesh. The room was like a large Faraday cage. Anything that was said in this room was just about impossible to be overheard outside.

The door closed and Senator Sheraton moved to an empty seat. Every one of the *Back Nine* were here. Many of them had canceled meetings, dinners and other affairs to be here.

Sheraton looked around the room, and for a change, no one was talking—which for this group was amazing. His eyes stopped on Liz Tyler the Senator from Texas. "Liz, any idea what happened with your boy?"

> Liz almost seemed to uncoil from her seat and hissed back, "He is **not** my boy. You and Andrew told me to hire him—remember?"

Liz was known for her quick strikes and hissing sounds as she spoke. Behind her back others had laughingly nicknamed her Cobra.

Sheraton had grown immune to her bite. "Liz, you knew exactly what you were getting. William Collins was the brightest deal maker any of us have ever seen."

"All of us have watched him and had him work his magic on us. He's good. But something happened. I thought he was with us?"

Andrew Carlin was serving his fourth term as a Representative to the House.

"I understand he had an accident, followed by an epiphany of love or religion. And he didn't choose us. Does anyone know what was leaked?"

Sheraton began analyzing each face in the room.

Andrew spoke up pulling the attention back to the problem. "Sheraton, it looks like he dumped just about everything, dates, meeting notes, agreements, conversations, and from what I have read so far…he didn't miss anything."

"And it seems he had enough foresight to make all of his notes, recordings and everything else electronic. He then posted it to several servers with a timer to begin sending out emails with attachments to every possible media source he had in his address list."

Andrew wrapped up by saying, "Then apparently from what my sources tell me, he had several sites set up so as you go online the email and files automatically download. Hell, he even has a YouTube site listing download sites. Twitter was carrying his feeds as he made his announcements."

Morris Yancey was sitting in the shadows of the room, just away from the table to keep his face hidden. "We knew this guy was good, but this attack makes the Normandy invasion look like amateurs planned it. My FBI contacts said they have never seen anyone spread information faster. He had to have had this planned for a long time."

Liz seemed calmer now that the focus was on Collins and not her. She shook her head saying, "I don't think he was planning this very long. He just used the very network he set up for us to open the doors to our files."

"I just spoke to the Homeland Security agent in Texas who was supposed to intercept Collins. The agent told me they were about fifteen minutes behind him. Collins had already stood up in front of this mock tribunal and announced all of the download sites."

The room began to rumble as the *Back Nine* thrashed around in their seats, realizing the impact of the electronic media bomb that had just exploded.

Liz continued, "The agent for Homeland security said when he walked into the auditorium it sounded like a horde of crickets as everyone in the room seemed to be typing on a computer, or cell phone. I spoke to one of our cyber people at Homeland a few minutes ago. They are monitoring all the internet, and social media feeds on this Tribunal. They said when Collins made his announcement the internet almost crashed. None of them have ever seen this much cyber activity. Apparently, this Mock Tribunal already had several internet feeds set up. By now, the Collins files are being downloaded all over the world. As we speak every intelligence organization in the world is analyzing the information."

Again, the room went silent.

Sheraton was looking at the grain of the oak table in front of him. "Has anyone heard from the President?"

Gregory Waters nodded his head and added, "I got a call from Victoria…" and with this, several of the *Back Nine* closed their eyes hoping they had not heard her name. Victoria was well known to them. She was the confidant of the President, and many felt she was the real power behind the throne. "She said she was going to go brief him and we had better have a good story for her to tell."

"She has called a couple of times since. I've just not taken her calls."

And taking her call was a task no one in this room wanted.

Sheraton leaned forward. "We need to focus on finding Collins and getting this leak under control. I suggest we all go work our resources and meet in the morning."

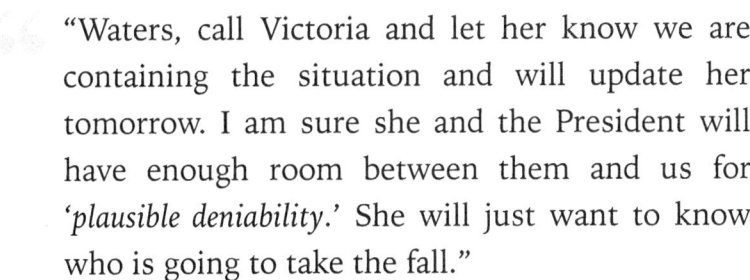

> "Waters, call Victoria and let her know we are containing the situation and will update her tomorrow. I am sure she and the President will have enough room between them and us for *'plausible deniability.'* She will just want to know who is going to take the fall."

The mumbles around the room masked their fears, and they slowly left the room, leaving Sheraton and Liz alone. Once the room had emptied, Sheraton turned to face Liz and asked, "Have you seen the information your boy leaked?"

Liz stiffened and nodded. "It looks like he leaked everything we asked him to do for the last couple of years and some things I did not know he knew."

Sheraton rolled the wedding ring on his finger. "I am afraid this is going to cost all of us more than we can afford and still be able to stay in office. I got a call from a couple of our lobbyist friends."

Liz, twisted in her seat, and preemptively said, "I am not taking the fall for this alone."

Sheraton nodded. "They are planning to distance themselves from all of the *Back Nine*. They are already working on replacing us. We need to get our staffs together and spin this to protect ourselves. I doubt any of us will all be able to muster any support from our lobbyist friends."

"We can only hope that the courts that try us will use our judges. I suggest we all look at spreading this over as many people as we can, so we can deflect attention from ourselves."

"Have you got a couple of targets you can sacrifice?" asked Sheraton.

Liz was getting very uncomfortable as she knew she would be the primary target for any investigations as Collins had worked directly for her.

"I have a couple of people I can toss under the bus, but we will need the bus to keep moving so no one looks closely."

Sheraton got up from the table. "I'll make some calls, and we can meet in the morning. I think we have a committee meeting we can use for cover."

Sheraton left Liz sitting alone. She shivered as she felt the chill of the coming days. These would be dark days for many inside the dome.

CHAPTER 8

THE WHALES WAS A TYPICAL COLLEGE restaurant/bar. They hired a lot of students and served great burgers and steak fries. The little-known fact about The Whales was that Professor Ramirez was the real owner. Michael O'Brien ran The Whales for Ramirez and gave every indication that he owned the place, which was what Ramirez wanted.

The Whales was Ramirez's diversion. He liked to sit and talk with people, and this was a good way to do it. He enjoyed the image of being one of the students. He held classes at The Whales, and the students thought it was great. Ramirez had learned a long time ago that a casual setting with food and drinks was more productive than most classrooms. So, most of his senior seminars found their way to the back room of The Whales.

As Ramirez pulled up in Dr. Tanager's car, he had a hard time finding a place to park. Finally, he pulled around back and parked in the loading zone.

As he got out of the car, a police patrol car drove by and slowed as if they were looking for someone. Ramirez ducked in the back door and waved at the dishwasher. He stopped at the door to the back room and looked through the service window of the door. No one was inside, so he pushed open the door and turned up the lights.

Ramirez walked over to the phone on the wall and called over the intercom to the bar.

Four rings into the call he heard Michael O'Brien's voice.

"I wondered when you would surface."

Ramirez was puzzled. "Why do you say that?

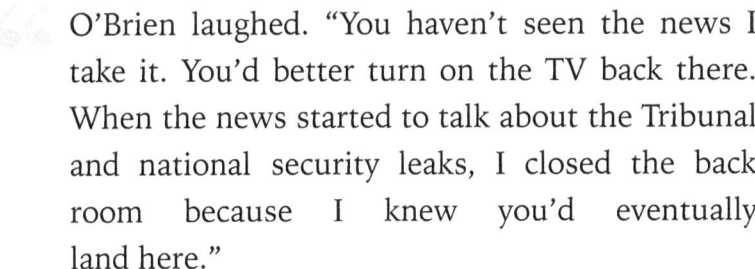

O'Brien laughed. "You haven't seen the news I take it. You'd better turn on the TV back there. When the news started to talk about the Tribunal and national security leaks, I closed the back room because I knew you'd eventually land here."

Ramirez walked over to the large screen TV and pressed the power button. "Any particular channel, or did we make them all?"

O'Brien walked in the same service door that Ramirez had

entered still holding the wireless phone. He pressed the off button on the phone and looked at Ramirez.

"It's on every channel. They're reporting that a government aide is wanted for leaking National Security information. The way they make it sound he has placed the entire country at risk."

"Your name came up a couple of times as they are naming names, showing photos and giving out tip lines for people to call."

"I think you really stepped in it this time."

Ramirez hung up the phone and sat down in one of the booths.

"Michael, there will be a number of my senior students showing up here. Can you keep an eye out for them?"

O'Brien had an interesting past, and because of it, he was one of those people who didn't ask many questions.

"I figured once they started showing up without you and seemed to be hiding in a booth in the back, that there was trouble. Then the TV started covering the problem at the school."

"I know a good conspiracy when I see one. I took them a pitcher of beer and told them to stay put. They keep looking at their phones and texting. I knew you would show up sooner or later. I think there are about six of them out there. Do you want me to bring them back or send them home?"

Ramirez took a deep breath, pulled out his phone and saw thirty-five new text messages.

"Can you send them back here—*quietly*? Tanager is supposed to meet me here."

"If you see Collins, get him back here quickly, and quietly as well."

O'Brien nodded. "Which Collins? Daniel or William?"

"Both when they show," answered Ramirez.

O'Brien added, "Should I call the IRA or are you planning on leading this rebellion yourself?

Ramirez, scanning his text messages stopped on the one from Anna Ramirez.

It read: "What did you get yourself into?"

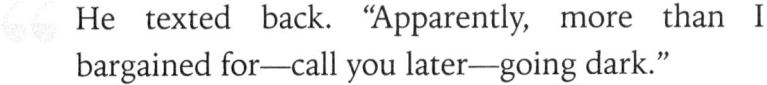 He texted back. "Apparently, more than I bargained for—call you later—going dark."

O'Brien had a talent for knowing what people were doing just by observing them. "I assume that was Anna. She called twice looking for you. She said you tried to call her, but she was on a conference call. I told her you were still unaccounted for, but I would let her know when you showed."

Ramirez also noted several texts from the College President that would prove challenging to answer.

"Michael, I expect several different law enforcement representatives will be checking to see if any of the Tribunal members are here. Just quietly let me know when they start showing up."

Michael turned and headed back to the bar. "I'll get your usual order sent back. Cathy is working tonight, so she'll bring back your tribe and keep watch."

"Do you want me to let Anna know you're here?"

Ramirez nodded yes. "Thank you, Michael. You're a good friend."

Michael backed out of the door and said, "It will be interesting," and he started singing an old Irish song, "Up the republic...."

CHAPTER 9

Two blocks away Dr. Jeffery Tanager had been pulled over by several police cars, marked and unmarked. One particularly menacing black SUV hung just back from the others, but no one got out.

The officer that pulled over Tanager was polite but tense. He never took his hand off his gun.

As Tanager lowered the window of Ramirez' truck, he asked the innocent question, "What was I doing officer?"

The officer looked at the photo on his cell phone and asked. "Can I see your license and registration?"

Tanager, reaching for his wallet and replied, "This is a friend's truck, I just borrowed it to use tomorrow to move some things."

He handed him his license, and the officer gave it to his sergeant who had just joined him.

With a reflex-like reaction to the now seven police officers standing around the truck, Tanager lifted his hands over his head.

The sergeant who had taken his license was in a heated conversation with someone on his cell phone.

Tanager, heard him say, "It's not Ramirez, just another teacher who borrowed his truck. Hell, I know this guy, he's taught two of my kids."

"No, there's no one with him…and look I'm letting him go. If you want him, you go find him."

The sergeant walked over to the truck. "Dr. Tanager I'm sorry. They are looking for Dr. Ramirez after that mess over at the school."

"If you see him, please tell him to call the station. They want to talk to him about the Tribunal thing they were doing at the school. Apparently, the guy who interrupted the meeting is wanted for questioning."

Tanager took back his license. "Of course. If I see Dr. Ramirez, I will let him know to call you."

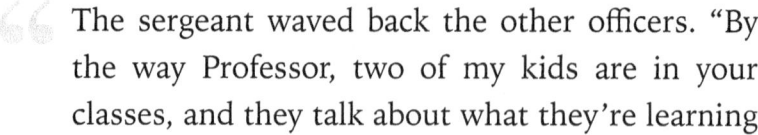

The sergeant waved back the other officers. "By the way Professor, two of my kids are in your classes, and they talk about what they're learning

—they really seem to be interested in what you have to say."

Tanager tried to catch the sergeant's name tag, but the shadows blocked it. "Well thank you. I appreciate the feedback. It's nice to know some of my students are paying attention."

Tanager started the truck and decided he would make a couple of stops on the way home. Maybe he was a little paranoid, but it couldn't hurt to be careful. He planned an evasive route and headed to a local drug store. Tanager looked in the rearview mirror and smiled as the black SUV followed him. "Well, maybe I'm not paranoid. So boys, let's go get some aspirin and then a stop at the grocery store. I hope you boys have time for me to shop." Tanager made sure he obeyed the speed limit and used his turn signals. Tanager was enjoying himself and he couldn't wait to tell Ramirez about his adventure.

CHAPTER 10

DANIEL AND WILLIAM DROVE PAST THE WHALES and parked in the back of another restaurant just down the street.

As Daniel turned the car off, his brother smiled. "Good thinking. If they spot your car here and raid this place I bet, we will still hear about it in The Whales.

Daniel nodded. "You know college towns, anything that attracts police attention spreads through the students like the smell of smoke. Anyway, I think the authorities will be looking for you. And maybe me, as I am now the brother of a notorious fugitive."

William dropped his head looked at Daniel. "Really. Then, you explain all this to mom." They laughed and got out of the car looking to be sure there were no police cars around.

While outside, Daniel pulled William's backpack and laptop from the back seat.

"Daniel, I didn't mean to get you into this. Hell, I didn't want any of this to happen. I just keep hearing Shelly ask me *who do I want to be*. Then I guess I heard God saying *it's your choice*. When I started running through the list of things I had done and was doing, I began to get sick."

"I need to make things right. I know it's not going to be easy."

> Daniel was leaning on the roof of the car, he held out his hand. "I'm here for you. Whatever you need to do I'll stand with you. Dad always said we were stronger together than alone."

William reached across the car roof and took his brother's hand. "Let's get something to eat before we start. I can't remember when I last ate."

They walked down to The Whales staying off the street behind the other buildings.

As they got to the door, Daniel handed William his backpack. "Wait here and let me see if it's ok inside…"

William nodded and drifted off to the side of the building.

Daniel opened the door and had to push his way inside. The place was packed.

He looked around to see if anyone from the Tribunal was

here. As his eyes crossed the bar, he saw Michael O'Brien. He started walking towards him when Cathy, one of the waitresses, hugged him and whispered in his ear, "Hug me back and then walk outside with me. Ramirez wants you to come in through the back."

Daniel hugged her, and she took him by hand and walked back out the door.

Once outside, she linked her arm in his like they were a couple and began walking him around the building. "Is your brother with you?" she asked.

Daniel was new to this type of role-playing and was still struggling with being this close to Cathy. She was beyond cute, and every guy who entered The Whales had a crush on her. In this state of confused puppy love, he managed to say "Uhh..." and with that William surfaced and said, "I'm William, Daniel's brother."

Cathy linked her other arm in Williams and continued walking them to the back of the building. As they came up to the service entrance, she stopped.

"William, your picture is all over the TV. Everyone knows what you look like. Dr. Ramirez asked us to keep an eye out for you and try to bring you in the back quietly. I was just about to round up the rest of your fellow conspirators when Daniel walked in. I figured it would be best to get you out of there before everyone saw you."

She opened the service door as the boys followed her. Daniel was having trouble speaking and kept mumbling, "Conspirators?"

Cathy laughed. "Just kidding, but you are in Ramirez class, and I think the Govey's are going to lump you all together and then maybe sort it out later." With that, she opened the door to the back room, and the boys walked in. Ramirez was eating his sandwich. Trying to wipe his mouth, swallow and get up to greet the boys, he started coughing and stopped to get a drink.

He took a deep breath. "My wife is always telling me not to eat so fast. You would think I would have learned that by now."

"Sit down boys, are you hungry? What do you want? How about something to drink?"

Cathy smiled and interrupted. "Doc, you may own the joint, but you're trying to do my job. Now sit down and finish your dinner and I'll take care of the boys."

She turned to Daniel and William as they sat down across from the professor. "Now, what can I get you, boys?"

Daniel trying to overcome his earlier mumblings looked up at the clock on the wall. "How about a Whale burger and fries?"

"Great, what do you want on it? The works?"

Daniel nodded. And before she could ask, he looked directly at her and asked, "Can I have an iced tea, unsweetened?"

Cathy grinned, the grin of all good waitresses, and said, "You bet honey and what about your *most wanted* brother—what would you like?"

William who had brokered deals that would make the devil jealous found himself under the same spell that Cathy had cast over Daniel.

With his most intellectual response, he managed, "Uh, I'll have the same."

Cathy said, "Two Whales burgers, loaded, fries and ice tea."

"Doc, do you need anything else?"

Ramirez smiled as he watched Cathy work the magic of a good waitress. "Not unless you can quietly escort the other members of my class back here. Michael says they are hiding in a booth.

Cathy, standing at the service door with a great view of the main dining room said, "Currently there are 4 or 5 of them crammed into one booth. They keep looking at the door every time it opens. If you were a cop, you would arrest them just based on their guilty looks."

Ramirez nodded. "Can you get them back here without attracting too much attention?"

Cathy grinned. "This one will cost you Doc. One strategically dropped tray of empty dishes at the other side of the room coming up!"

And with that, Cathy backed out of the room leaving only the memory of her smile and the twinkle in her eye.

Ramirez laughed as the boys watched her exit. "And that gentlemen is why the only thing the Bible says for men to run from is a woman."

 "Relax gentlemen. Cathy is one of the best waitresses I've ever met. She makes everyone feel warm and friendly. I've seen her stop bar fights with just a smile and a gentle walk to the door."

Daniel and William let out a deep breath and tried to return to the present.

Ramirez nodded toward the TV on the wall as William's picture showed on the screen with the following caption: *Congressional Aide wanted for espionage.*

William just looked at the news tickers rolling across the bottom of the screen.

Ramirez could see the weight of the situation settling on him.

"William, I don't know what you want to do, but I think we need to get you somewhere quiet and talk this over so that you have a chance to defend your actions."

William turned back from the TV. "I think maybe I need a lawyer."

Ramirez nodded. "Do you know any outstanding lawyers?"

William looked at the table, studying the marks and scratches typical in any college hangout.

"I know a couple, but most of them have ties to someone on the hill."

Ramirez nodded. "Do you know Ben Langley?"

William and Daniel both nodded. Daniel finally coming out of the *Cathy spell* managed to say, "Isn't he the guy who defended the whistleblower last year?"

Ramirez finished his last bite of sandwich, nodding. "Ben is an old friend and classmate. If you agree I am going to call him and see if he will help. For now, I want the two of you to slip through that door in the corner. That is Michael's private office. It's small but your classmates are about to show up, and I think it's best if we keep William and you out of sight."

Ramirez got up and hurried the boys through the door. "Just stay in here, I will have Cathy bring your food to you. I need to talk to the rest of your classmates and get a feel for which side of this fence they are going to land on."

Daniel and William found themselves in a small room with a desk full of papers and a couch. William took the couch, and Daniel turned the chair around and sat on it leaning forward on the chair's back.

"William, I think Professor Ramirez is right, you are going to need an outstanding lawyer."

William got that faraway look that people get when they start realizing how their actions are now going to impact those they love.

He looked up at Daniel. "What am I going to tell Mom and Dad?"

Daniel shook his head. "Dude you don't have a choice, just tell them what happened, stick to the truth—it's your best defense. Dad is going to be really mad for a while Mom will just tell us it's going to work out."

William looked at Daniel. He had heard his brother including himself in this problem. "Daniel, you don't have anything to do with it. I want you to stay out of this."

Daniel was ready to argue when Cathy opened the other door to the back office.

"So, you guys trying to change tables to get a better waitress?"

Cathy slid into the room and placed the tray of food on a stool. The beguiling waitress persona slipped away. "Ok, guys, you need to eat. Doc wants you to eat and rest. I will check back on you in a little while—stay in here. The place is crawling with people, and both of your pictures are on the TV."

"Don't make any calls. Michael is going to get a couple of burner phones for you guys. Think who you need to talk to, parents, girlfriend, or pastor. You know those you talk to before they hang you. Then make your calls on the burner phones. When you finish throw them away."

And the waitress persona was back as she put on her smile, winked and walked out.

Daniel reached for a plate. "She was kidding about the hanging thing? Right?"

William took the other plate. "I hope so, but right now, I'm starving."

Daniel was already a full bite into his burger as he managed the male equivalent of a food review by nodding and grunting, "Great burger."

CHAPTER 11

RAMIREZ WAS SITTING IN THE BOOTH SO HE COULD see the door to the main dining area. The door opened, and five students stumbled in. They all turned as they heard the door lock behind them.

Ramirez took a mental roll call of the class. There were ten in the class...

Daniel Collins, present but in hiding.

Andy Clayton, present. Andy was Judge number two. He will be a good attorney someday.

Barry Weinstein was missing; He was the Defense, second chair and typically, was best at whining about almost everything.

Angela Thompson was present. Angela was Defense lead.

She was a good student. She was astute at spinning her position, so it always made her look good.

Tanya Landers was missing. She was Prosecution, third chair. She wanted to be a corporate attorney. She was just taking this class because she needed it to graduate.

Gregory Justin was missing. He was Defense, third chair. It was disappointing that he didn't show up. He was probably more worried about what his parents think than anything else. Too much family money tends to breed out character.

Mary VanDort was present. Mary was Tribunal Judge three. She should be a better student. She was very liberal in her interpretations of the law, but ready to support a better argument—though it had better be a better argument than hers.

Timothy Balinson was present. Timothy was Tribunal Secretary and charged with being sure all sides, and the judges adhere to the rules and laws. Timothy may be the most judge-like student Ramirez had seen in a long time. Timothy weighed the facts against the laws. He had impressed Ramirez from their first meeting, which was why Ramirez had put him in as the rule keeper for this Tribunal exercise.

Diana Jeffers was missing. Prosecution second chair. She was a good student but so quiet that you didn't know what she was thinking or which side she was on.

Baruti Madise was present. Baruti was the Prosecution lead. He was an outstanding student of the Constitution. One of the best Ramirez had ever seen. He had a passion that was lacking in most students. Ramirez believed that this was because half of his family had been slaughtered in Rwanda. He had fled with what was left of his family to America. Now he was passionate about freedom from any form of tyranny.

Finished with his mental roll call Ramirez said, "Glad to see you made it out of that mess. Please grab a seat. Have you eaten? How about something to drink? Then we can talk and figure out what we need to do."

The Tribunal students took their seats around Ramirez as if they were still in class when the door opened, and Cathy escorted Diana Jeffers through the door. Cathy smiled, closed and locked the door, causing everyone to look at the door and Diana.

Ramirez noted that this was the first time Diana seemed rattled. She just stood there.

Ramirez walked over and took her arm to escort her to a seat.

She looked at him and said, "I had to go feed my cat."

Ramirez nodded. "And how is your cat?"

Diana sat down and looked at him and seemed to relax slightly. "He's okay. Socrates gets crabby if I'm gone too long and knocks stuff over to let me know he's mad."

Ramirez decided to use Diana's late arrival as an opportunity to put the class at ease. He needed to determine the position of each one of them. Who would continue to support the

Tribunal? Who would fold? And who would seek asylum for immunity? These were all lawyers in the making, with their careers in front of them. At least he hoped.

"So, Diana, was Socrates alright?"

She nodded. "He just knocked over some stuff on the counter. I cleaned it up, gave him his favorite food and left his music playing so he should be ok for now."

Ramirez moved to the middle of the room so he could see all of the students and the service door behind them.

"Well, we're all glad that Socrates is alright."

"Have any of you seen the rest of the class?"

An exchange of questions among the class began as they mentally looked for their missing classmates.

Angela spoke first. "I saw Barry and Tanya when we left the building. Barry said they were going to his parents until this blew over."

Ramirez made a mental note to follow up on that later.

Baruti raised his hand. He was always the most polite of the group.

"Yes Baruti," Ramirez acknowledged.

"After the Homeland Security agent broke into the meeting, I heard Gregory saying he didn't need this, that his family would never forgive him. He said he just wanted out and ran out the door with the crowd."

"Well, let's review what we know so we can figure out what we need to do." Ramirez looked at Baruti, "Can you help with the facts?"

Baruti nodded and took out a pad and pen. One thing you could count on when Baruti finished, there would be an accurate record of who said what.

Mary Van Dort raised her hand.

Ramirez acknowledged her raised hand just as if she was in class. "Yes, Mary?"

"Has anyone seen Daniel?"

Ramirez looked around the room as Angela jumped in. "I saw him as I left. He was sitting on the stage talking to the guy who interrupted the proceedings. I think that guy is his brother?"

The class nodded and started talking. "Ok," Ramirez interrupted, "So we have four missing, and you are correct, that was Daniel's brother, and hopefully they will both turn up soon."

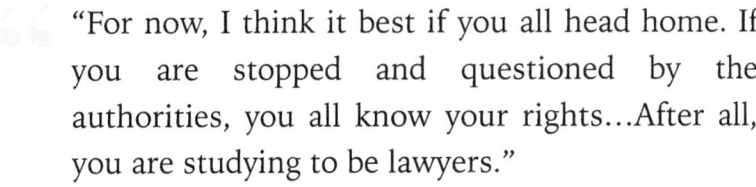

"For now, I think it best if you all head home. If you are stopped and questioned by the authorities, you all know your rights...After all, you are studying to be lawyers."

"If any of you need assistance call my office and I will see if we can get you additional legal help."

Timothy Balinson stood up. "Professor! What about the Tribunal? Are we going to proceed with it?"

Ramirez was surprised. He looked at the class. He couldn't tell where they stood.

Baruti put his pen down. "Professor, I would like to continue with the Tribunal. Especially now, I believe that we have an obligation to continue."

Timothy was still standing and starting to rock from side to side. Ramirez had noted this was a habit when Timothy was in deep thought. The words started to pour out.

"I believe Baruti is correct. I was not sure about the Tribunal as a valid exercise when we started. But I have been thinking about it a lot. I had a chance to talk it over with my Grandfather who's a retired judge. He told me I had a duty to do this."

"My grandfather is old school in his thinking; He can trace our family all the way back to when they came over from the old country. He can even tell you about which of our family was on what side during the Civil War."

"He asked me to reread the Constitution and then decide if the Tribunal was worthwhile. He asked me if it would help people learn about the Constitution and why it was important to our ancestors and this country. And then he asked me if I thought I could put the Constitution in perspective with today and see if we had veered from its intent. Are we better off or should we turn back towards it to protect the future generations?"

Still rocking back and forth, Timothy, suddenly stopped and faced his classmates. "I think we owe it to those who wrote the Constitution to test it in front of the public. We have all seen how much interest has grown for people wanting to observe this exercise. Now that it has been interrupted I think it is even more important that we continue."

Andy Clayton turned in his chair. "I don't know if any of you have had a chance to look at the information that Mr. Collins submitted to us, but I downloaded the files and read about 20 of them."

"I need more time to read all of the files, but if even ten percent of what Collins has submitted is accurate, then we have a responsibility to make it public through the Tribunal."

Mary VanDort shifted uncomfortably and started her rebuttal with her trademark vocal interjection. "Umm, I think we may get a lot of resistance from the government and the school. I don't think they will let us continue. And I doubt this would be good for our careers."

Ramirez moved back to his seat and sat down. The class was deciding their next action. Would they step forward as a group and take on this fight? Or would they fold and run?

Diana Jeffers picked some cat hair from her sweater and said, "I would like to proceed. If we want to be attorneys, then we should get used to standing up for what is right and not suppressing the facts. If the school doesn't let us go forward, then I think we should find another venue. After what we saw this evening, it is obvious that someone needs to bring this forward and present both sides, so the people can decide."

"If we don't do anything but accurately present the two sides of this argument to the public, then we have done what we were called to do. I want to go forward. I expect it will cost all of us, but that is what our founders did so how can we do less?"

Ramirez wanted to hug her. She got it. As a teacher, he believed in empowering his students, teaching them to understand cause and effect. To be responsible for their actions. He wanted them to stand for something, and this looked promising.

Ramirez sat up and tapped the side of his coffee cup with a spoon, calling the group to order.

"This is your call. I will support whatever decision you make. If you want to walk away from this, so be it. If you want to take it on, then I will help you every way I can."

"I believe if you go forward this will be a test of everything that you believe. You will find yourselves in a very uncomfortable spotlight. Most likely you will be threatened by several agencies of the government. They are not going to want this information or the Tribunal to become a public record. So ultimately, the decision is one only you can make."

Diana stood up. "I'm in."

Baruti joined her in standing. "I also want to do this—no matter the cost."

Andy stood up. "I don't have a choice. If I don't my grandfather will disown me. Let's do it."

One by one the remaining class stood agreeing they wanted to proceed. Except for Angela, who said, "I need to think about this. I will call or email your office tomorrow professor —right now I want to think."

Ramirez stood up. "Ok, why don't you all take some time to think about it and if you still want to go forward, call me or email me. Now, quietly get out of here and go home. I am sure you will all encounter some representative of our Government in the next few hours. Tell them what you know. However, I would leave out your intent to continue with the Tribunal."

"We will know how to proceed in the next day or two. Be careful and avoid the Media. You do not want to let them trick you into saying something that will be public record forever. Consider this a test of your skills as future attorneys. Practice your best delaying tactic and say, *no comment.*"

The class got up as if the bell had rung signaling the end of class. Cathy must have been monitoring from outside as the door unlocked they filed out the door and left Ramirez alone with a cold cup of coffee.

CHAPTER 12

TANAGER DROVE DOWN THE STREET WITH THE obvious black SUV tailing him. He looked in the rearview mirror and chuckled. "Wow, talk about the elephant in the room. You would think they could use a less obvious vehicle to follow people." Tanager picked up his cell phone and called his wife. On the third ring, Jill Tanager answered. "I figured you would be late after catching the news reports on the Tribunal. It's on every channel."

Jeffery turned into the parking lot of the local drug store. "Yeah, the campus is in complete chaos. Do you need anything? I'm going to pick up a couple of things on the way home."

Jill was slow on her reply. She had talked to Jeffery several hours earlier and let him know she had picked up the groceries on the fridge list. She responded slowly listening for what Jeffery was trying to tell her without saying it. "No, I think we're good, just get what you want."

Jeffery smiled. Jill was one of those rare gems of life that could read between the lines. He knew they had talked earlier and they didn't need anything. Now he needed to fill in the gaps for her without actually saying it in the event the SUV or someone else was monitoring his call. "I need a couple of things from the drug store. I was also going to pick up some lunch meat and bread—just sandwich stuff."

"And for safe measure," he added, "Oh, I borrowed Patrick's truck so that I can pick up the stuff for the garden."

Jill pulled the phone from her ear and looked at it. Then she walked to the front door and looked out. "Ok, that sounds good. Why don't you get some aspirin, I'm getting a headache."

Jill knew something was wrong. Jeffery looked at yard work as an equivalent to a sentence on Devil's Island. But she picked up on his borrowing Patrick's truck and kept the conversation moving.

"Jeffery, I'm going to take the dog for a walk, do you want me to fix you something to eat?"

As Jeffery got out of the car, he looked around and headed for the store.

Entering the drug store, Jeffery turned down an aisle that let him see the front door. And sure enough, a guy in a suit walked in the door and began walking the aisles. Jeffery knew for certain he was being followed.

He continued to try and fill Jill in without letting his paranoia get the best of him.

"No, don't worry about it. I think I might stop at The Whales and get a burger. With all of this commotion, I'm sure the students are worked up. Maybe I can help calm some of them down."

Jill nodded and snapped the leash on their Boston terrier. "Hang on a minute, Jeffery. I want to switch to my headset." She pushed her headset on her ear and put her Smith & Wesson Crimson Trace in her jacket holster.

"Ok, Jeffery I'm going to take Sadie for her walk."

Jeffery pushed his cart to the checkout. "Be sure you take your friend with you."

Jill smiled. Jeffery had encouraged her to go through the concealed carry class after a couple of incidents in their neighborhood. "Yes, I have Sadie and my friend."

Jeffery signed the credit card receipt and walked to the car. "Ok, I'm headed to the grocery store so we can talk while you walk. Besides, I think I have a friend with me as well."

Jill had locked the front door and was starting around the block. "What friend?"

Jeffery pulled out of the parking lot and headed west. The grocery store was about a quarter mile away. The SUV pulled out and followed him. "It seems that driving Patrick's truck has earned me an escort."

Sadie was busy leaving her mark on their trip around the block. Jill began casually looking around to see if anyone was following her. "Jeffery are you sure?"

Jeffery turned into the grocery store parking lot. As he parked the truck and headed to the store entrance, he saw the SUV park two aisles over. The same guy got out of the SUV.

"Yep, I'm sure. When I took Patrick's truck from the school lot, I got stopped by the police. After I had assured them I had just borrowed it to use tomorrow, a black SUV followed me to the drug store. A guy followed me into the store, and now the same SUV and the same man is grocery shopping with me. I can't wait to see what he buys."

Jill and Sadie were on the back side of the block. Jill was now on full alert watching for any sign of someone following. "Jeffery, why are they following Patrick? I saw the news, but they were looking for some guy named Collins."

Jeffery spoke to the clerk behind the deli counter, "I need a pound of hard salami, a pound of sugar cured ham, and a half pound of the smoked turkey." He then pointed at the earpiece and said, "Yes dear, I got the lunch meat."

He stepped back from the counter and looked at the potato salads. Jeffery caught his shadow by the cheese counter out of the corner of his eye. "We'll have to talk about that later, Babe. It seems my shadow is too close for us to talk about it. I think Patrick is going to get a lot of unwanted attention. He certainly didn't expect Mr. Collins to use the Tribunal as a conduit to expose a lot of very sensitive documents to the *worldwide web*."

Jill was almost back to the house when she noticed two guys sitting in a car on the opposite side of the street from their home. "Jeffery, it looks like driving Patrick's truck may be getting you more attention than we both want. It seems we have two gentlemen sitting across the street from the house."

Jeffery nodded to the Deli Clerk as he handed him his lunch meats. He turned and went directly to the cheese counter almost bumping into his shadow with the grocery cart. "Excuse me," Jeffery smiled as the shadow tried not to make eye contact and headed off disappearing behind the bread aisle.

Jeffery picked up packs of pepper jack and onion cheese. "Be careful, Babe, I think everyone who knows Patrick or any of the Tribunal crew are going to be getting a lot of attention."

Jill unlocked the door and let Sadie off her leash. Sadie headed for her food bowl to see if there were any new tidbits. Jill locked the door and turned off the light in the foyer. The car was still there. One of the figures was smoking as you could see the light of his cigarette. "Are you still going to The Whales?"

Jeffery had used the self-checkout aisle. He noticed his shadow had picked up a couple of bottles of water and was using the express checkout.

"Yeah, I think I should drop by and just see if I spot anybody."

Jill took off her jacket and headed for the kitchen. "Why don't you bring me something, I think it's going to be a long night."

Jeffery opened the passenger door of the truck. He put the groceries inside and walked around to the driver's side. The shadow had gotten back into the SUV.

"Do you want the usual?"

Jill poured a glass of wine. Tossed a couple of treats to Sadie and headed for her office. "That would be great, one greasy burger with everything…and fries. I'm going to check the tube and the internet and see what's going on."

Jeffery pulled out of the parking lot and headed back past drug store on his way to The Whales. The SUV followed. "If you see anything call me. I should be about a half an hour. I'll just order it to go and see what's going on."

Jill sat down at her computer. The left monitor was playing the local news channel. "Wow, Jeffery if the media coverage is any indicator of how big of a mess this is, then get ready for a big storm. You should see the number of people gathered outside of the auditorium. It looks like every news station in town is over there, and the place is swarming with windbreakers from every Govey team you can imagine."

Jeffery turned into the parking lot of The Whales. It was packed. He drove around the building and saw his car parked in the loading area. The SUV had followed him into the lot. "What's going on?" he asked Jill.

> Jill was writing on a pad. "Well, so far I have seen a DEA, FBI, Homeland Security, Police and ATF windbreakers. So, either everyone is working on this, or they're going to a bowling tournament."

Jeffery pulled the truck in front of the dumpster ignoring the "NO PARKING" sign. It was Patrick's truck, so anyone who knew Patrick would recognize his vehicle and shouldn't tow it.

"You might want to email Jenny. I think Patrick is going to need her help."

Jeffery locked the truck and walked around to the front of The Whales. The SUV was still looking for a place to park. As they drove by, Jeffery waved and opened the door to The Whales. The noise was overwhelming. "It's too loud to talk Babe. I'll call you when I leave."

Jill could barely hear him as the noise of The Whales seemed to swallow his voice. She barely heard him say he'd call when leaving. She glanced at the clock on her screen.

The timer began in her head. Ten minutes for Jeffery to get to the bar, exchange *hellos* with everyone. Ten more for him to find out who was there who was hiding and place an order. Twenty minutes if he was lucky to get his order and if he didn't get stuck talking to someone. Then she might still get warm fries before midnight.

Jill fired off an email to Jenny asking her if she had time for lunch and wasn't it terrible that the Tribunal was getting so much negative attention. If Patrick hadn't already contacted Jenny, she would know to call Jill. After all, she knew Patrick and Jeffery were thick as thieves, and if one of them were in trouble, the other would be right there trying to help.

She looked up at the news channel. They were now showing pictures of both Collins boys and talking about how they were wanted for questioning. Another photo flashed on the screen. Patrick Ramirez was also wanted for questioning as the sponsor for the Tribunal.

Jill sighed. It was going to be a long night. Sadie grumbled and lay down on the couch, burrowing under her favorite blanket. Jill turned on the big screen, tuned to another news channel and joined Sadie. Might as well catch a nap, once Jeffery got home they would compare notes. Sadie started to snore as Jill lay down.

CHAPTER 13

JEFFERY HUNG UP THE PHONE AND HEADED FOR the "Carry Out" sign at the bar. Cathy waved at him as he made his way through the crowd. Michael O'Brien was handing a pitcher of beer to one of the waitresses when Jeffery got to the bar.

He sat down on the one remaining bar stool, in the "Carry Out" space. Michael grinned. "And what can I get you before they arrest you?"

Michael and Patrick were longtime friends and shared a common past which neither ever discussed. Jeffery had come to know both of them over the years and just accepted them as friends. "How about an iced tea and an order to go?"

Jeffery saw his shadow come in the front door. He was

wearing a windbreaker over his suit. Jeffery watched him in the mirror behind the bar.

> Michael placed a glass of iced tea in front of Jeffery. "Is the windbreaker watching you or should I be letting Patrick know that the walls have been breached, and the heathen are among us?"

Jeffery took a drink. Only Michael could sound so Irish and conspiratorial. "I'm sure he's following me. I borrowed Patrick's truck, and they've been following me all evening." Michael nodded. "Patrick parked your car in the back about an hour ago. I've been waiting for the riot squad to show up and raid the place ever since."

Jeffery looked around to see if he recognized any of his students. "Patrick is here?"

Michael handed an order to Cathy as she swung by the bar. "Tell Patrick Jeffery is here, but he has a tail. I don't think he should see him."

Cathy nodded. "You mean the windbreaker in the corner drinking water?"

"Aye, that would be him..." Michael looked at Cathy and winked. "What can I get you, Jeffery? Your usual order?"

Jeffery nodded. "Yeah, two loaded burgers and fries. Jill loves the fries."

Cathy smiled and picked up a half-empty glass of beer. "I'll let Patrick know you're visiting but can't stay. I also plan on spilling this beer on your shadow."

Cathy danced across the floor as only a good waitress can.

Jeffery tried to keep track of her but lost her in the crowd. "She was kidding about spilling the beer?"

Michael grinned. "I think we'll know in a moment."

With that, a commotion broke out where the shadow was perched. A waitress could be seen trying to help the shadow wipe the beer off his windbreaker.

The telephone behind the bar rang. Michael turned to answer the phone; he looked back at Jeffery. "I'll bet it's for you." As he punched the button for the intercom, Jeffery could just barely hear him say, "Yes, he's here, hang on."

Michael handed the wireless phone to Jeffery. "Hello."

Patrick started pacing around the back room. "Jeffery, Cathy just told me you were out front. She said you have a tail?"

Jeffery turned to watch his shadow head for the restroom. "Yep, it seemed like a good idea to swap my car for your truck. But I didn't realize it came with an escort service. The local police stopped me right after we left the school parking lot. Luckily, I was able to convince them that I had borrowed your truck and that I was not the notorious Professor Ramirez."

Patrick felt old as the weight of this mess kept getting heavier. "I am sorry Jeffery, just leave the truck and take your car. You don't want to be involved in this. I'm afraid it's going to get very bad."

Jeffery stirred the lemon in his ice tea, trying to sink it unsuccessfully. "Patrick, I think you and the kids from this Tribunal project are going to need all the friends and help you can get. Besides, I rather enjoyed Cathy's beer baptism of my shadow."

 Patrick walked over to the door that led into the bar and looked through the peephole. "Cathy is a most resourceful young lady. But don't ever get on her bad side."

Patrick went back to pacing. "You really should get out while you can Jeffery. I've been watching the news, and the stuff Collins put in our laps is radioactive. Anyone near it is going to get burned."

Jeffery was trying to watch the door to the bathroom using the mirror behind the bar.

"Patrick, Jill's been watching the media coverage and says they make it sound like the Tribunal and this Collins kid were in cahoots—that all of you are suspected traitors or heroes. They just can't figure out *which*. I expect anyone who knows you will fall under scrutiny. Jill said we already have a car outside our house with a couple of guys watching."

Patrick could see Jeffery at the bar. "I am sorry. I shouldn't have sent that stuff to your office. Is it still in the truck?"

Jeffery spotted his shadow coming out of the bathroom. He was still trying to dry the windbreaker as he headed back to his perch. "It's in the back of the cab. I can't touch it without being seen by my shadow and his friends."

Patrick watched the shadow resume his perch. "Jeffery, I see your shadow has spent too much time sitting behind a desk. He sure doesn't blend in here. Why don't you slip Michael the truck keys and ask him to move the stuff and tell him what kind of car your shadow is driving."

"OK, hang on…" Jeffery took the phone from his ear and pulled his keys out of his pocket and laid them on the bar. "Michael, there is something in the back of Patrick's truck that he would like you to move."

Michael refilled Jeffery's ice tea and palmed the keys. "Be back in a minute. You said it was a black SUV your friend came in?"

Jeffery nodded. "Michael is going to get the stuff. How bad can it be?"

Patrick moved back to his seat and his coffee. "I don't know yet, but the amount of stir it's causing already is significant. I think we're going to need all of the friendly press and legal counsel we can scrounge."

Jeffery noticed his shadow was talking on his cell phone. "We better cut this short my shadow is on his cell phone and keeps looking at me. I think we might be getting company. You need to get out of here. I asked Jill to reach out to Jenny. She's probably at her cabin."

Patrick swirled the remaining coffee in the cup. He wondered just how black the next few days would be. "Thanks for reaching out to her, I was going to do that, but I've been busy trying to take care of my class. I still have to figure out what to do with the Collins boys."

Jeffery almost shouted but controlled himself to a slight whisper. "You have them here?"

Patrick drank the last of his coffee. "Yes, they showed up right after the Tribunal blew up. I have them in the back office. No one knows they're here but Michael and Cathy. I met with the rest of the class but felt it best to keep them out of the mix. When we finished, I sent the class home."

Jeffery looked in the bar mirror. The shadow was holding one hand to his ear trying to block the noise of the bar and talk on his cell phone. "Patrick, I think you need to get those boys and yourself out of here. I have a bad feeling this guy is calling for help."

Patrick got up and started looking around to see if he had left anything out. He knew Jeffery was right and they needed to move quickly. He thought to himself, "I guess we'll head towards Jenny's."

"Ok, I will see if I can get the boys out of here."

Michael returned to the bar and sat a *ToGo bag* in front of Jeffery. "I think you should go *now*."

> Michael reached for the phone. "Patrick, Michael said I should leave, I will try to make enough noise, so my shadow goes with me, but you need to go. Go to Jenny's cabin at the lake. I'll let her know you are coming and to expect guests."

He handed the phone back to Michael and placed a twenty on the counter. Jeffery picked up the keys, his order and headed for the door.

Michael took the phone. "Patrick I'm sending Cathy back, it's time to take your drunken friends home." He hung up the phone and waved at Cathy.

Patrick knocked lightly on the door to the office. William was sound asleep on the couch. Daniel had been dozing with his head on the desk. The plates were empty and stacked to one side on the floor. Daniel still had the imprint of his watch on his forehead. "Sorry, professor, I guess we fell asleep. What's going on?"

Cathy burst through the other door. "Good, you're awake. Now we need to get moving. Michael thinks we're about to be raided. We believe they're looking for all of you—at least that is what the news is saying. By the way Patrick, you're suspected of being a ringleader in this conspiracy against the Government."

Patrick started to turn on the little TV in the corner of the room.

"No time for that Patrick!" She tossed a hoodie at William

and an apron and ball cap at Daniel. "Daniel, you are going to take out a couple of bags of trash and then go to my car—it's the Red Camry directly across from the dumpster. Here are the keys."

"William, you are going to put on this hoodie and help me get your drunken buddy Dr. Ramirez to my car. Daniel when you see us come out. Start the car, and we will come to you. Once we get you all in my car get out of here. Michael suggested you go to Jenny's cabin. He and several others are trying to let her know you're coming."

Daniel had put on the apron, and as Cathy turned to head out the door, she stopped. "Give me your keys Patrick, Michael is going to take Jeffery's car. I will take Michaels car and if you need something, call my phone not his."

With that, she turned and headed to the back door. She pointed towards a couple of trash bags and shoved Daniel out the door. "As soon as you hear us coming out the door, duck down until we get him to the car. If anyone is watching they'll just see us loading a drunk and his friend into their car."

Daniel headed to the dumpster and tossed in the trash bags. Then he headed towards the back of the parking lot and the red Toyota. He clicked the unlock button on the car key and slipped in. As he looked around, he saw a couple of police cars parked in the empty lot three doors down.

The noise at the back door brought him back to the mission Cathy had given him. You could hear her talking as if she wanted everyone to know what they were doing. "Ok, Hon, let's get you to your car, you said it was the red one. Ok, now you take him home and don't let him drive." They opened the back door, and the professor crawled in. William slipped into the front seat and Daniel started the engine.

"Be careful," Cathy said as she closed the passenger door.

Daniel backed out of the parking spot, headed out the back of the parking lot into the alley. He turned away from the police cars and headed east.

Professor Ramirez peeked over the seat and whispered, "You are going the wrong way—we need to head west to the highway."

Daniel looked in his rearview mirror and saw The Whales parking lot was lighting up with red and blue lights as half dozen patrol cars and other cars with lights pulled into the parking lot. "I think we need to get away from here first, Professor."

William and Ramirez looked back at The Whales. The building was lit up by Police car headlights and spotlights. "It looks like they're going to storm the place." Daniel turned and looked at William. "Dude, can you imagine if they do that to Mom and Dad at the house?"

William sank lower into the seat. "Yeah if they do that, I just got disinherited."

Patrick shifted in the back seat and found the backpack and the laptop. "I guess Michael and Cathy took care of getting it out of my truck...Bless 'em for thinking. I almost forgot about it."

"Daniel, when you can, get on 35 going north. We will turn off at 157 and go east. How are we on gas?"

When they drove far enough from The Whales, Daniel turned back and headed towards 35. "We should be on the highway in a few minutes. Gas looks good—the tank is full."

Ramirez sat back in the seat. "Now if I could just call my wife and let her know we're ok."

William reached for his backpack. He dug around for a minute and handed Professor Ramirez a cell phone. "Here. He said I got used to carrying a couple of burner phones while I was making deals in D.C. It was easier to use one for a couple of deals and throw it away than worry about some whistleblower tracking me." William laughed. "Now, I am one of the whistleblowers. God has a real sense of humor Daniel—remember what mom used to say?"

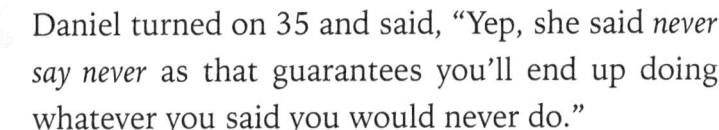 Daniel turned on 35 and said, "Yep, she said *never say never* as that guarantees you'll end up doing whatever you said you would never do."

Ramirez turned on the phone and began to dial his wife's cell phone. William turned to look at Ramirez. "I would keep the call short and then give it to me when you finish so I can take the chip out of it. I am sure they have put taps on everyone involved with the Tribunal by now. If nothing else, I can bet the *Back Nine* is pulling out all stops to find out what I have on them."

The phone rang in Ramirez's ear. He heard Anna Ramirez answer. "Hello?"

Patrick sighed as he heard her voice. She was always the port he turned to in a storm. Anna could look at any storm and see a guiding light through it. "Anna, it's me. I just have a minute, so bear with me. Everyone is ok, but I'm going to go somewhere and see if I can get my head wrapped around this..."

Anna was quiet. Patrick knew something was not right. "Professor Ramirez, you need to get back here right now, the police and Homeland Security are looking for you."

Ramirez was surprised as Anna never called him *Professor Ramirez* but quickly realized she must be trying to tell him they were listening into her call. "Anna, I will call you when I figure this out." He pressed the disconnect button on the phone and handed it to William.

"I think the police were listening to the call."

William pulled the phone open, took out the chip and tossed the phone out the window.

Patrick sat back in the seat. "Well that confirms it, we need a safe place to go and strategize what we need to do next. We need to recruit some help. I hope Jenny won't throw us out."

William looked out the window. "Well by now, anyone who is interested has downloaded the files I released at the

Tribunal. At least this way D.C. won't be able to block the information. The public will have the opportunity to decide if they have been fairly represented or not. D.C. won't be able to stop this from getting out."

Daniel was staying exactly at seventy miles an hour hoping not to attract any attention. "Won't they just block the servers you uploaded to and pull the files?"

William smiled. "Little brother, you know me better than that. I set it up to rebroadcast the files every twenty-four hours for the next two weeks. I figured I might need extra protection if this thing went south." Daniel chuckled. "Yeah you could say it *really* went south."

Professor Ramirez tried to get a feel for where they were. He caught the sign saying the 157 turn off was five miles ahead. "Daniel when you pull off on 157 you might let me drive—it will be easier for me to get us to where we're going."

Five minutes later, the red Camry exited 35 and at the top of the ramp two car doors opened, and Daniel and Ramirez switched places.

Ramirez turned on 157. "It's about a half an hour from here...William can you find a news station? We need to hear what they are saying."

William turned on the radio and began station hunting.

CHAPTER 14

Michael saw Cathy come out of the kitchen carrying a tray of food. She nodded as she went by mouthing the words, "They're gone." She reached the table associated with the tray of food she was carrying and had just put the last plate on the table when the front door burst open. The windbreaker teams began pouring in the door. FBI, Homeland Security, and local police entered with guns drawn.

Agent Patterson was yelling, trying to be heard over the music and general noise. Michael walked over to the volume control for the music and turned it off. Agent Patterson shouted, "We are looking for William Collins, his brother Daniel and a Professor Ramirez. If anyone has seen them, raise your hand so we can talk. Otherwise, stay seated as we're going to search the place."

Michael raised his hand as agent Patterson walked to the bar. "I'm the manager, and by now I am sure you know Professor Ramirez owns this joint. If you would you like me to walk you through the building, then maybe you won't have to kick down any doors as I have the keys to every door."

Patterson nodded. "That will work," he motioned to a couple of agents by the door to join him.

> Michael waved Cathy over. "Can you take over the bar so I can show these gentlemen the facilities? Oh, and Officer, do you think you could have your people put their guns away—it's hard to eat when someone is pointing a gun at you."

"It's agent, not officer. He waved at the other agents and officers to lower their guns.

"No one leaves until we check everyone's I.D."

Cathy, who just couldn't resist, smiled as she slipped behind the bar. "Well, that should be good for business. Do you think you can keep them here until breakfast?"

Patterson started to say something when Michael touched his arm. "Let's start with my office and the storerooms."

CHAPTER 15

THE COLLEGE SECURITY CHIEF HAD OFFERED Agent Tillis the use of a conference room on the first floor of the auditorium building to establish the Homeland Security command post. Tillis thanked the Security Chief for his cooperation and then proceeded to take over the entire first floor and the auditorium. The Security Chief had objected but lost to the needs of Homeland Security.

Agent Tillis and the various other agencies were busy setting up the command post and using every room available for the ever-growing number of agents pouring into town.

Tillis was exhausted. He hadn't slept in the last 36 hours. He stared at the board in front of him with the pictures of William Collins, his brother Daniel, Professor Ramirez and the other members of the Tribunal. The focus of last night had been to find William Collins. Then hopefully they would be able to stop the leak of sensitive information.

So far Tillis hadn't succeeded in apprehending William Collins or stopping the distribution of his files. Everyone in D.C. was letting him know how they felt about his failures by email, voicemail, and text.

At 6:00 AM Tillis changed the focus of the local investigation. Now, they were looking for anyone connected to the Tribunal with the hope they would lead them to Collins. The Campus Security office had offered to let Tillis use their camera network with their face recognition software to locate the Tribunal members. None of the Tribunal members had shown up at their dorms or their off-campus residences.

They had searched Professor Ramirez's office and his home. Both were now under surveillance. Agent Tillis's face still stung where Professor Ramirez wife had left her palm imprint. She had quite a right hand. One thing Tillis knew. Anna Ramirez was not going to help them find Professor Ramirez.

His phone rang. He looked at the caller I.D., closed his eyes and prayed for strength. Bracing himself, he pressed the answer button.

"Yes sir," he answered as the voice on the other end started the questions that Tillis knew he couldn't answer.

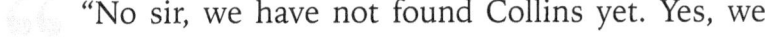"No sir, we have not found Collins yet. Yes, we

have everyone looking. Yes sir, the college has their security cameras running face recognition software. We hope to pick him up and the rest of the Tribunal team—especially his brother and Professor Ramirez."

"Yes sir, I know the information has been broadcasting every hour. We have people working on it. As soon as it shows up we are shutting down the site."

"Yes sir, I do know how serious this is. Yes sir, I have seen some of the material Collins has released. I am sure the Hill is very angry."

"Yes sir, I would expect the White House is also upset. No, I don't think that is necessary sir. We have almost a hundred people working on this. I am sure we will have Collins in custody soon."

"Yes sir, I will call you as soon as we know anything. Yes, I know how important it is that you hear about any arrests before the media..."

Tillis took the phone from his ear. He pressed the end button and wondered if this was also the end of his career. Fifteen years as an agent and here he was chasing college kids and a congressional aide. He wasn't chasing killers, terrorists, bank robbers...just a bunch of kids.

He resisted the desire to throw the phone and instead dropped it in his pocket.

Agent Patterson was walking towards him carrying two cups

of coffee. Patterson held out one of the cups and said, "Decaf with cream."

Tillis took the cup. "Thanks, I just got another motivational call from D.C. If we can't find Collins by noon, they are going to send in another team to help."

Patterson pulled up a chair and sat down. "So, by help you mean they show up and take over and tell us all of the things we should've done?"

Tillis looked out the window and wondered what his wife and kids were doing. "How are the troops holding up?"

Patterson kicked off his shoes. "You don't want to know. Most of our people are asking, '"why are we chasing this guy?"' Have you read any of the information this Collins guy sent out?"

Tillis looked over the room mentally calculating the agents that he could trust if this thing went farther south than it already had. "Yeah, I spent about an hour looking at it, and every one of our people has pretty much said the same thing. We're chasing the wrong ones."

Patterson looked around to be sure no one was close enough to overhear. He leaned forward and lowered his voice. "Brad, this stuff is bad. The press is howling as their analysts tear this stuff apart. The word treason against the American people is becoming a common description of our elected officials. They're starting to promote this Collins guy as a patriotic hero who had enough guts to stand up to the *D.C MOB.*"

Tillis nodded. "I know. We should be back in D.C. arresting everyone on the Hill associated with this and seizing records like mad."

Patterson swirled the last of his coffee. "Can you imagine how many shredders and hard drive failures Collins has caused? I can just see the rats running down the hallways from office to office just trying to find a safe place to hide!"

Tillis leaned forward. "Be very careful about your notes. We're going to have to be ready to deflect on this one. Make sure you have a backup of your notes. I'm back to a paper notepad and a voice transcript."

"Brad, we have worked together a long time, I think you need to record all the calls you get just in case. I'll have the guys set it up and record for your review only."

Tillis leaned forward so that the two of them could talk without being overheard. From a distance, it almost looked like they were praying.

"I am worried about what happens when we do catch this guy. Make sure everyone knows this guy is not dangerous. Don't let anyone shoot him. We need to be sure when he's in our hands he's alive."

Patterson looked around the room. "I thought about that.

Have we been assigned anyone new or is there anyone joining the hunt that might have a different set of rules?"

Tillis checked his watch and stood up. "It's time to check on the face recognition team. The students should be starting to stir. Hopefully, we'll get some results."

Tillis paused and looked around the room and then lowered his voice. "Watch and see if we get any help sent in that might not have the same objectives you and I have. You know what to look for. We should be able to spot anyone who might be problematic. Now let's go watch and see how the face monitoring is going."

They walked out of the conference room and down the hall to the video surveillance room. Tillis and Patterson were amazed at how this team could drop into almost anywhere and setup so much equipment in so little time and be fully functioning. It did help that the campus security and college staff had been able to get the camera feeds into them so quickly.

The monitor wall in front of Tillis was capturing facial images and running them through the face recognition software. Tillis spoke to the backs of the techs.

"How's it going, guys?"

A voice answered, "So far it looks like we're getting good shots of the students. The school has a lot of cameras in place. We don't have a lot of students up and moving yet, but that should start in the next fifteen minutes or so."

Another voice spoke, "Hey Tillis, when are you going to come over and help me set up my video game." There were several snickers from the techs.

"Funny guys, you know no one wants me to help with anything electronic. Now if you have some electronic thing you want me to shoot and put out of its misery, I'm your man."

One of the other techs shifted the team back to work. "We're also monitoring the school's email and the internet—the chatter is picking up—the whole school knows we're here and watching. If the Internet chatter is accurate, the school will be a drug-free zone for a while. There seems to be a lot of stuff being flushed down the toilets in the dorms."

Tillis watched the monitors as the students started moving to their first class.

> Another voice spoke, "They know we are watching. Some guy named Gator has sent out a tweet to tell everyone the Feds are watching. He has declared it the day of the Hoodie."

Another voice from the far side of the room commented, "It looks like the hoodie notice is going viral—the internet traffic just spiked."

Tillis looked at Patterson. "It's going to be a long day."

Patterson turned to walk with Tillis as he started for the door. Tillis called out as he was walking. "Keep me posted if this hoodie thing catches on and if you need help call Patterson. I'm busy."

"Will do," echoed from several voices.

Patterson followed Tillis into the hallway. "Brad, we need to look up this guy Gator and see if he is connected. The last thing we need is for the students to rally behind this hoodie thing. A demonstration of support for this Collins guy is not going to help us find him."

Tillis leaned against the wall for a minute. He soaked up the cool feeling of the tile on the wall. A fleeting thought of a soft tropical breeze and a remote beach passed through his thoughts. "Keep an eye on this and let me know what you find. I'm going to see the Campus Security Chief and maybe the school Administrator. We need to get them to help us keep this thing calm. Call me if you get anything."

Tillis walked out the door of the auditorium towards a campus security car that had parked in front of the auditorium. He could see the Chief of Campus Security talking with one of his agents at the top of the stairs.

CHAPTER 16

LIZ TYLER WAS HIDING IN HER OFFICE. HER STAFF had surrounded her blocking phone calls, reporters, a myriad of lobbyist, and supporters who wanted to talk to her.

Her staff was starting to show the effects of the ongoing pressure. Three of her key staff had resigned. The rats were deserting the ship. The three that had left all had inside knowledge of deals and meetings which would be damaging and inconvenient if that information came to light right now. Liz called on the intercom and asked someone to get her another cup of coffee. Her cell phone rang. She looked at the caller ID. It was her husband, probably whining about how much money he was going to lose. She pressed the answer button and put the phone to her ear. "Yes George, what is it?"

Liz and her husband shared the marriage that many of the

D.C. insiders had developed. It was a marriage of convenience and photo ops. They shared two children that they drug out for photos and special events. Then they put them back in school and let the schools look after them.

> George sounded panicked. "Liz, the house is surrounded by reporters. I called my office, and Cindy said reporters keep showing up there looking for me.

"When are you going to get this thing fixed? My phone is constantly ringing. People are canceling their contracts with us and saying they don't want any part of this scandal. What did you do?"

Liz looked at her fingernails. She had chewed the polish off of her nails and ruined her manicure. Her stomach was screaming as a staff member walked in with two cups of coffee. Liz nodded thanks and waved him out of the room. "George, there is nothing I can do. If you think you're surrounded, you should come over here. The Hill is crawling with reporters, lobbyists and everyone that didn't have anything to do but come and protest government corruption."

"There is nothing I can do, stay home, and stay off the phone. Don't talk to anyone. Do you understand?"

"Liz, I'm going to be ruined," George whined, "I called our attorney, and his secretary told me he would get back to me. What are we going to do? The kids called and said the school suggested they come home. I don't need them here right now —we have enough to deal with."

Liz took a sip of the coffee which was hot and burned her mouth. Her stomach growled as she dumped more acid into an already overloaded acidic stomach.

She wondered again why she ever married George—he was such a coward. He had been easy to manipulate and had served her well as the photo op for her career. He was kind of like the big dumb dog they had adopted to show their support for abused animals. Of course, the housekeeper took care of the dog, and he was never allowed anywhere but the kitchen and laundry room. Oh, how she wished she could let the housekeeper take care of George the same way.

"George, you need to send the kids to your mother's. We don't want them being questioned by the press. Just tell your mother to keep them out of sight. Don't make any more calls —just sit tight. I'm trying to work this out."

George had gone over to the window and peeked out from behind the drapes. "Liz, you need to call *her* and get some help. Get *her* or the *Back Nine* to do something. You guys are always making deals—*do* something."

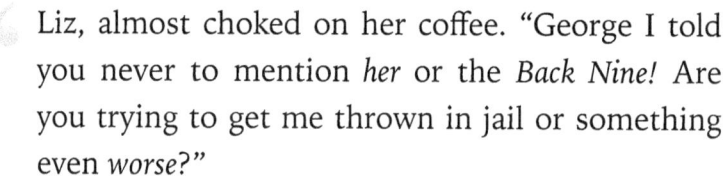

Liz, almost choked on her coffee. "George I told you never to mention *her* or the *Back Nine!* Are you trying to get me thrown in jail or something even *worse?*"

"Do not ever mention *her* or the *Back Nine* again...especially on the phone. My God, what if we're being recorded?"

George began looking around the room. "Do you think they bugged the house? *She* wouldn't do that, would *she*? I didn't do anything but what you said we should do—I don't want to go to jail."

Liz resisted the urge to throw the coffee against the wall, but instead sat it down on her desk and pulled out her crisis voice as she spoke to George. "George, I want you to hang up the phone. I will send one of my staff to sit with you. Let them handle the calls. Just go watch TV. Don't email or even look at your email. I will take care of this, and we will be fine. But don't ever mention *her* again or the *Back Nine*. Can you do this George?"

George seemed to calm down just enough to respond. "Ok Liz, I'll wait here. Maybe Juanita can make me a sandwich." Liz rolled her eyes. George's answer to any crisis was a sandwich and excessive amounts of beer.

Liz continued in her special events voice. "That's good Honey, just stay off the phone, I have to go. Remember what I said..." Liz hung up the phone and pressed the intercom button on her office phone. Janice her longtime secretary answered. "Janice, how bad is it out there?"

Janice looked around the room so she could judge what volume her voice needed to be so the staff didn't overhear her. She smiled a reassuring smile at a young intern sitting across the room. The intern was texting someone and crying.

Janice lowered her voice. "Liz, it's not good. The staff is barely holding off the wolves. We've had to call security four times already. Several of the interns have called in sick. The few left look like they won't make it past lunch. Outside of that, what can I do for you, Senator?"

Liz smiled. Janice had been with her a long time. She knew where most of the bodies had been buried along the campaign trail. She also knew who could talk to Liz and who had to be stalled or passed off to one of the handlers. "I need someone to go babysit George before he does something more stupid than normal."

Janice looked around the room and sighed as the mental list of staffers rolled through her head. "Maybe Bill? He could use a break from the front line, and George likes him."

Liz had sat down at her computer and started looking over her inbox. "Bill will work. Tell him to go in the back door at the house and keep George off the phone. If he needs anything have him call me."

Liz, stopped, her eyes focusing on one email in particular. "Take care of it Janice I have to make a call, I just got an email from *her*."

Janice was a survivor. She recognized it was time to step aside. Few things had scared her in her journey with Liz. But, Liz's involvement with the *Back Nine* and any contact with *her* was enough to make anyone seek asylum in another country.

"I'll get Bill out the door—good luck on your call." Janice hung up the phone and stared at it.

Janice had always been able to smell trouble. That call smelled of a bad ending.

Janice looked at the door and wondered if she should retire. The last thing she wanted was to end up on the wrong side of the table during an investigation. There is no way to win one of those fights. Maybe she should check her "hole cards" when she got home. She liked Liz, but she liked being home with her grandkids more. From the looks of things, grandkids were a better option.

CHAPTER 17

SENATOR SHERATON HAD DECIDED IT WAS BETTER to work from home today. He looked out the window and saw the expected group of reporters waiting to catch him if he left his house.

He looked at his email. Well, it seemed like the Titanic was taking water and everyone he knew was trying to find out just how long it would be until they sank.

He had shipped his wife and son off late last night, sending them to her parent's home to wait out the storm. No sense putting them in the line of fire if he could help it.

His cell phone vibrated again. He had lost count of the voice messages and texts. He picked it up to see who it was this time. He read the simple message.

"Call me. I need to know where we are."

The caller ID just read *blocked*. He opened his desk drawer and took out a new burner phone. It was one of those *she* had given him. Sheraton plugged in the SIM card and powered up the phone. He only had two more phones left. He would need to get more as he was sure this mess was not going to be something that ended quickly.

Sheraton looked at the bar in his office. He kept a well-stocked bar for his visitors. Few of them knew he had quit drinking years ago. He kept a bottle filled with tea, so it looked like he was joining them, but he hadn't had a drink in five years.

He dialed the phone and said, "Heres to one more day sober." The phone rang twice. *She* answered, "How may I help you?" It was the safe way for *her* to answer the phone. Anyone calling *her* would either know *her* number or would identify themselves immediately. It was all part of the plausible deniability that they had so carefully constructed.

Sheraton responded, "It's me, Sheraton."

There was a very awkward moment of silence as he heard *her* shut a door. "Have you stopped the leak yet?"

 Sheraton could feel *her* presence through the phone, and even though he had only met *her* once, that was enough. There were many rumors about *her*, but those were only spoken in very low voices. Anyone who knew *her* was afraid of *her*.

"We have everyone in every law enforcement agency looking for Collins. We have our best IT guys trying to get ahead of his timed data releases. He seemed to know we would be looking for his releases on the hour, so early this morning he shifted patterns."

She cut through the rest of his defense. "So, you have nothing?" Sheraton waited afraid to say anything. "Very well, we will add some help to your efforts."

Sheraton wanted no part of *her* help. The only kind of help *she* ever offered was the type where no one survived. "Just give us till noon—I'm sure we will have Collins in custody by then."

The silence was chilling. Sheraton started to sweat, waiting for her to respond. "Very well, you have until noon. I will advise the President, so he can have his press secretary make a statement." Sheraton had been holding his breath as *she* responded. "Thank you. I will let you know as soon as we have anything."

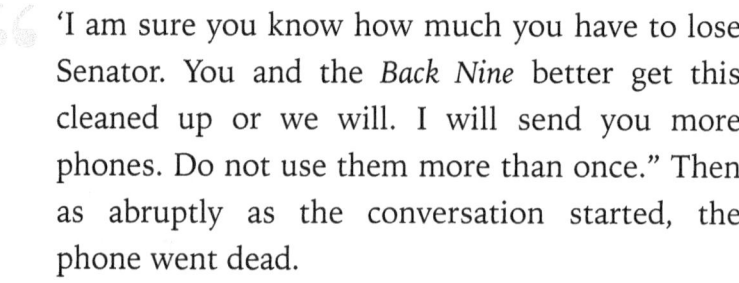

'I am sure you know how much you have to lose Senator. You and the *Back Nine* better get this cleaned up or we will. I will send you more phones. Do not use them more than once." Then as abruptly as the conversation started, the phone went dead.

Sheraton sat just holding the phone. Why had he ever let himself get drawn into working with *her*? He took the phone apart and removed the SIM card. He ran it through the shredder behind his desk as instructed and then placed the burner phone in a mailbag. He would drop it in a mailbox next time he went out. Those were the instructions he had received with the phones, and he was very careful to follow them. Sheraton looked around the room and wondered if he should have it swept for electronic bugs again. Last time they swept the room, he was told they found nothing, and then *she* told him never to do that again.

With the noon deadline to locate Collins racing towards him, Sheraton picked up his other phone and began dialing. It was time to share the pressure.

CHAPTER 18

JENNY DROVE UP TO HER LAKE HOUSE. IT WAS A place she spent as much time as she could. It was peaceful, out of the way and a place where she liked to work. As she drove up, she saw a car parked under the carport. She didn't recognize the car. Being cautious she pulled off the road where she could watch the house. Having a house away from everyone and everything had advantages, but it also had disadvantages. Over the years, Jenny had made some enemies by reporting on things that some wanted to remain undiscovered. Those reports had caused her a couple of close calls.

After a couple of threats, one of her friends who had worked on some undisclosed operations had taught her how to use firearms. She had gone through all the classes, including a couple of self-defense classes. She was cautious. Jenny picked up her cell phone and called the lake house. She was still old school in that she liked having a real phone at this house. The phone rang three times. A voice that was easy to recognize answered. "Hello?"

Jenny sighed. "Patrick, if you are going to hide out, you need to work on disguising your voice. I assume the car in the carport belongs to you?"

"Yes, I was just making coffee." Patrick peeked out the front door.

Jenny started the car. "Hang up the phone I'll be right there."

Jenny pulled the car into the second spot under the carport. She got out and triggered the trunk release.

Patrick and two others joined him as they walked out the side door. Jenny looked at William and said, "Grab the groceries and my bag gentlemen. Then you can tell me what trouble you are in and I can decide if I want to play in this mess that you've made."

William picked up a bag and handed it to Daniel. With groceries and her bags in hand, they entered the kitchen.

Jenny took her bags and headed towards her bedroom. "If one of you were using my bedroom, I'm pulling rank and kicking you out. The rest of you put the groceries away and pour me a cup of coffee with a little cream."

Ramirez started to follow her, apologizing as they went down the hall.

Once in her room and out of earshot, Jenny threw her bag on the bed. "Is that the Collins kid half the world is looking for?"

Patrick needed a shave and a fresh change of clothes. He hadn't slept, and he was starting to worry about what he should do. "Yes, and the other one is his brother who was heading the Tribunal project where this thing erupted. I didn't know where to go with them. Jeffery suggested you, and naturally, we just drove up here to wait for you."

Jenny opened her bag and started putting clothes away. "How did you know I would come here?"

"Michael was supposed to call you and let you know we were coming." Patrick sat on the edge of the dresser looking down the hall to be sure the boys were still in the kitchen.

Jenny nodded. "Yeah, I got the call. I was just checking to make sure I know everything before I jump in this river. Remind me to get even with Jeffery later. What do you want to do with these two? Right now, the three of you are on all the latest wanted lists. They say they are searching for you in regard to National Security interests."

> "I know, and I am sorry for involving you in this. I just needed some time to think this out and help these boys build a defense." Patrick stood up and followed Jenny down the hall.

As Jenny reached the kitchen, Daniel handed her a cup of

coffee and offered to pour the cream he was holding in his other hand.

Jenny took the cup and nodded as Daniel poured the cream. "Enough. I still like to taste the coffee." Grabbing a steno pad and a pencil, she headed for the kitchen table. "Ok boys, tell me a story..."

For the next hour, Ramirez and the Collins brothers told her as much as they could remember. Jenny took notes and cross-examined them on several points.

After an hour, Jenny sat back and realized her coffee cup was empty. While walking to get another cup, she looked at William and asked, "How damaging is the information you posted on the internet?"

William got up and retrieved his laptop and an external hard drive. He sat it on the table and plugged them in. As the laptop booted, he said, "I think it's the worst collection of back deals anyone in this country has ever seen. I've been negotiating for Senator Liz, and on behalf of a secret group, they call the *Back Nine*. I can't even tell you how far reaching this stuff is. I was in the middle of most of the deals. Most of what I negotiated was not good for the American People."

Jenny had returned to the table with a fresh cup of coffee and pulled the laptop in front of her. She was quiet for a couple of minutes while she scanned the various files and emails.

Finally, she sat back and pushed the laptop away from her and looked at it as if it would bite.

"Patrick, you need to get legal counsel immediately. You are going to need all the legal protection you can muster. If half of what I am seeing is true, nobody in D.C. is going to want you guys found alive."

Daniel looked at his brother. "They wouldn't kill us for this would they?"

William pushed back from the chair and started pacing. "I didn't mean for anyone to get hurt, I just kept brokering deals, and they just kept getting bigger and darker. No one was ever supposed to find out what we were doing."

Jenny cut through the drama. "What did you think was going to happen when this came out?"

William turned to face her. "I never thought it would come out. I was as involved as everyone, but then that damn deer ran in front of the car, and Shelly was hurt, and I don't know...I just heard a voice asking me if I could live with what I had been doing."

Jenny looked at Patrick. "I think we need to be sure he doesn't mention hearing voices again. If anyone picks up on that, he is going to wind up in some hospital practicing better living by prescription for the rest of his life."

Patrick nodded. "William, I would leave the part about hearing a *voice* out of future statements. Just let them know you had a change of heart or that you felt compelled to come clean."

Patrick looked at Jenny. "I asked Michael to reach out to Ben Langley and see if he would consider helping."

Jenny smiled. She liked Ben they had all been friends for years before their careers had led them down different paths.

As if on cue a vehicle pulled up in front of the house. Jenny headed for the door. "You guys head to the back room—*now*."

Jenny opened the door and watched as a young man in a windbreaker got out of the car. Everything about him announced he was law enforcement. The young man asked, "Are you Jenny Albright?"

Jenny was not easily intimidated. "Who are you and why do you want to know?"

The back door of the SUV opened, and a tall, lanky man in a sports coat stepped out. "Nice to see you haven't changed."

Jenny stepped off the porch and headed to the car. "Ben, how did you find us?"

Ben hugged her and then pushed her back. "You are slipping. You just admitted you have company."

Jenny punched Ben in the arm. "You will never change, and I'm glad you don't." She took his arm, and they headed for the door to the cabin. The other two car doors opened, and two more people followed them towards the house. Jenny looked over her shoulder. "I think we're going to need more food. I wasn't counting on a party."

Ben patted her hand. "I believe that we are going to need a lot of things to help us get through this *if* what I have read is any indication. I brought some of my staff to help. They are all used to a good fight, although this one may be one for the history books if we don't all disappear. Is Patrick here?"

Jenny pushed through the front door with the rest following. "Patrick, it's Ben and company. Better bring out the boys, and I'll make some more coffee and iced tea. It's going to be a long day."

Jenny turned to the driver. "You might want to put the car out of sight. Pull it under the trees. It will be harder to see in case we get visitors."

The driver looked at Ben. "That's a good idea, David. Move the car out of sight." Ben looked around the front room. "Jenny is it ok to set up in here?" Jenny looked at Parick, and the Collins boys and shook her head yes. "My house is your office. We're going to need more coffee." Jenny headed to the kitchen mumbling. "So much for a peaceful weekend."

Ben, laughed. "David, see what you can do to help Jenny but watch out, she will put you to work. Now, let's get moving. I have a feeling we are going to be very busy."

David nodded and headed out the door to move the car. The other two were unpacking laptops and hunting for electrical outlets. They had set up on the couch using the coffee table for a desk.

Jenny smiled. "The outlets are just behind the couch. Plenty of electric—I like to plug in where ever I sit." She turned to Ben. "Not their first rodeo, is it?"

Ben smiled. "They have been with me for a while."

Patrick and the boys came into the kitchen area. Ben walked over to Patrick. Patrick was overwhelmed and hugged Ben. "Thank you. I wasn't sure you would come."

Ben held Patrick at arm's length and looked at him. "I owe you so much, how could I not come? Now introduce me and let's see what we have to work with."

Jenny and David took turns bouncing in and out of the kitchen bringing food and drinks. David seemed to have many talents—one being a great cook. They had been going at it for hours, and now that it was dark, Ben stood up and said, "I think we need to try and get some sleep. In the morning, we should consider making a deal for you three to turn yourselves in at a press conference. That way we can get as much public exposure as possible."

Ben turned to his two assistants, Diane and Walt, and said, "See if you can draft something up that we can go over in the morning. Once we've had some sleep, we should be able to finalize our first public move."

Jenny was handing out bunk assignments and blankets. "It's going to be close quarters, and one or two of you might end up on the floor." Jenny was pushing the boys to the sun porch and a couple of couches.

Patrick waited until the boys were out of earshot. "How bad is it Ben?"

Ben looked at Diane and Walt. "What do you guys think?"

Diane took off her reading glasses. "I've read about half the files from Collins. If the public takes it seriously and any of the media pursues the information, at least half of D.C. will be facing prosecution for a long list of offenses. You might even make a case for several of those mentioned that have been making deals with leaders in other countries to be tried for treason."

Walt sat back on the couch. "Diane is right. If what we are reading in Mr. Collins files is accurate. I'd expect at least half of the existing members of Congress and their staffs are looking at the threat of prosecution on numerous counts. It also looks like most of those at the top of the Department of Health, Education, and the others will be seeking deals to protect themselves. The next election could see over half of the Congress replaced."

And the White House appears so deeply entangled, they won't be able to deny their involvement. There is so much evidence. I don't know how anyone at the White House will survive the investigations. This could cause an overthrow of the government if the people get behind it..."

Diane picked up from Walt. "The trick will be for us to keep this public and not let them hide the evidence or Collins. It is going to be very bad for a while. Are you sure you want to take this on Ben?"

Ben looked at Patrick and asked, "What do you want to do? I won't kid you. It will be expensive and probably the worst fight of our lives. I'll want you to help as legal counsel. I know you have things in your past that we can't discuss in open court, but just knowing you are helping represent the boys and yourself should cause some of those other secret keepers to wake up and maybe help."

Patrick did not talk about his life before being a Law Professor. Few people had any idea what he had done. Patrick stood up. "I will need to speak with Anna. I am sure she will agree, but I owe her that. I won't leave these boys to the wolves or the rest of my class for that matter. I won't let them be destroyed for doing what is right."

Ben turned to David. "Can you get a phone in Anna's hands so Patrick can talk to her?"

David nodded. "It will take a couple of hours. Do you want me to deliver it, or one of the staff we left in town?"

Ben got up to stretch. "Have Mindy do it. She can pose as a neighbor or friend and penetrate the screen around Anna."

"Let's have Mindy drop by first thing in the morning." He looked at David. "Pastries and a shoulder to lean on?"

David nodded and reached for his phone.

Jenny was standing in the doorway with more blankets.

"Diane, I can give you your own room, or you can share the bed with me. The boys can fight over the last three beds and two couches in here."

Diane stood up. "Thank you. I could use a little sleep." She shut down her laptop and followed Jenny to the back.

Ben headed down the hall towards one of the other bedrooms.

Patrick walked outside—he needed to think and pray. He was about to make a decision that would impact all their lives. Most people who knew him never thought of him as a believer in anything but the law. He had often been baited by students to get him into a discussion of is there a God or not. Patrick would listen to their questions and then quietly point out, "Who and What you believe is a right I will defend. What I believe is personal. Someday when we die, we will all know one way or another if there is a God." But right now, Patrick was going to seek counsel from a higher authority.

CHAPTER 19

BACK AT THE CAMPUS, TILLIS AND PATTERSON HAD gone to a local restaurant to find something to eat that didn't come wrapped in foil or a Styrofoam container. Tillis picked at his spaghetti and meatballs. Patterson watched him push the meatball around the bowl. "At least it's not fried…"

Tillis smiled and put the fork down. "Thanks for dragging me out of there. I couldn't decide if I should shoot the Campus Security Chief or myself. Can you believe we may have triggered the first nationwide hoodie protest?"

Patterson laughed for the first time in a couple of long days. "I wish you could have seen your face when he told you they had banned hoodies on campus. What did it take, a half an hour before everyone was wearing a hoodie and protesting the face recognition cameras?"

"And then the reporter who was shooting his local color shot with you guys in the background—that was priceless."

Tillis smiled he liked working with Patterson. He could always find something to laugh at, even if it was himself.

> "How well do you think it went over in D.C. when that reporter said the students were outraged over being told they could not wear a hoodie on campus?

"I thought that was awesome when that reporter looked into the camera and said, '"Sometimes we just have to support what's right."' Then he pulled the hoodie over his head and walked over to the Campus Security Chief." Thank God, I pulled you out of there before the Campus Security Chief went off on the reporter.

Patterson leaned forward. "Just remember, I saved your career when I pulled you out of camera range. The only thing that reporter captured was the Security Chief!"

Tillis smirked. "Thanks, now can you pull me out of this mess?"

Patterson shook his head. "I've had a dozen calls that the Hoodie protest is now nationwide. I got a call from the New York office. They said the Mayor was livid as the whole town seemed to be wearing hoodies. In fact, the newly printed hoodie says, 'Support the Collins Tribunal.'"

Tillis looked at his plate. "I'm going to get fired or shipped off to Afghanistan to draw fire if this thing doesn't turn around soon."

"I know it's bad. My phone stopped ringing an hour ago."

Patterson looked up and saw one of the agents waving them to come outside. "Looks like something is up. Portland is waving at us to come outside. You go, I'll get this stuff wrapped and take care of the check."

Tillis nodded, grabbed his phone, and headed for the door. He heard Patterson tell the waitress to wrap up the leftovers.

 Agent Portland from the FBI was waiting outside. He smiled at Tillis. "Thought you might like to know that the Hoodie movement is nationwide. Our Chief of Campus Security has issued a campus-wide ban on wearing hoodies."

Tillis' shoulders dropped. "Patterson has already informed me this is now a nationwide protest."

Portland nodded. "You bet. In fact, the reporter who covered the hoodie interview with the Chief is now wearing one of the new *Support the Collins Tribunal* hoodies. Since it aired during the dinner hour, it's gone national."

"It's a good thing Patterson pulled you out of camera range, or you would be joining the Chief in notoriety."

Tillis started walking back to the auditorium as Patterson joined them. Portland filled him in as they walked. After Patterson was done laughing, Tillis asked, "Has anyone heard from the school administration? Surely they won't let this guy continue with the ban?"

Portland seemed to be wired into the local events. "Already checked and the Dean is letting it stand for now as they wish to appear as if they are cooperating with law enforcement."

"Oh, I also got a report that when they announced the "Hoodie Ban," the local internet chatter went off the wall. There are rumblings of another protest tomorrow. Some guy named Gator showed up in the chatter. Apparently, he's pretty wired in, and the chatter is hitting every college across the country. Tomorrow should be fun."

They entered the building tactfully avoiding the Campus Security Chief's car. Tillis took off his jacket and hung it on the back of his chair. "Patterson, figure out who we have that is savvy enough to talk to the press if this thing comes up. We need a story that this is a local call and not something that the Feds are behind. I know we will get blamed for it, but let's try to be ready to deflect if we can."

Patterson nodded. "Let me talk to Rebecca Stinson. She is one of the best info spinners we have. She should be able to wrap this around the Security Chiefs neck and make everyone believe he beats puppies, hates children and Christmas while she convinces the media we support the students, the flag, and motherhood."

Tillis' phone rang. He picked it up and saw who was calling. His stomach tried to reject his half-eaten dinner. "That sounds good, try to keep me up on this new event. I have to take this."

Tillis answered, "Yes director, what can I do for you?"

The call was fairly one-sided. The director asked all of the usual questions that occur during any investigation.

"Where are we?"

"Why haven't you caught them yet?"

"What is taking so long?"

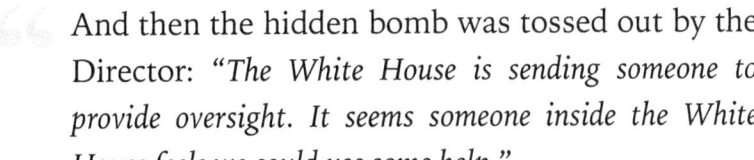 And then the hidden bomb was tossed out by the Director: *"The White House is sending someone to provide oversight. It seems someone inside the White House feels we could use some help."*

Tillis knew that his career had just turned over and was spiraling out of control. "Do we know who is coming?"

The director's voice softened. "Brad, I know you are doing everything you can, but this mess is going to leave a lot of casualties. The call I got said *she* and the President are not happy. They are sending a personal liaison to provide direct feedback to the White House. I am sure the President isn't picking the person, and I only hear rumors where *she* is concerned. Just give them whatever they want and keep me informed."

"You can't believe the impact these files are having. How much of them have you read?"

Tillis looked at the growing stack of paper on his desk and the floor. As each document printed, someone was going over it and providing a briefing page by page. The result was the growing pile of paper staring back at him. "I've only read a dozen or so, and that's enough to launch a couple of decades of investigations."

The Director sniffed, and Tillis could hear him blowing his nose. "I started keeping track of the retirements and sudden leaves of absence. We are at twenty-two retirement announcements and about thirty requests for a leave of absence. I understand if you walk through the Hill, all you can hear are shredders working round the clock. I have a feeling it is going to get really bad here in D.C. The Attorney General is supposed to make an announcement tomorrow. The White House keeps saying that they are keeping up on the investigation."

"Watch your back and let me know who shows up."

The director hung up before Tillis could respond.

CHAPTER 20

JENNY TRIED TO SLEEP, BUT THE FILES KEPT calling to her. She would get up and read a couple of Collins' files. Then she would get tired and try to sleep. Then she would roll over and have to go read another file and so the night drug on, a little nap, another file until 6:30 AM.

Jenny got up, took a shower and quietly moved to the kitchen to start fixing breakfast. There were bodies everywhere trying to sleep. She doubted anyone was getting any rest, but as they woke up, she would at least try to get them all fed. She looked in the fridge and calculated how much food she had on hand and how many mouths she needed to feed. Well, a little of this and a little of that she could probably stretch breakfast, but someone was going to have to go pick up stuff for lunch.

She got the coffee pot going and turned on the kettle for the tea drinkers. She never understood tea, whether it was supposed to be iced or hot.

She started to cut potatoes when she saw car lights coming down the road. She turned off the kitchen lights and moved to the window.

Ben's SUV pulled up in front of the house, and David stepped out. He walked to the back and opened the tailgate. Jenny met him at the door, speaking in whispers, "I wondered who it was…for a second I thought we were going to be raided." She took a grocery bag from David.

> "Sorry Mam, I just figured with this many people, you were going to need a lot more food. My *momma* would have handed me a grocery list and tossed me out the door. I guess I just did what she taught me."

Jenny sat the grocery bag down and looked at David. "I like your Momma. She trained you right."

David blushed. "Thank you, Mam. I have a couple of more bags in the car."

Jenny began unpacking the groceries as David brought in four more bags.

"David, what time did you get up?"

David helped Jenny unpack and sort the groceries. He

seemed to sense what she needed and handed it to her. "I don't sleep a lot Mam. I rolled over around five and figured Ben would want to get a phone in Patrick's wife's hand first thing. So I drove into town and made a few calls." He grinned. "I did wake, Mindy—she wasn't very happy—but she should be at Professor Ramirez's home around eight with pastries and a phone."

Jenny stopped and looked at David. "Can I adopt you or are you stuck working for Ben?"

David began cutting onions to go with the potatoes. "I like working for Mr. Langley. I see gaps and fill them in for him. He says I just seem to know what the team needs before they do. I like working with him and the team."

Jenny smiled. David was rare, a young man that knew his gifts and how to use them. He would be the type of asset anyone would treasure. "So, I'm guessing your Momma taught you to cook. What did you plan to feed this crowd?"

"I know pretty much what the team eats. So that means Mr. Langley is partial to bacon, Diane likes a frittata with potatoes, onions and sausage and Walt will eat anything. Is there anything you think we should fix?"

Jenny turned on the oven. "Tell you what, I'll start a batch or two of biscuits and help with whatever you need…"

David smiled. "Yes Mam, I could use some of those gypsy peppers cut up for the frittata."

Jenny pulled out a mixing bowl and began the biscuits. "I will get on that as soon as I get the biscuits in the oven."

The next hour was spent passing out coffee, tea, and juice as Jenny's houseguests began to wake and head towards the breakfast smells coming from the kitchen.

CHAPTER 21

MINDY MATTHEWS WALKED DOWN THE STREET towards the Ramirez home. She noted two different vehicles with people sitting in them. She smiled as she passed the one vehicle. A quick glance in the car and it was easy to see the two people inside had been there a long time. The seat was tilted back for the one who was trying to nap. The other was making notes and had several empty cups stacked in the cup holder.

Mindy had noted the license number and repeated it so David could hear. David's voice carried through the cell phone headset. "Nice to see our government employees are working hard."

Mindy laughed. "David, you know what surveillance is like…" She turned and walked up the path to the Ramirez front door. "Better get the Professor on the line, it will help for her to hear his voice."

Mindy knocked on the door and pulled the little sign from under the pastry box. To anyone watching she was just a neighbor in her jogging outfit taking pastries to a neighbor.

Anna Ramirez opened the door. Mindy held the sign up in front of the pastries.

"Hi Anna, I was so sorry to hear about all of the problems on the campus."

> She waved the sign carefully, and Anna looked at it and read: *Patrick asked me to bring you a phone. Invite me in. He is on the line and wants to talk to you.*

Anna was slightly confused and waved Mindy inside. Mindy stopped and hugged Anna for the those watching and then went through the door. She whispered, "We have an audience —act like I am an old friend so we can sell this."

Anna was a quick learner. She hugged Mindy back and almost yelled, "Thanks for dropping by! Would you like something to drink?"

Anna closed the door, and Mindy handed the cell phone earpiece to Anna. "Patrick is on the phone. Here is the burner phone, put this in your pocket and let's go to the kitchen."

Anna stuck the earpiece in her ear and whispered, "Patrick?"

Mindy was already in the kitchen opening the pastry box and looking for a plate to put them on.

Anna had followed her and almost stopped as the earpiece filled with a worried voice. "Anna, it's me. Mindy works for Ben Langley. Hes going to be our attorney and is helping me sort out this mess. Are you Ok?"

Anna sat down at the counter. Mindy handed her a cup of coffee and placed a plate in front of her. She whispered, "Act like you're talking to me and eat something."

Anna nodded. "Patrick, what is going on. Are you safe? Where are you? How did Ben find you?" Anna caught Mindy's gestures to slow down. Mindy winked at Anna and mouthed, "Take a deep breath, relax."

 Patrick started his defense statement to Anna. "Babe, it's going to take a while to figure this all out. Ben did not want me to call you direct as we're sure you are being watched and probably monitored."

Anna smiled at Mindy and took a pastry as she continued her part of the play.

"You bet they're watching. I spotted two cars this morning when I went out to get the paper. The Dean has called twice looking for you, and I quit answering the phone unless I know who it is. Your students are in a panic if the messages left on the phone are any indication of their mental state. And some idiot was looking over the fence from the house behind us trying to take pictures. I squirted him with the garden hose."

Patrick stepped outside to sit on Jenny's porch. It was quieter out here, and he just needed a little privacy. "I'm sorry Honey. It wasn't Roger that you squirted was it?"

"No Patrick, it wasn't Roger."

"Ok." Patrick knew he needed to get back on track even if the image of Anna hosing down the neighbors was an image he would'nt be able to forget.

"I don't know what we're going to do. Ben and his staff are working on a plan. He's going to call Peter and advise him what is happening so Peter can communicate directly with you as our personal attorney. That should help if you need to get a hold of me."

Anna couldn't taste the cherry tart she was eating. It was just a mechanical act. She caught the flash of light as the idiot behind their house tried to hide his camera. Anna looked at Mindy and then at the patio door. Mindy nodded, saw the neighbor and quickly was out of her seat and out of the neighbor's field of vision. The drapes swept shut, and Mindy smiled and returned to her seat.

"Patrick, are we in danger? I've been reading the files the Collins kid released, and they are staggering. It seems like most of D.C. should be in jail."

Patrick looked out across the little lake. No wonder Jenny liked it here, it was peaceful. "I'm afraid that the genie is out of the bottle. We've been looking at the files and talking to William."

Anna stood up and caught herself breaking character. "Patrick, are you with the Collins kid? My God, half the world is looking for him! They're calling him everything from a patriotic whistleblower to a terrorist out to take down D.C."

Anna moved to the sink and filled a glass with water. She knew by the reaction her stomach was having to her third cup of coffee and the sugar in the pastry it was time to switch.

Patrick could sense Anna was on the move. When she got excited, she would start moving, cleaning, picking up, and placing things in order. It was her way of coping. "Yes, I am actually with both of the Collins boys. It seems the three of us have been lumped together, for better or worse. The media is connecting the Tribunal Project to this as well. It seems some creative media types have thrown out the idea that the Tribunal was a ploy to get this information out and that we are all part of a grand conspiracy to take down the Government."

"I fear this is going to be a life-changing event. You need to let the kids know I am ok and they should go on the defense. No comments and stick to that as the only course of action for now."

Anna took a pad from the desk in the kitchen. She started writing down the names, phone numbers, and addresses of their two children. She wrote at the top of the page: *Our children, please contact and tell them "NO Comment" per Dad.*

She slid the paper across to Mindy who read it and nodded. She folded the paper, and it disappeared into a pocket of her jogging jacket. "I'll let them know Patrick. I think Mindy can help as it seems I am the center of attention while they are looking for you."

"Anna, I'm sorry. I wish I could be there with you. Just cover us with your prayers, and I'll let you know what is happening as we figure this out. Ben is going to make contact with the authorities and let them know he is representing the three of us. I guess it may end up we have to defend everyone in the class. It looks like the whole world is focusing on the Tribunal and the Collins testimony."

Patrick watched a hawk floating in the air as he patrolled the lake looking for a fish that might have gotten too close to the surface. "Can you imagine what would happen if we got to run the Tribunal and the public got to see Collins testimony out in the open—and uncensored? It could change the whole face of our Government. The secret deals would be exposed, and maybe the voters would turn out and force a change."

Anna closed her eyes. She could see Patrick dusting off his armor getting ready for a battle. There was no doubting it was part of why she loved him. Years ago, he had decided the only way to change things was to begin educating the next generation to think and stand for something.

Patrick had said that too many generations had traded their lives and freedom for another social handout. While others simply stopped caring. We have let those with more greed than honor move into positions of power. Then slowly through what Patrick referred to as "Bureaucratic Terrorism," they invaded and took over the halls of government. Anna had heard the call to arms—Patrick was going to take on the fight.

"I love you, Patrick. Pray about it and be sure. I will stand with you even though it's going to come with a cost."

Patrick was deep in thought. "I love you too. I'll let you know what we're doing as soon as I can. Please thank Mindy for me —Ben's staff is wonderful. I can't tell you where we are and I am sure we are going to be moving. We just have a lot to work out. If you haven't, you had better get some cash. I am sure our bank accounts will be targeted if they haven't been already."

"I have to go. We have a lot to do."

Tears were building as she could hear Patrick preparing to go to battle. She felt like so many wives who had seen their spouses go to war not knowing if they would ever see them again. Anna knew this was either going to be a battle on American soil like none other or it was going to be a slaughter and those taking a stand would be destroyed and swept away. Either way, the path was set. Patrick was preparing to take the fight public. "I love you, wild man. May God be with you."

Anna handed the phone back to Mindy. Mindy shook her head and said, "Keep this one. I'll get you another in a day or two. The only calls you should get on this phone are from Patrick or one of us on Ben's staff. We will only call you to keep you updated."

Anna took her hand and squeezed it. "Thank you."

Mindy had worked a lot of cases with Ben. She had developed a sense about people. She looked at Anna and said, "Your husband is going to take this on isn't he?"

Mindy had done her homework and read the background on Patrick Ramirez.

Patrick was one of three children. His father legally immigrated to Texas and had been a strong advocate for legal immigration. Patrick was proud that his father never took shortcuts. He had taught Patrick to love the law. Patrick remembered hearing his father counsel many of those who wanted to immigrate and how to do it the right way. He had developed a love for Texas and the US.

He had married a woman who claimed her Irish heritage went back to immigrants coming into the United States through Ellis Island from Ireland.

Both of them had been typical hard-working parents raising their children and teaching them their heritage from both sides. Patrick quoted his mother as saying her children were trilingual. They had taught them English, Spanish and Gaelic. She had raised them to be passionate about their heritage. And who could be more passionate than the children of a hot-blooded Latino and a red-headed Irish Colleen? Naturally, their children would never be afraid of a fight

Patrick had been quoted in an article about immigration as saying, "The strength of America was in the blending of the steel of different cultures, much as the forging of the blade of a sword. If you blend steel from different areas in the fire of freedom, you will forge a powerful sword."

Mindy stood up. "I'd better go. Are you going out today?"

Anna looked around. "No, I can work from my office here today. If I do go out, I know the *'no comment'* rule, and I'll expect to be followed."

Mindy nodded. "Why don't I pick you up for lunch tomorrow about noon and I can update you then. She pulled out a mini iPad from under her Jacket. You can use this to send us emails. The account is already set up. Your email name is Mindy. The instructions are taped to the back. This way it will just look like traffic from me. If you send me an email, it will just look like I am sending reminders to myself."

Mindy and Anna had migrated to the front door. Anna hugged her. "Thank you—you're a blessing. If you see Ben tell him I send my love and tell him to try and keep Patrick in check."

Mindy took Anna's hand. "I'll pick you up tomorrow. If you need me, I am number one on the speed dial on the phone I gave you. David is number two. He can get you to whoever you need."

Mindy opened the door and stepped out, continuing the theater for the audience. "I'll pick you up tomorrow!"

She turned and walked away as the door closed. She walked back the way she had come deliberately passing the watchers. She waved as she went by and then jogged off to her car.

CHAPTER 22

Patrick was still holding the phone. He and Anna were best friends, married and happy together. Patrick smiled and thought about the Bette Midler song he kept on their playlist in the kitchen. He could hear the echoes of Midler singing, "You're my favorite waste of time…"

The door opened and Ben stepped out. "How's Anna?"

Patrick got up. "She's ok, just getting ready for the siege."

Ben was holding a glass of iced tea. He looked out at the lake. "Patrick, I can hear the rumble of what you're thinking."

Ben could see the light in Patrick's eyes. The call to Anna had triggered a change. Last night Patrick was concerned and unsure. Now he was steady and focused.

 "Because the Sovereign Lord helps me, I will not

be disgraced. Therefore, I have set my face like flint, and I know I will not be put to shame."

Patrick turned to Ben. "Isaiah 50:7?"

Ben nodded. "I see you have set your face like flint and you have a plan?"

Patrick smiled. "I have an idea that might bail us all out of this."

He opened the door, looked at Ben and asked, "You coming?

Ben muttered, "Why do I feel like the fly being invited into the spider's web?"

As Patrick closed the door, he continued with a sheepish grin, "Of course, the other side of this debate is that we all go down together."

Jenny was perched cross-legged on the counter with her laptop in front of her. She looked up over her reading glasses. "What are you two plotting? I only caught something about we all go down together. Is that crash-and-burn or just buried alive?"

Ben shrugged and sat down in the recliner. "I think we're about to find out. Patrick is working on an idea to get us out of this."

Jenny looked at them both. "I'm just harboring several wanted fugitives...I don't have any idea what they were doing...They just spent the night your honor..."

Ben pushed back in the recliner. "Nice defense, but I don't think it will stand. Alright, Patrick, the suspense is killing me. What are you plotting?"

Patrick looked around the room. His teaching persona took attendance. William, Daniel, Ben, David, Diane, Walt, and Jenny. All present. He stood by the door so he could face all of them as if he were getting ready to lecture the class.

> "It came to me while I was talking to my wife. If we play by their rules, we'll just be censored. William will disappear in a cloud of national security challenges. And nothing will change but a few retirements to keep things quiet."

Jenny piped in, "Four retirements and counting. The national security threat is continually associated with William's name."

Patrick turned to Jenny. "Thank you, madam." He then turned back to his class. "So how do we slip past the censors and get our story out?"

Patrick paused as no one from the class commented. "I propose we go forward with what we started." He wanted to see if anyone had jumped the gap yet.

Ben had closed his eyes and looked like he was napping. He opened one eye and looked at Patrick. "You aren't thinking about what I think you are thinking about?"

Patrick nodded. Everyone was watching the verbal tennis

match as their heads followed each volley. Jenny stopped them mid-sentence. "For those of us still on this planet, will you kindly tell me what you two are talking about?"

Ben sat up and said, "I think Patrick is planning on continuing with the Tribunal and using it to get William's information in front of the public."

Patrick bowed. "Precisely. If we can get a wide enough audience, it will be impossible to suppress the evidence. William can be kept in the public eye and possibly survive the attacks."

Daniel raised his hand. Patrick acknowledged him as if still in class. "Professor, how do we do that? No one is going to let us conduct the Tribunal now. And even if they did, we would never be allowed to use the information William has. I would bet the school would not allow any public coverage."

The gleam in Patrick's eye was glowing. "You're exactly right. The school will probably not let us do it openly. William, you obviously had some technological help in releasing your information. It keeps going out and keeps moving. Correct?"

William nodded. "I had some help. They probably won't be able to shut it down for a couple more days."

Patrick began to lay out his plan. "What if we started taping the Tribunal. We will present the information from Williams's files as evidence. We try the case exactly as we had planned. Except, we release it over the internet in segments.

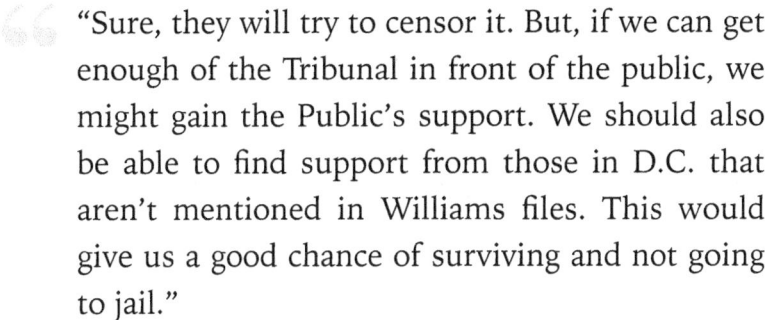

"Sure, they will try to censor it. But, if we can get enough of the Tribunal in front of the public, we might gain the Public's support. We should also be able to find support from those in D.C. that aren't mentioned in Williams files. This would give us a good chance of surviving and not going to jail."

David was making the rounds with a fresh pot of coffee. "Professor, you want to use the internet, the darknet, and social media to present your case?"

Patrick moved to the counter where Jenny was seated. David refilled Patrick's cup with coffee. Jenny watched Patrick as he went to the fridge for cream.

"You're nuts—you know that? They are going to go after you with everything they can. I've been reading the files and watching the media. The media is scared. They don't know if they should report on this or just do their usual and roll over and read the D.C. script of the day."

David looked at Ben. Ben caught his look. "What are you thinking David?"

David had returned to the kitchen and was standing next to Jenny. "It should work. The fastest way to spread any information is to tell people not to spread it. Every college campus in the world is filled with people wanting to challenge the system. Most of the people in power today used to be those people in the 70's. They protested everything. Now they're in power. They just forgot where they came from. The students will use every trick in the book to get the word out. It will be the new underground movement.

Look what happened yesterday with the hoodies."

Patrick turned to David. "What happened with a hoodie?"

David smiled. "Sorry sir, I forgot you've been busy. It seems the campus security people linked up with the federal authorities and were planning on using face recognition software to locate you and your Tribunal class. The underground protest groups got wind of it. Can you believe the Campus security guys were so dumb that they used students in the media department to help run the cabling and bridge the face recognition software on the campus network? They honestly thought the students wouldn't get wind of it."

David looked at Ben. "The student underground is faster to distribute news and rumors than all of the media outlets combined. The word was out before they got the system in place. The underground put the word out that the campus security and the feds were going to use the face recognition software to identify the Tribunal students."

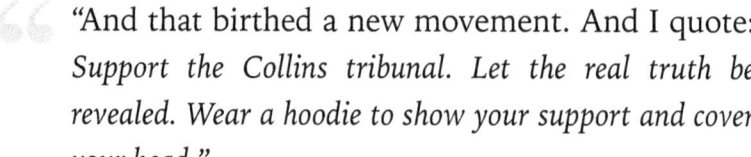

"And that birthed a new movement. And I quote: *Support the Collins tribunal. Let the real truth be revealed. Wear a hoodie to show your support and cover your head.*"

Ben sat up. "Patrick, I think it might work."

David interrupted. "You should see the media coverage—it's priceless. The students showed up wearing hoodies. The word has already spread, and over half of the colleges are reporting a rash of people on campus wearing hoodies. Lots of them are saluting the cameras as they pass them…if you know what I mean."

"But it gets better. One local reporter went to the campus and put on a hoodie and tried to hide his face and interview the Campus Security Chief."

David paused, still grinning that mischievous grin of someone who knows something others don't.

Diane broke the silence. "David if you don't tell the rest of it, I will forge your letter of resignation."

David knew how to keep an audience in suspense. He smiled, took a drink of water, looked at Jenny and said, *"Check the web address www.collinstribunalsupport.com."*

Everyone in the room near an electronic device started typing.

Jenny looked at Ben. "My God! You can buy a Collins Tribunal Hoodie online."

Ben stood up. The front room was a little crowded for both Patrick and Ben to be pacing and talking, so they just faced each other and began the verbal duel.

Ben fired first. "So, we already have public support from the students…"

Patrick returned fire. "Some of the media is showing support even if it's only humor."

David interrupted. "I think you have more support than you know. It seems New Yorkers are joining the protest against face recognition surveillance. A couple of reporters are filing stories on the increase in Tribunal support hoodies sales in New York and the new salute as they pass a camera. The mayor of New York is livid. It's reported he is considering banning hoodies in the city.

"Not to be outdone the local Campus Security Chief already issued a ban on wearing hoodies on campus."

Both Patrick and Ben turned on David. Ben began, "David, you better get it all out before I strangle it out of you..." He knew David was an exceptional storyteller. He enjoyed holding everyone in the palm of his hand.

Jenny punched David in the arm. "Spill it!"

David faked being hurt and continued. "The Mayor of New York joined the Campus Security Chief and tried to issue a ban on hoodies. But it failed when the sanitation workers started wearing hoodies. Then the street vendors began selling hoodies with the Collins Tribunal support logo."

"The local College Dean is ducking the issue trying to figure out whom to listen to... The students, the money people behind the college, or the Campus Security and the Feds."

Jenny turned her laptop around. "It looks like they stopped the hoodies, at least locally, but you will love this..."

Patrick and Ben stood in front of Jenny reading her laptop. William called from the couch. "What is it?"

 Patrick turned and said, "We have support."

Ben smiled as he watched the video on Jenny's laptop. "They banned hoodies on campus. The underground and students countered. Today is cowboy hat day to show your support. The video on the laptop was playing a video clip of the 'hoodie reporter' from yesterday. He still had on his hoodie and was posed with the Campus Security car behind him."

His dialogue started, "The local campus security has banned the wearing of hoodies and especially the Collins Tribunal hoodie that I'm wearing. But in the spirit of Americans standing up for truth, justice, and the American Way, we continue the Protest."

 "And he put on a cowboy hat and started towards the campus security car. The coverage continued as it showed photos of students wearing cowboy hats and anything with a big brim to hide their faces."

Ben looked at Patrick and then at Jenny. "Did he just quote the Superman lead in?"

Patrick was almost dancing as his Spanish blood began to stir. "Yes. He just quoted the opening of the old Superman series!" Patrick deepened his voice and took on the pose from the old series. "Standing for Truth, Justice and the American way…"

William, Daniel, Marie, and Walt just looked at them. Being unfamiliar with that version of Superman, they just waited quietly to see what was next.

Patrick and Ben were back to facing each other and shooting ideas back and forth. Jenny seemed to be excited, and they started to develop a plan.

Ben turned to David. "We need butcher paper or a whiteboard." David smiled and pulled out a roll of butcher paper and a pack of markers.

Ben grabbed the paper and headed for the dining room table. Patrick followed. A war was brewing, and it needed a plan.

Jenny turned to David and furrowed her brow in question. David flashed that smile that he used before speaking. "He likes to draw out stuff, so we just keep a roll of butcher paper and markers. He draws out diagrams and plans, and we hang them on the wall, and a plan develops."

David held up a roll of masking tape. "And we won't make a mark on your walls…" He headed for the new war room. The rest of the Collins Tribunal defense began to take their places in the war room.

Jenny called out to David, "I still want to adopt you if you get tired of Ben!"

CHAPTER 23

AGENT TILLIS WAS WATCHING THE DOOR expecting any minute for someone to walk in and take over the investigation. He was sure his career was on the last gasps before life support was disconnected. His boss had called earlier and told him to cover his butt. The agencies in D.C. were all being worked over by their particular favorite supporting bureaucrat. Threats were running from agency to agency as the blame game was working from room to room.

The President's press secretary kept giving out statements on everything *but* the Collins Tribunal leak. It was interesting how quickly the Tribunal had gotten saddled with Collins actions. As far as any of those working in this room had figured out, the only connection between Daniel and William was, they were brothers. William appeared to be on his own and had used his brother's school project as a stage to open the worst Pandora's Box D.C. had ever seen.

They had been checking out all of the students and teachers associated with the Tribunal project and had not found any connections to William Collins other than their family relationship.

There was the police report about the accident with Williams's fiancé and the deer the week before. When they had interviewed his fiancé, the only thing she said was, "Maybe he is going to change." Then her parents had asked the agents to leave.

Tillis and Patterson had gone over her testimony. The only thing anyone could come up with was that Collins had had enough and wanted to make a clean break. He wanted to get everything he had done in the open. The hard part was the people he worked with were going to bury him. Too many careers and fortunes were in danger of toppling. The media was already busy projecting how many seats would be up for special elections and the impact on the next term.

Blood was beginning to run in D.C. Two members of the house had already asked for immunity. Several DOJ high-ranking officials were talking about retiring for *personal* reasons.

After reading more of the Collins files, Tillis hoped they could get back to D.C. and make a few *real* arrests instead of chasing college students and one whistleblower.

Patterson stuck his head in the door. "Brad, you're going to want to come out here and see this."

Agent Tillis got up and headed out the door. Patterson escorted him to the front door. They saw two students being handcuffed by the Campus Security. A woman standing on a bench was holding a sign which was dancing in the wind. Patterson and Tillis waited inside the door watching this drama. Tillis asked, "Can you read the sign?"

 Patterson moved to one side trying to read the waving sign. "Oh great, it says *We Surrender*. I guess we better go find out why they are surrendering. Do you recognize any of them?"

Tillis had memorized most of the photos of the Tribunal team. "Yeah, I think it's Tanya Landers and Barry Weinstein. I can't for sure say it's Tanya, but it looks like her. We better go help before the Chief starts a riot."

Patterson held his arm up blocking Tillis from going out the door. "Maybe we better wait—catch the reporter behind the Chief's SUV."

Tillis watched as the reporter and his cameraman hurried towards the now growing crowd. The Chief and one of his men were dragging the two kids towards the SUV. The crowd was growing, and a rock flew through the air and hit the Chief's vehicle.

Patterson looked at Tillis. "I think we should watch this from inside the command post unless you want to be in the news for helping to start a riot."

Tillis turned and hurried to the command post. They needed to get the word out that things were going bad—and needed to do it quickly.

CHAPTER 24

OUTSIDE, THE CAMPUS SECURITY CHIEF HAD shoved Barry Weinstein in the back seat of his SUV. The woman holding the sign was screaming at him. Officer Jordan had just pushed Tanya Landers around the back of the SUV when a crowd of students swept over him, knocking him to the ground. He rolled under the back of the Chief's vehicle trying to avoid the protesting feet as the crowd kicked him and disappeared with Tanya Landers still in handcuffs.

The hoodie reporter was shouting at his cameraman to get this shot and get that shot over there. Too much was happening for one cameraman, especially as close as they were. The crowd had swirled around the SUV and had begun rocking it and pounding on it. The chief was on the passenger side and didn't have the cars' keys. The keys were under the vehicle with Officer Jordan.

The rear passenger door was opened by one of the swirling crowd, and Barry Weinstein disappeared in the flowing ocean of students.

The Chief was trying to call for help on his radio, as the crowd surrounded the SUV and began venting their anger like the unrelenting waves of a storm. The windshield gave way. Several students had made it to the roof of the SUV and were jumping up and down.

As the sound of approaching sirens began, Chief Wendell Peters ended his career with a shot fired through the roof of the SUV. The shot permanently ended the academic career of Mason Ballard. The bullet entered his groin in a vertical trajectory, passing through various organs including his heart and stopped in his throat.

> The gunshot caused the crowd to scatter, knocking the woman with the sign off the bench and over the ledge where she landed on several large rocks striking her head.

The arrival of several campus police and local police cars dispersed the crowd except for two victims. The first being Mason Ballard who was lying on the roof of the SUV. The second body wasn't found for several minutes. The police were busy hauling the Chief out of the crushed SUV and trying to keep the growing number of media trucks and cameras out of the way.

A rival news channel to the hoodie reporter was trying to get a different angle on Mason Ballard's body lying on the Chief' vehicle when she and her cameraman came across another body still holding the sign *"We Surrender."*

The reporter began shouting at her cameraman "Get the shot with the sign on her body." The Campus police, the other reporters, and their camera crews stopped. Once they heard there was another body, they all turned to rush towards the newly discovered body. The campus police didn't know about the second body. There was little they could do now but get in the way as the media continued shooting photos of the woman still holding her sign. The local police began showing up and took control of the situation. They started by establishing a perimeter and moving the press back.

A news cameraman sitting on top of his news truck captured one of the most grotesque displays of rivalry between reporters as several reporters tried to rearrange the body of the woman with the sign to get a better shot of her face. The nightly news coverage would be shown over and over as they immortalized the deaths of Mason Ballard and the woman with the sign. The woman would later be identified as attorney Wendy Carlson, representing Barry Weinstein and Tanya Landers. The first and second of the official casualties of the Public Tribunal.

CHAPTER 25

Inside the command post, almost every phone started ringing as the news coverage displayed the chaos just outside their door.

Patterson and Tillis watched the replay. The video was jumpy because the crowd was jostling the cameraman. They watched the crowd destroying the car. They both flinched as they heard the gunshot. The video would forever freeze Mason Ballard's last moment in life as he stopped jumping on the car roof and suddenly collapsed.

The still photo of Mason starting to fall became one of the images that would show up on T-shirts across the country calling to support the Collins Tribunal.

Tillis looked at his cell phone as it vibrated on the desk.

Patterson was answering his phone. Tillis heard the second-guessing starting.

Tillis picked up the phone with the same heart of any man walking to certain doom. He pushed the button and answered the call. "Yes Mam, I am watching the news coverage."

He paused for the question he knew he would answer over and over in the weeks to come. "No. There was nothing we could do." He then began to detail what had happened and why he had decided not to enter the mob. Everyone in the command post supported his decision not to rush into that crowd. But Tillis knew the bureaucratic quarterbacks sitting thousands of miles away, would be judging and second-guessing every decision Tillis had made.

After twenty minutes of nonstop questioning, Tillis hung up the phone. Patterson had taken three other calls while Tillis was enduring the verbal beating. Patterson handed Tillis a cup of coffee. "It's the strongest thing I have."

Tillis looked up. Tears clouded his eyes, and he started second-guessing his own actions. Patterson read the look. "There was nothing you could have done. We both saw it unfolding. The only thing we would have done was add fuel to the fire, and it might have gotten worse. The chief should never have cuffed those kids and tried to haul them off like that."

 Tillis nodded. "I know. And we both know

anyone who goes through something like this can't help but replay it trying to second guess what they could have done to prevent it from happening."

Tillis took the cup, sipped at the hot coffee and looked out the window. "I've been relieved of command pending an investigation of my failures on this assignment."

Patterson sat down and looked out the same window. It seemed so peaceful. The room was very quiet as most of the staff had left the command post. "It reminds me of the quiet just after a tsunami sweeps over some island destroying everything in its path and then just quietly washes back to the ocean."

Patterson continued, "My boss just told me the same thing. It seems I am also responsible for the deaths of the two people outside and everything that is happening in D.C."

"I wonder what it's like to disappear on a long vacation. I guess I'd better go call my wife."

Patterson got up and walked out the door to find a quiet place to talk to his wife.

Tillis was still looking out the window. He picked up his phone and hit the speed dial for Mattie Tillis. As she answered the phone, the backwash of emotions filled Agent Tillis as he heard, "Are you ok? I'm here. Do you want me to fly out there?"

Tillis was having a hard time talking. Tears flowed as the days of pent-up frustration, and the unneeded loss of life tore at his soul. "I'm all right. I'm coming home. The boss just relieved me of command. I'm done."

CHAPTER 26

DAVID WAS PREPARING LUNCH. THE COLLINS WAR council surrounded the dining room table as they planned a strategy to conduct the Tribunal. Hopefully, their plan would allow William Collins to survive the attacks from D.C. David had been monitoring the news as he was stirring his marinara sauce.

The news began showing the arrest of the two students. David called out as he stirred the sauce. "Ben, you had better come quick—the situation just got worse."

David turned up the volume, as the reporter announced that two people had died in the Collins Tribunal Protest. They then began replaying the video showing the campus police dragging the two students to the SUV.

Patrick and Daniel both recognized the two handcuffed

students. Patrick gasped, "My God! That's Barry Weinstein and Tanya Landers. They're part of the Tribunal class."

The video continued, showing the crowd growing and then turning into a riot. The mob swept Tanya away from the officer.

"Tanya got away." Daniel pointed at the screen. He watched Tanya disappear into the mob. Then they watched as Barry was pulled out of the car and disappeared into the mob.

> The gunshot made them all jump as they watched Mason Ballard die on screen again. Jenny cried out, "My God they shot him!"

The report continued, and they all stood in silence, unmoving, except for David who was still stirring the marinara sauce.

As the story ended, they showed Wendy Carlson body sprawled across the rocks still holding the sign. The reporter made sure everyone knew the sign read, *"We surrender."*

Ben shook his head. "I didn't know her personally, but I knew she had a pretty good reputation for corporate law. I don't know how she got involved in this."

Jenny turned the volume down as the reporters droned on and on covering the same photos and speculating on things that they knew nothing about. "This is the part I hate about my media colleagues. They are worse than mindless gossips. Their whole day is spent trying to catch a producer's ear with their witty evaluation of a disaster or tragedy. It's pathetic what the media does for market share."

The videos had shaken Patrick. Everyone in the room could see William was not doing well either. Patrick opened the door and called out, "William, let's take a walk and get some fresh air."

William welcomed a chance to flee the room. He was suffocating from guilt as he had begun blaming himself.

Patrick, closing the door on his way out, stopped, and leaned back in the room. "Ben, I think we need to get some more help. This thing is spinning out of control. These deaths are going to stir up the public. Who can we bring into the mix to get the right spin on this? Just think about it. I'm going to take a walk with William."

Ben nodded as the door closed. He walked back into the dining room and sat down in front of his laptop. Walt and Diane joined him and sat their laptops on the table. The only sound was the three of them firing off emails.

Jenny looked at David, and he nodded toward Daniel. "I could use some help getting lunch ready. Daniel, can you give me a hand?" Daniel got up as the video played over and over in his head even though he didn't know Mason Ballard. "Yes, Mam, what do you want me to do?"

CHAPTER 27

PATRICK CAUGHT UP TO WILLIAM AS THEY WALKED down the path to the lake. Rocks covered the shore at the edge of the water. Patrick picked up a smooth rock and tried skipping it across the water. The first rock made two hops. "I was never very good at this." He picked up another rock and made three hops before the rock dove beneath the water.

William picked up a rock and watched the circles of ripples from the three hops spread. As they dissipated to calm waters, he threw his rock he counted, "One, two, three, four, five, six..."

Patrick sat down on a bench looking out over the lake. "I concede, you win."

William tossed another rock but this time he didn't try to skip it, he just threw it as far as he could. Almost as if he wanted to throw the last several days and especially the last twenty minutes as far from himself as he could. He sat down next to Patrick.

"I think I've made a mistake."

Patrick took a deep breath and looked across the lake. "Jenny's right. The air is cleaner and fresher here. It does seem to make things clearer. William, I don't think you made a mistake. Yes, it's tragic that those two people lost their lives. But you had nothing to do with it. You were here. You didn't kill them."

> William was having a hard time with his mind. Patrick could see the duel going on inside him. "Professor, if I hadn't brought this stuff out in the light, none of this would have happened."

"William, I've found that following every tough decision are three nagging little voices trying to tell you what you should have done, what you could have done and what someone else would have done in your place."

William was leaning forward looking at the ground. "Yeah, I have heard those three a lot in the last couple of days. I think I've made the right decision and then it's like someone whispering in my ear and then I start questioning."

"You know William, I have personally debated all three of those little whispering demons. They are good at debating, and they are relentless. Once I held a debate with them for almost three days."

William looked at Patrick. "So who won?"

Patrick smiled as he recalled that debate. "I had decided to do something that I thought was right. I had talked it over with my wife, and she agreed. So, I acted on my decision, and several people lost their jobs. I got some phone calls and had several encounters with people who didn't like my decision, and they let me know it. I was told about the personal losses these people suffered and how their families would suffer and asked why didn't I just mind my own business..."

William looked at him. "And then when it was quiet and dark the debate started didn't it?"

Patrick continued. "Yes, they like to whisper when it's dark or when you're alone. I became so involved in the debate that I was sitting in the family room about two o'clock in the morning talking out loud. I was arguing all sides of my problem, what I should have done and why it was the right decision. I guess my debate got kind of loud."

William added, "I know what you mean. I almost shouted at myself last night. So, what happened?"

"Well, I was sitting in my favorite chair in the family room, and I was in the middle of a great argument and Anna smacked me on the back of the head and said, "Will you tell those three to get out? You were right. Now quit second-guessing and go to bed. You're keeping me up.""

"You know, I hate when Anna is right, but she was. So, I stood up, walked to the door, opened it and shouted, "The 'should have,' 'could have' and 'would have' debate is over. I stand on my decision, now get out!"

"I closed the door. I went and made a sandwich, watched an old movie and slept without a single whisper."

Patrick put his hand on William's shoulder. "I've been reading the files you are releasing. You made the right decision. Standing up for the truth is never easy. I will tell you I am proud of your decision, and so is everyone in the house. We have chosen to stand with you, and I am sure we will all pay a price. But you made the right decision. The truth can't be hidden forever. It will always find a way into the light. Now let's go have lunch or I am liable to start preaching."

William stood up. His eyes had cleared. He looked at the Professor and held out his hand in gratitude. "Thank-you sir."

They shook hands, and as they walked back up the path, Patrick began to strategize with William. They began to prioritize the information. They needed to figure out what were the things D.C. would most want to cover up and what would have the most impact on the public.

Jenny was standing on the porch as they arrived. "I was just coming to get you. Lunch is ready and Ben wants to start going public."

Patrick looked at William. "We're ready—it's time to start this fight."

CHAPTER 28

THE RENTAL CAR PULLED UP ON THE SIDEWALK AND drove in front of the auditorium. The tow truck was trying to pull the Chief's SUV on the truck so that it could be moved to the police impound yard for processing.

The voice from the back seat said, "Park it here. I don't want to walk all over this campus looking for a place to park."

Tyler Winston pulled the car to one side trying to park out of the way. As he put the car in park, he heard the rear two doors open. Tyler turned the car off, hit the trunk release and tried to catch up with his boss Lisa Millington.

Lisa was already heading for the auditorium as a Campus Security officer started shouting for her to move her car.

Bailey Valentine hurried to cut off the officer flashing his DOJ credentials. The last thing he wanted was for this poor guy to challenge Lisa Millington. He had seen it happen before. Someone would cross Lisa, and then their life would take a plunge down a very dark hole.

> "Officer we are with the DOJ. Deputy Director Millington will be taking command of the Collins investigation. We're on our way to the command post to assess the situation. Can you tell me who's in charge here so we can get up to speed?"

Lisa breezed by the officer without even looking at him. The officer followed her with his eyes, turning to watch as she walked down the stairs toward the auditorium. He turned and looked at Bailey. "I'll radio the Dean and let him know you're here. They haven't appointed a replacement for the Campus Security Chief so as of right now we're all helping out. It's a mess. The students are wound up and angry. The college administration is in a panic. The media is swarming over this place looking under every rock for an interview. If you guys want this one, you can have it."

The officer turned and went back to trying to get the SUV on the tow truck and out of sight.

Bailey stopped and looked around trying to get his bearings. He had seen the news clips and had replayed them in his mind over and over. Bailey envisioned the crowd swarming the Chief's SUV. He could close his eyes and see the students on top of the vehicle. He could almost hear the echo of the gunshot that ended Mason Ballard's life. His eyes shifted to the bench where Wendy Carlson had been pushed by the crowd losing her balance and falling to her death. He walked over to the bench and looked at the rocks. You could still see the blood and the evidence tape marking where she had died.

The area was cordoned off with tape marked *"Police Line."* The nearest students were about thirty feet away. He noticed that most were wearing hoodies with the hood up or cowboy hats. The emotions on campus were electrically charged and ready to explode—it would take very little to re-ignite this powder keg.

As he turned to head to the auditorium, he prayed that Lisa would pour water on this situation and not gasoline. Lisa Millington was not known for taking prisoners but instead, leaving a wake of bodies and destroyed careers behind her. When the Director told him he was sending Lisa to take over this mess, Bailey Valentine had asked his boss, *Why*. Bailey was almost Lisa's equal in rank and had been working on another very sensitive investigation of his own.

The Director had looked across his desk, folded his hands and paused. After an uncomfortable silence, Director Brent Underwood cleared his throat a couple of times. "The White House has directed us to send Lisa to clean up this situation."

Bailey knew the score in D.C. He was more career than one of the part-timers. *"Part-timers"* were what the career types called the political appointees that drifted in and out with changing seasons of Presidencies. "The President or just the White House?"

Brent shot a sharp look at Bailey. "You know who it was. The President is out playing a round or raising money. Hell, he may not even know anything is going on yet."

Bailey nodded. His intuition was right. The infamous *one* that no one spoke of publicly was calling the shots. "So, what do you want me to do on this cleanup mission?"

Brent picked up a pencil and began drawing on a scrap of paper. Everyone in D.C. knew when he started doodling he was worried. "I need someone on the ground I can trust if this thing goes as badly as I think it will."

"I was told to send Lisa on this and give her free reign to clean it up. Lisa will report directly to the White House."

Bailey shifted in his seat. He felt his career begin to wave in the breeze of bureaucracy covering itself. It was not a good feeling.

"Brent, am I the fall guy in this? Because I don't plan on ending my career in some college town in Texas."

Brent got up and walked around the desk. "Look, I'm already losing chain of command on this. I'm sending you and Tyler to try and keep me in the loop. She is going to find someone to blame for this disaster. We've already relieved two or three of the lead agents from Homeland and the FBI. No one is happy. The media is in full circus mode. They just don't know if they are supposed to cover this up with other stories or if they should release the dogs and tear this town apart. On top of that, we're starting to face public sympathy for this Collins guy. Several websites have already popped up supporting him and free speech.

"Everyone from the left, the right and the middle are taking sides. The big government powers want this to die-off quickly. The small government factions are howling for the truth. They want to use Collin's material as the way to clean house and wipe out the corruption that the files have exposed."

Bailey settled back in his chair. He wasn't afraid of a fight. He just wanted to know whose side he was on and who was on his side. "I've been reading the Collins files. They show up every couple of hours. I made a copy and am about a fourth of the way through them. Brent if any of the stuff this guy is uncovering is true, DOJ will be very busy either providing cover or helping the media crucify the guilty. And it looks like there are a lot of guilty parties."

Brent had earned his reputation for being non-political. He liked to judge the case based on the evidence and the law. But this administration tended to use the law to justify their objective or just ignore it. "I am hopeful the country will survive this. It could be the thing we need to bring a little integrity back to D.C. We both know D.C. is bloated with bureaucrats and lobbyists. A change would be good, but right now we need to focus on making sure it happens legally and above-board. We may not be able to show any of this publicly. But we need to record it if for no other reason than for our own protection and defense. That's why you and Tyler are going. I trust you guys to do what's right."

> "Lisa is on a mission to protect the elite. It won't matter who she destroys in the process. Let her call the shots, but keep me informed. I need you and Tyler to make sure this is done by the book. That may be the hardest part of this assignment. What you do may save the country. It may also be our defense if it goes wrong down there."

"I don't want to see on the tube that Collins was shot and killed in a gunfight. We will need him alive if we have any chance of getting to the truth."

Bailey got up and started towards the door. He stopped and turned towards Brent. "Thanks for trusting me. I assume you've officially *not* talked with Tyler?"

Brent got up and moved back behind his desk. "Yep, I never had this talk with you or with Tyler. Now get out of here and keep me informed. If I can, I will try to send you some help through the other agencies. We still have a few good guys in the ranks, most of them are just laying low waiting for the next change in the part-timers."

Bailey walked out of the Director's office. His secretary never looked up. It was her way of saying this meeting had never happened.

Bailey pulled out his cell phone and called home. "Hi, babe looks like I'm heading out. I have to grab some stuff and will be home to pack. Do you want me to pick up something to eat? I want to have dinner with you and the kids before I leave. This trip may take a while."

CHAPTER 29

JENNY'S DINING ROOM WALLS WERE COVERED WITH white paper and drawings. The TV in the family room had been shifted so they could see it from the dining room. Jenny sat back and thought how much Ted would have loved this. She and Ted had been married for ten years. They had worked together most of those ten years, writing and reporting. It was an ongoing romance and love affair with life and each other. Jenny smiled. She had only two regrets. First, losing Ted to cancer. And second, for not taking the time to have children. It would have been wonderful to have seen Ted as a father. They had built this place, as their private hideout where a family could grow up. But, *the cancer* had a different plan.

After Ted found out he was sick, they had spent a lot of time trying to work with the doctors to see if there was a cure.

The trauma of trying to get through the new health plan was almost as bad a nightmare as was *the cancer*.

As the diagnosis became clear, the treatment options dwindled to nothing. She still remembered talking with one of the doctors while waiting for Ted to get through some test. The doctor was a friend of a friend, and he had taken Jenny to the cafeteria for coffee and a talk.

She remembered how angry he was as he told her. We can't get treatment for Ted. They had turned everything into the new healthcare process and then learned that Ted didn't qualify for cancer treatment. It would be too expensive, and they needed to cut costs.

Jenny had almost started a war right there in the cafeteria. The doctor told her he could not say anything, but he urged her to try and get some help outside the country.

Unfortunately, this cancer had a different timeline. Jenny and Ted had spent many hours talking about it. Ted decided he would rather spend time with her than trying to fight a losing battle.

Lots of tears and hugs were now a part of this house. She and Ted had spent his last days here working on a project together. A tear escaped and ran down her cheek.

Patrick turned to go and get something to drink from the kitchen. He spotted the tear and put his hand on her shoulder. She took his hand, and he squeezed her shoulder. He looked at her and said, "Ted?"

She nodded and caught the tear on her fingertip. She looked at the tear and patted Patrick's hand on her shoulder. "I can just see him in the middle of this... ready to stand on the front lines for these boys."

> Patrick kneeled down, so they were face to face. "I know. I thought about him when I was down at the lake with William. Ted would have relished this Tribunal battle. He so loved the truth and anyone who stood for it."

Jenny nodded, trying not to give into the longing to just have another day with Ted. She got up and said, "Well, let's go get some fresh drinks for them so I can keep it together."

Patrick nodded. "Let's go." He turned and looked back at the table as Ben looked up with concern. He knew Jenny and Ted and had seen the tear from across the room. His face asked the question *Is she alright?*

Patrick nodded and waved for Ben to keep going. Ben nodded. Sometimes friends just need to be around those who don't ask a lot of questions. The discussion picked up, and Patrick and Jenny headed for the kitchen. Patrick smiled as he thought about Anna. They were blessed, and he made a promise to let her know how much he missed her.

David who was on constant alert turned up the TV. The crawler at the bottom of the screen identified Deputy Director Lisa Millington. Her voice stopped everyone in the dining room as they turned to listen. Millington announced that she was there to take charge of the situation at the direction of the White House and that William Collins and his co-conspirators would be brought to justice. She was there to make sure this situation did not claim any more innocent lives.

The reporters started their spin and interpretation. After all, they needed to tell the public what she had just said. The media knew the American public was obviously too dumb to understand a statement like Millington's for themselves. David turned the volume down.

Ben looked at Walt. "Isn't she the one that crucified that prosecutor last year?" Walt nodded. "That's her—don't you remember she's the one who ran that other investigation on union corruption and found no justifiable grounds to pursue the inquiry…"

Diane was typing on her laptop pulling up files on Lisa Millington. "Ben, she is the one rumored to have demoted those two whistleblower agents in Immigration."

Ben sat back in his chair shifting from four legs to two. "Oh, yeah, what was it they called her? The White House attack dog? They only bring her out when they want someone silenced. Wow William, congratulations—you just made the White House hit list!"

William turned red. This was not the recognition he had hoped for. "I remember hearing her name. In fact, I think she's in the files. She was brought in to handle something for Senator Liz."

Ben lit up. "This could be helpful. Diane, see if you can find any references to her in William's files. Perhaps this could be the ace we keep up our sleeve."

Patrick and Jenny returned to the war room and looked at Ben. "So, if we are all in agreement, we are going to try and hold the Tribunal in secret. We will video it and then release it in pieces to gain public support and exposure."

Ben leaned back on all four legs. "That's good. I will make a statement that I am representing you and the Collins boys. Patrick, do you want us to represent all of the Tribunal members?"

Patrick sat down his iced tea. "I think we first have to contact each of them and see if they are in or out of the fight. I wouldn't blame any of them for not wanting to be involved."

Daniel had been quietly listening to the plan. "I think Barry and Tanya have already decided. And I am surprised none of the others have turned up on the news."

Patrick grinned. "I guess some of them were listening when I said you might someday need a place to disappear to for a time. Now we just need to figure out how to get to them and see if they want in."

Walt was still typing. "And we are going to need a place to hold the Tribunal and record it. One or perhaps several places where we can lay low. Boss, once you go public, we have to avoid you."

Ben looked hurt. "Walt, what are you saying? Do you think that the authorities would try to follow me after we make a public statement?"

David appeared in the doorway. It was something they were all getting used to. David just appeared when he had something to say. The rest of the time he was busy doing this or that.

"I think I know someone who could help locate the missing members. And he might be able to help us get the word out when we want to start releasing the videos."

Jenny turned to David. "I can't wait to hear this."

David grinned at Jenny. "There's a guy I know who is an organizer for hire. He's working here under the name Gator. He's the one rumored to have triggered the fire alarm and organized the hoodie and hat demonstrations."

Ben was continually amazed by David. Outwardly, he acted as Ben's driver and gopher. Few realized how much more David did for Ben. Ben counted on him and his unique skill sets. "David, how do you know this Mr. Gator?"

David shifted over to lean against the wall. "Gator is the name he's using on this job. His real name is Morris Schwartz. I ran across him a couple of years back when we were investigating demonstrations in Seattle. We suspected a very wealthy outsider funded the protests with a very real agenda of his own. We noticed several protests broke out, but they all had similarities to them—like a signature. I was asked to go find out if someone was behind them."

Ben interjected. "Let me guess. You infiltrated the demonstrators?"

David smiled. "Actually I led one or two of the demonstrations. It was the best way to prove I was one of them. Anyway, I got to know Morris. He has set up a network process you wouldn't believe. If you need a demonstration or a commotion somewhere, you can hire him and his group. They choose code names and fly into the area. They set up and recruit a bunch of locals to help. Recruiting local help is much easier than I thought it would be. Morris uses a cell-based organization structure. That way none of the locals know anything but code names. They use cell phones, texting and a couple of other tricks which I might tell you someday."

"Anyway, they are very well funded. You've seen Gator's work in several prominent activist protests. If you thought about it, you could guess who hires him and who funds his work. You would not believe how connected he is. Gator poses as some guy living on the streets, but he's loaded. His network also does a lot of legit marketing, and spread-the-word type campaigns that people don't even realize are happening."

"I was at one of his houses once. He has a wife and a couple of kids. They think he's in advertising and travels a lot. He was a lot of fun to work with."

Ben looked concerned. "Do we need to refresh your background check or maybe your work contracts?"

David knew Ben was kidding and responded, "Honestly boss, the statute of limitations will run out on those things one of these days. Do you want me to reach out to him?"

Patrick and Ben exchanged looks. Both nodded, and both spoke at the same time. "By all means do so,"

Ben asked, "What is this going to cost?"

David shook his head. "Knowing this guy—he'll probably do it for free. He loves a challenge, and you can bet he'll find a way to make a profit and probably bill "the deep pocket guys.""

"I saw him work one of those media laundering groups once. He took a couple of events from the news that we were nowhere near or involved with and convinced them we had made them happen. They, in turn, paid him and told him how great he was."

"Morris is interesting to watch, and if he ever runs for office, I am either voting for him or leaving the country."

"I'll be gone for a little while. I need to go see if I can track him down and we need more groceries."

Ben called as David headed towards the door. "Don't forget receipts."

David waved and left.

Jenny shook her head. "That boy is starting to scare me."

Walt looked up. "You don't know the half of it. I tried to do a background check on him once. What information that wasn't redacted just didn't exist. He is as close to a ghost as anyone I've ever met."

Jenny stared at Ben. "I'll buy the wine if you will tell me his story."

Ben tested his best Sargent Schultz voice from Hogan's Heroes: "I know nothing."

Jenny turned to leave the room. "I'll get it out of you one way or another Ben. I still know where some of your bodies are buried."

Walt and Diane both stopped typing and looked at Ben. Diane piped up, "I might buy the wine to hear that story."

Walt chimed in, "Me too."

Ben looked at them and quipped, "You're both fired, now get back to work."

CHAPTER 30

SENATOR SHERATON HAD BEEN ABLE TO GET FIVE of the *Back Nine* to join him in the secure meeting room. The missing three were not responding to anyone's calls.

Sheraton looked around the room. "Andrew, have you heard from our missing friends?"

Andrew Carlin was a fourth term Senator. He had grown up in politics. His constituency loved him but mostly because they had no idea how much money he and his family were making from "quiet deals" as they were known in the *Back Nine*.

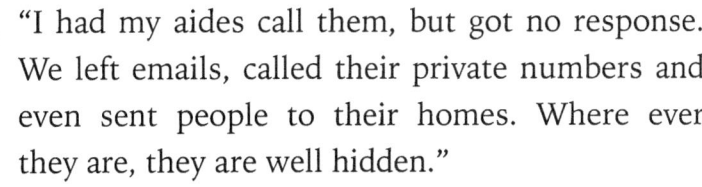

"I had my aides call them, but got no response. We left emails, called their private numbers and even sent people to their homes. Where ever they are, they are well hidden."

Donald Winslow had been in the DOJ for many years. He had survived one administration after another by feeding information to his partners inside the group known as the *Back Nine*.

"The Administration is torn on whether to let the public go after everyone named in Collins documents or try to shut it down. Their concern is how much damage it will do to the White House and those aligned *with* the White House. I know they just sent Lisa Millington down there to take personal charge of the investigation. I think she is just waiting to hear who she needs to sacrifice. Then she will feed them to the public."

Sharon Liston was a relative newcomer. It was her first term. She had been brought in because of her family connections. There were lots of skeletons in her family's closets. "How much of the Collins Papers have you all read? I had the files digitized so we could start scanning them for keywords. I've no doubt why we are missing our other four members. Their names show up on almost every deal and every one of our behind closed-door ventures."

Sheraton was surprised. He hadn't thought about digitizing the papers so they could search through them. Maybe he was getting too old for this stuff. Sheraton was not a tech guy. The science and technology briefings he had to attend were so over his head he didn't know how to respond. "Can we get copies of your digitized versions so we can have our staff look at them?"

Sharon nodded. "I'll have my people deliver you a hard drive with the data. I've suspended sending emails except for superficial exchanges. I think we all remember the IRS drama with email. I've instructed my staff to try and make any inquiries about the Collins papers personally."

"The biggest problem they're having is with the media. It seems they have a pool of reporters following everyone associated with anyone listed in the Collins papers. They're ahead of us in their analysis of who is involved and just how guilty everyone looks."

Gregory Waters was obviously uncomfortable in his chair. He kept squirming like something was biting him. Maybe it was his conscience. He had barely survived the scandal last year about voter fraud and donations. "I think I'm going to go home and wait for this to blow over. This stuff never lasts long."

Sheraton knew Gregory had several homes, most of them offshore and at least one in a non-extradition country. "Are you planning on being available if we need you, or do we just guess where you're going?"

Gregory knew what Sheraton was implying as he raised his voice. "I don't think that is any of your business! My wife is not taking this well and I need to move her to a quiet place to recover."

Morris Yancey seldom said anything but when he did it was usually pointed and short. "Greg, that's the same line you used last year. I know your wife—she is as tough as nails.

Hell, she has stuck with you through three or four affairs and how many other scandals?"

"If you're going to skip out, just say so, and we'll deal with it."

Greg was boiling. He had planned to skip out as soon as this meeting was over. His wife had already left for Miami. He had a private plane standing by and planned on collecting some cash from a couple of safe deposit boxes before he joined her. "I don't have to tell you anything. I'm not going to stand for this…" Greg got up and stormed out the door.

Sharon was tracing circles on the table with her finger. "He must have read a couple of the Collins files about his wife's brother's investments. Once the public figures out how much money he's been moving to his private holding companies, he's liable to be hung in his own backyard."

Sheraton was concerned. The *Back Nine* had usually protected each other and kept an eye out. But Sharon's comment concerned him. Sheraton had no idea about Greg's wife's activities. "How damaging is the information on Greg and his wife?"

Sharon stopped tracing and looked at Sheraton. He had never realized how cold her stare was. He felt like a shark had just sized him up and was deciding whether to have him for lunch or swim on. "If the DOJ, or the ethics committee, or anyone wants to prosecute him, he'll be lucky to ever breathe a breath outside of a jail cell."

"Greg let greed and stupidity get the best of him in his decisions over the last several years. His name has shown up a half dozen times in the ethics committee. The only reason nothing has occurred is half of the ethics committee are linked to one or more of his deals. Only three of us are clean where Greg is concerned, so we've been ignoring the inquiries saying *they lacked proof*. If it comes up now, he's cooked."

Yancey got up. "I suggest you all better get with your attorneys and develop a strategy. The word we get is the White House is about to climb on the White Horse of Justice and go after corruption in D.C."

Winslow nodded. "I heard the same thing just before I came over here. The word is the President is scared and wants to deflect as much as he can. Apparently, *she* has received instructions and is letting the President run with this. The unofficial word is *she* is about to distance herself from him and may even be taking a vacation. I read that as the first signs of *Everyman for himself*. Man, the lifeboats and pray."

"I'll try to let you know if I hear anything else, but for now, I agree with Yancey. Get counsel and be glad this Tribunal thing didn't happen. If they ever fully presented this stuff and the public started watching, there is no way the media could suppress it. The White House would have to start World War III to get traction."

"My boss at DOJ is preparing for the worst. We're going over everything looking to see how bad this is going to hit DOJ. Keep in mind the DOJ has been very selective about what we pursue. I think public opinion is about to change that."

Winslow headed for the door with Carl and Yancey right behind him. Sharon quietly walked out leaving Sheraton alone.

Maybe he should try and stop by the White House before he found himself alone without a friend. *She* still owed him a favor. He hoped he still had a few chips that he could use to bargain with her. This would certainly be the time to collect on them. He got up and left the room putting his mental list together.

White House, then home.

CHAPTER 31

DAVID WAS SITTING IN A LOCAL COFFEE HOUSE. HE had changed clothes and was wearing jeans and an old hoodie from the Seattle campaign. He was reading emails and thinking about another cup of coffee when a familiar voice whispered in his ear.

"If I were a cop, I would have had you. I thought I taught you never sit out in the open? Always put your back against a wall and watch the entrances."

David stood up, and Morris Schwartz hugged him. "You look good man! How long has it been?"

David grabbed his coffee and his phone. "Let's move to the back table. It looks like it's finally empty. And you are still one ugly dude."

Morris always managed to look like he'd been sleeping on

the street even though his status quo was five-star hotels and twenty-four-hour room service. "What are you doing here? Are you working on this Collins thing?"

David slid into one side of the corner booth. "Do you want a coffee or something?"

Morris slid into the other side of the booth. "I ordered for us when I came in. Billy is getting it and will bring it over when it's ready. You still drinking decaf lattes. Right?"

David nodded. Morris had an incredible memory. It seemed he remembered everything and almost always had someone with him in case someone had to "take a fall." He always had someone who would get in the way while Morris just disappeared.

"I got asked to look into this thing after it happened. What are *you* doing here? This isn't your usual gig." Billy swung by dropped off the coffees and moved to another table so he could watch and block if necessary.

Morris sipped his coffee, always black and full strength. "I'd picked up chatter about this Tribunal and thought it would be fun to watch. I convinced the "money well" that this could be a good location to put a network in place. They agreed. So, I put a small group together. You know a couple of them. Anyway, we were kind of taking a vacation and testing a couple of new approaches. Then the Feds raided the place, and someone set off the fire alarm."

 David knew Morris. He looked him in the eye,

and *the stare and don't blink* game began. "If my memory serves me right, you always like to sit next to a fire alarm if possible. What was it you used to call the fire alarms?"

Morris tried to look innocent and didn't blink. "I have no idea what you mean...I have heard fire alarms referred to by some as *the escape switch*. But, I have no idea what they mean by that."

Neither of them broke the stare, nor blinked. Finally, David shook his head letting Morris win the staring contest. "I wondered if you were here when I heard the fire alarm had broken up the Feds raid. I guess the smoke bomb outside was also yours?"

Morris looked shocked. "David, what are you saying? I was just an innocent bystander. I had no idea what was going on."

David liked Morris. He was fun to be around, and he could work a crowd like no one else. He used other people to take the spotlight, but if you knew where to look, you could see the conductor directing the various parts of the play. "How about the hoodies and hats thing?"

Morris grinned. "It's hard not to take credit for something so well executed. Wait till you see what's next. The school and New York City government have both come out very strongly against people hiding their faces from the cameras. It could be considered breaking the law."

" David saw the mischievous side of Morris coming from behind the mask. It was a side of Morris few got to see. But David and Morris had become friends. They had great respect for each other. "So, I understand you are using Gator as the name for this gig?"

Morris nodded. "You know, each gig, different code names for the crew. It makes it better if we have to bug out and leave the locals in a pinch. Watch the news tomorrow around noon—you'll enjoy it."

David swirled his coffee and looked Gator in the eye. "What do you think about this Tribunal gig?"

Morris leaned forward. "Why are you asking?"

David knew this was the pivotal moment of their conversation where Morris would decide to stay and help or simply bolt. "I just wondered if you might be interested in helping make the Tribunal an underground event?"

The hook was set. Morris hunched over his coffee. "I really wanted to see the Tribunal happen. I did some research, and this Professor Ramirez is the real thing. He teaches his students to think. When people leave his class, they all say the same thing: *He taught them how to look at issues and discern the truth.* You know how I feel about that. The schools are full of hypocrisy. They don't teach anything anymore. They just try to program the students and distract them. So, I take the money from the ones that want to sway opinion and create distractions. I give them what they want and try to find a few who want to make *real* changes."

"What do you want from me, David? You didn't come to say *hello*—we both know you have a motive for this meeting. Don't get me wrong, the Tribunal would have been good theater and fun to watch. The Collins guy is the wild card that moved the whole threat of exposing the D.C. powers to the front page. So why are we here? I'm sorry he can't get his files in front of a real Tribunal and the public. It might be the catalyst needed to wake up this country."

 David nodded. "So, if there was another way to get the Tribunal in front of the public, and if you were going to mastermind an underground Tribunal with Collins as a real witness, how would you do it?"

Morris lost his smile, and his eyes dimmed. He held up a hand, and Billy swung by the table dropping a pad and pencil in front of him. Then Billy returned to his seat to watch.

Morris started an outline talking to himself. He looked up at David. "I assume you would have to record the Tribunal and release it in segments. The Feds would never let you do it live—they would be all over you."

David nodded. "Think of holding the Tribunal somewhere very protected with about fifteen people. It might take a couple of days to get the proceeding taped. Then you need to release it in pieces so it gains enough public support and assure those involved wouldn't disappear down the DOJ's rabbit hole..."

Morris stopped, the pencil was still writing. "You are serious?"

Morris' eyes got huge as he read David's face. "You've got Collins and Ramirez?"

David knew Morris could not resist a gig of this size. He shrugged. *"Maybe."*

Morris put the pencil down. *"If* you're serious, it would take a very secure place big enough to house fifteen to twenty people and not attract attention. We would have to activate all of the campus networks to keep the feeds going out. Much like that Collins guy did with his notes. You know they still haven't figured out how to shut Collins down. His files are still going out. Even *Daddy Money* asked if I knew how Collins was doing it."

David almost lost his poker face. He had only heard Morris mention *Daddy Money* once before. "Why would he care?

Morris slipped back to the conspirator role. "I wondered the same thing. Generally, he never asks questions. Usually, someone just tells me about something they would like to have happen and sends money. I think those mentioned in the Collins files may have some links that lead back to him. All I know is this is the first time he sounded worried."

David would have to think about this information. Maybe,

Gator's operation was bigger than he thought. "Morris, could you pull off getting the Tribunal to the public?"

> Morris grinned. "I already have a place you could use to stage the Tribunal. You would have to have everyone stay put once they got there. Traffic in and out could attract attention. But you could get it recorded, edit it and then we could start releasing it immediately."

Morris looked at David and then looked around. "You *really* have Collins and Ramirez don't you?"

David smiled. "Are you in?"

Morris smiled, held up his hand and Billy appeared again. Morris, indirectly speaking to Billy said, "I need a phone for Rabbit. Get a hold of the crew and let them know we got a new gig. Get the big building ready—we're going to have company."

Billy handed David a phone and took out another phone and began to text the alert out to the crew.

David smiled. "*Rabbit*? I'm surprised you remembered."

Morris was excited as he drained his coffee. "You know me, each gig different code names. I need a couple of hours. I'll call you when we're ready. Get me a body count. I'll arrange transportation to the site. Bring clothes and all your files. Once in, we stay till we're done. Then it goes national."

Morris stood up. "This will be fun. I can't wait to see how

the media and D.C. deal with this. Man, it's good to see you."

David stood up. It was time to go. He hugged Morris. "You know this puts a target on your back for working with Collins?"

Morris turned to leave. "What's new? It's just more amateurs taking shots at me."

Morris and Billy ducked out the back door. David walked out the front door to his car. He looked around just to be sure he was alone. He started the car and headed indirectly to the grocery store in case someone was following.

Time to pick up food for tonight. The group would need a good meal. He knew the kind of pressure they would be under to get the Tribunal recorded and pushed out to the public. He just hoped they could count on the other members of the Tribunal to join them. He pulled over and used Gator's phone to text the question: *Can you find the other Tribunal members, and can you pick them up?"*

He pulled out a pad and started a list of groceries. Steaks would be good tonight, baked potatoes, salad.

The phone beeped, he read the text. "Have six located. Two don't want any part. Let me know who to pick up, and we will do what we can."

David typed out another text. "Send you names in an hour."

As he drove to the grocery store, he called Diane. He needed to give her a heads-up.

CHAPTER 32

BEN WAS DICTATING A LIST OF QUESTIONS TO WALT while Jenny and Patrick kibitzed. Diane picked up her phone and answered. "Yes dear, did you forget something?"

Ben stopped talking as Diane handed him the phone. He listened nodding. "Ok, you trust him?"

Ben got up and started to pace. Walt looked at Diane and mouthed, *"David?"*

She nodded.

The room was quiet as they listened to the one-sided conversation. Ben stopped and said, "See you shortly." He turned to face the waiting questions of the group. He raised his hand to stop them. "David's friend *Gator* is the one who set off the fire alarm which allowed you to escape the auditorium. He's going to help us tape the Tribunal and get it out via the internet. David should be here shortly, and he suggested we get ready to present the Tribunal as planned. He asked if you could identify which of the Tribunal members we should include."

Patrick was still working through the legal issues of what Ben had just said. He turned to Daniel. "I think we can omit Barry and Tanya— I'm sure they will not want to participate. What about the others?"

Daniel had been leaning against the wall trying to keep up. He was exhausted and hearing the Tribunal might be going underground was a lot to process. He stammered. "I think Baruti for sure, Andy likes a fight, and Angela would be helpful as she always has a different perspective. I don't know Professor...we don't even know where they are."

Ben interrupted. "David says Gator is tracking them down and already has a line on a couple of them. We just need to tell them which ones to contact."

Jenny turned to go to the kitchen. She looked at Ben. "I like that kid, are you sure I can't adopt him?"

Ben shook his head. "He's too old to adopt—go cook something."

Patrick had picked up a pad and started a list of the students that he thought would be interested in participating. He stopped and looked at Ben. "If we do this, and we can't get it in front of the public it's over. And if we can get it to the public, we still have to pray they watch the Tribunal and support it."

Ben smiled. "Thank you for those encouraging words, Patrick. Now if you're done we need to get things laid out."

He called Jenny. "David said we need to be ready to relocate for a couple of days. Once we go into wherever we're going, we don't come out until we finish."

William got up. "I think I need a shower," and he headed for the door.

Ben turned to Diane. "Make sure we pick up jury-suitable clothes for Patrick, Daniel, and William. We can ask Gator to be sure the Tribunal class brings Jury suitable clothes when he picks them up. Daniel, we need sizes for you and William. Patrick, are you listening?"

Patrick was deep in thought preparing for the trial of his life. He looked around at the people in the room. A smile crept carefully across his face. If he had to face the biggest trial of his life, this was a good group to do it with. He wished Anna could be here. He looked at his notes and began to add items by category. "Yes, let's do this."

Everyone was working. Jenny looked around and thought how good it had been to have them here. She felt alive again. Jenny emptied the dishwasher. Time to get ready to feed the herd. She wondered what David was planning for dinner. She had gotten used to his foresight and just enjoyed having him here. He was the kind of kid she wished she and Ted could have raised.

CHAPTER 33

AGENT TILLIS, PORTLAND, AND PATTERSON STOOD in front of Lisa Millington. She had taken over Tillis's desk. Patterson nudged Tillis and looked at a pile on the floor. Tillis raised one eyebrow as he recognized his laptop and the pile next to it which used to be sitting on his desk.

Millington kept looking at her computer screen. "As you know I was sent by the White House to clean up the mess you've made. I've read through all of your case notes, and now I need to hear what's not in them. Is there anything you wish to tell me? If not Bailey will take your statements."

Tillis felt that awkward silence one feels as they stand by a casket and look at the body of an old friend. In this case, the friend was probably going to be agent Tillis's career. "I believe everything is in my case notes Mam, is there anything else or can I go? I want to get checked out of the hotel and head home."

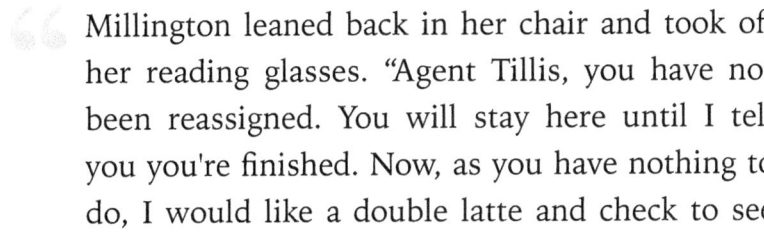

Millington leaned back in her chair and took off her reading glasses. "Agent Tillis, you have not been reassigned. You will stay here until I tell you you're finished. Now, as you have nothing to do, I would like a double latte and check to see what my staff would like. I am sure you are familiar with where to get coffee."

Tillis nodded and started to head for the door. He could hear her beginning what would be a lengthy interrogation of Patterson and Portland.

As he exited the room, Bailey Valentine followed him. Once outside the door, Tillis turned expecting another insult from her lackey. Bailey stuck out his hand. "Bailey Valentine, she's a charmer, isn't she?"

Tillis shook his hand cautiously. "I can think of many descriptive references, but *charming* is not one of them."

Bailey laughed. "I know. I asked my boss what I did wrong to be sent with her on this assignment."

Tillis relaxed just a couple of degrees. "What did your boss tell you?"

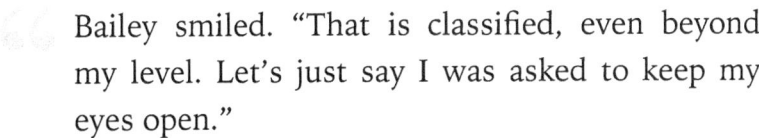

Bailey smiled. "That is classified, even beyond my level. Let's just say I was asked to keep my eyes open."

Tillis nodded. "Her reputation preceded her. I got several calls warning me she was on a head-hunting expedition and to be careful. Who sent her? My boss didn't know about it until she was on her way."

Bailey looked around to see who was listening. With no one visible, he lowered his voice and kept his stage smile in place. "It seems that certain parties within the White House set this up. We all need to be watchful while we are here. The target appears to be Collins and anyone who helped him. His files are causing the biggest panic in D.C. anyone has ever seen."

"The deaths of Mason Ballard and Wendy Carlson are just adding fuel to the public's anger."

"The media is describing the Campus Security Chief as a crazy old man who recklessly shot through the roof of his vehicle and deliberately killed Mason Ballard. Which then leads to the death of Wendy Carlson."

"You and I know this is one of those things where everyone involved has some blame, the Campus Chief, the students but no one should have died. But everyone wants someone to pay for the deaths."

"In this story, the Campus Security Chief is the bad guy."

"The media is just working the story for all they can get. Everyone is looking to use this tragedy. The anti-gun lobby is in full swing. Some are talking about disarming local police and only having guns in the hands of Federal law enforcement. You know the usual *distort the report to support your cause* strategy."

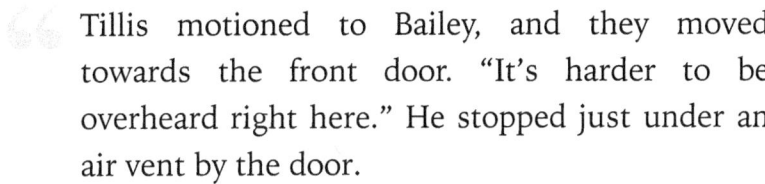 Tillis motioned to Bailey, and they moved towards the front door. "It's harder to be overheard right here." He stopped just under an air vent by the door.

Bailey looked up at the air vent. "Thanks, I'll remember that."

"We learned on day one that this foyer area has great acoustics and anything you say carries up the stairs around the corner and pretty much all over. I figured that out when I came out of the "John" on the second floor, and I could hear two of my guys talking downstairs. I thought they were pretty loud, but when I got to the steps, they were sitting on that bench talking in normal voices, but this place amplifies the sound."

Bailey looked around the foyer studying the layout. "That could be useful in case I intentionally need to be overheard. Thanks. I guess you should go for coffee now?"

Tillis smiled. "How do you want yours?"

"I'm good, just make sure you get something for the Madam —she pulled that on me twice. I made sure I found the worst coffee around. After a couple of bad cups, she moves onto making someone else's life hell."

As Tillis turned to go, Bailey touched his arm. "Be careful.

She doesn't care who she destroys. She just likes doing it. They use her when they don't care about prisoners or witnesses. Be sure if she sends you somewhere, that you take someone with you that you trust. You may need them as a witness. Pick your people carefully and be sure they all understand."

Bailey turned and headed back to the command post.

Tillis watched him walk away. Tillis had a lot to think about. Bailey seemed to be an unusually honest person, which was not the norm in D.C. Most of those in D.C. practiced building their careers by standing on the remains of someone else's career. Maybe Bailey was trying to distract him? For now, his mission was to find the worst cup of coffee around for the Madam.

CHAPTER 34

JENNY SLIPPED OUT TO THE SUNROOM WHERE IT was quiet. The others were all in the dining room working. She wanted someplace quiet to make a couple of calls. She needed to check with a couple of her contacts in the media and see which direction public opinion was blowing. She ran through three of them and was processing what she had heard. She saw David drive in and got up to help him unload.

As she opened the door, David was already at the back of the SUV removing bags. "David, you are going to make someone a great husband. You cook, you shop, and you seem to remember everything. It's a good thing I'm not younger. I'd be after you."

David laughed and handed Jenny a bag of groceries. "My momma believed everyone pitched in. If you weren't busy, she would find something for you to do. My sister and I got good at trying to outguess momma. We stayed busy."

Jenny pushed the door aside as they carried in the bags. "So, no one special in your life?"

David began unpacking the groceries and laying out dinner. "There have been a couple that might have become special. But I've been pretty busy following Ben the last couple of years. It's not the time for me to settle down yet. I know there's someone special coming, but I just want to wait for the right time and the right one."

Jenny was folding the bags from the groceries. "David, have you been listening to the media while you were out?"

David stopped seasoning the steaks. "Yes, ma'am. It sounds like public sentiment is growing for Mr. Collins and lots of people are talking about how they'd like to see the Tribunal happen.

Jenny turned towards the war room. "Come with me."

Patrick and Ben were debating some point or another when Jenny walked in and tapped the table with a pencil. Everyone stopped and looked at her.

"I just made some calls to some of my media colleagues to see which way public opinion was blowing on this mess."

"I wasn't sure about trying to go forward with this Tribunal, but everyone I spoke to has said the same thing. They see

Collins as the new warrior for the rights of the people who are standing up to the corrupt D.C. government. It was interesting that the comments were almost identical. Kind of like if you listen to the Sunday morning talk shows where the spin is already scripted, and the various media drones pitch the same story no matter what channel you watch."

She continued. "But the general public seems to want to see the Tribunal. They want the dirty details exposed."

> "Ben, I wasn't sure at first, but I think we have a chance. I want to begin leaking information to the media. I believe we need to carefully link Collins to the Tribunal and start a branding campaign."

"If you agree, I'll get started."

Ben blinked a couple of times as he was processing Jenny's plan. "Do you need help?"

Jenny shook her head. "No, I think I've got this one. If I need help, I'll just steal David."

Jenny turned, picked up her laptop and a pad of paper. She headed for the sunroom. She smiled and spoke to Ted. "Wish you were here Babe, this is going to be fun. We're going to shed some light and watch the rats run for cover."

CHAPTER 35

SENATOR SHERATON HAD SLIPPED OUT OF HIS office. He had sent his driver on a scavenger hunt to throw off the media that followed every car that left the Hill. He, in turn, had one of his staff drop him off at the metro. Then Sheraton caught the red line and headed to Shady Grove. The hat and old field jacket gave him just enough cover that people shifted away when he sat down and acted like he was sleeping. His sunglasses hid his eyes, so he could easily watch others.

He had called an old friend who lived near Shady Grove and asked him to pick him up. The metro ride was uneventful and gave Sheraton a little time to mull over the last couple of calls he'd received.

Sheraton had called his wife and assured her everything would work out. He had reassured her it was just a lot of typical D.C. bluster about nothing.

Winslow had called him from DOJ to let him know the debate at very high levels seemed to focus on who they were going to sacrifice to save the White House and give them the famous Presidential excuse of *"Plausible Deniability."*

Winslow told him that there was no mention of the *Back Nine* in the briefing. Winslow also let him know there were so many people poring over the Collins files that it was just a matter of time before someone put it all together.

Sheraton got off at Shady Grove, which was the end of the line for the Red route. Marty Spitzer was sitting in the parking lot in an old pickup. Sheraton opened the passenger door and hopped in.

"Sheraton, what the hell did you get yourself into?"

Marty was an old hunting buddy and didn't care for politics. He had worked construction most of his life. Now he just did little repair jobs and let his sons do the real work.

> "Marty, I really stepped in it this time. I need to get out to the hunting lodge and wait this out."

Marty looked in the rearview mirror. "I think it may be too late. Have you been watching the news?"

Sheraton slouched in the seat wishing he could hide—too many people knew him around here. "I was watching just before I got on the metro. Why?"

The traffic was light, and Marty was pushing the speed limit. "Then you don't know the Department of Justice is looking for members of a secret D.C. group called the *Back Nine*. They said one of the members of the *Back Nine* was a guy in the DOJ who just killed himself in his office. The media is saying that he had papers spread out all over his desk about this group called the *Back Nine*."

"Apparently, your name is on the list of those wanted for questioning. They say it's linked to this other mess—the Collins conspiracy? What are you going to do?"

Sheraton's phone rang. It was Liz Tyler. He turned off his phone. Now was not the time he wanted to listen to her whining. "Can you get me to the cabin? I need to make some calls and figure this out."

Marty looked at Sheraton. "I figured that's why you were coming. I picked up some food and had one of the boys leave a truck out at the cabin. I'll drop you off and then I don't know you."

Sheraton nodded. "I think that's probably for the best. If anyone does show up looking for me, tell them you haven't seen me. And you have no idea where I could be. If I come up with something I may have to call you, but otherwise, stay away from the cabin."

Marty turned off the main road and headed down a back

road. A few more miles and turns and they would be at the cabin.

The rest of the trip they made in silence. Marty had turned on the radio and Sheraton had tuned out. He needed to figure out who was left that he could trust.

CHAPTER 36

GATOR HAD BEEN ON THE PHONE SINCE HE AND David had parted. Billy kept handing him different phones. Gator had learned the art of walking in the shadows and Billy was part of that shadow world. Everyone he had checked with was interested in making the Tribunal real if they would use the Collins files. By now everyone had read them. The media was spinning to the left and then to the right. But the media could not sway the American people in any direction —they were tired of being screwed, and the people were uniting on one thing. The public wanted to find the guilty and prosecute them to the fullest extent of the law. They wanted to clean house no matter who was in it.

Several of the internet newsgroups were volunteering to help broadcast the Tribunal segments. No one was backing down, they all expected there would be fallout but the way things were going in D.C., everybody could sense the change coming.

Gator called the phone he had given David. It rang twice. David answered. "Ready when you are."

Gator smiled as he looked out the window of the van. "You're sure this is what you want to do?"

 David stopped preparing dinner. "Everyone here is committed. We still need to round up the other Tribunal class members and see if they are in or not."

Gator punched Billy in the arm. "Billy has it covered. The two that tried to turn themselves into the authorities won't play. The others are ready and willing. We already have them moving to the new office. They know they will be underground until this is over. Most of them became committed when that Ballard kid got killed. I think we need to dedicate the Tribunal to his memory. It will have a huge impact and draw tons of support."

David shook his head. "You never miss an angle, do you? Gator, we've been talking about it over here and thought we need to break this into segments that we can broadcast quickly. My boss thinks we need to strike while it's fresh in people's minds."

 "Believe me, David, it's fresh. You should watch the news about D.C. It looks like the plague of truth is sweeping through the city—it's hourly confessions and resignations. Three suicides so far and two of the resignations were in the White House. The story is, the President is screaming at everyone and threatening anyone who leaves."

"Once we start the Tribunal hearings, I think you will have everyone's ear around the world."

David began to season and wrap foil around the potatoes. They needed an hour to bake. David looked at the clock. "So, when do we move?"

The car came to a stop in front of the warehouse door. Billy keyed in a code on the remote control, and the door began to open. "We need about four hours, and then we'll need to pick up your crew. How many are we moving?"

David looked at the war room and began to count. "Walt, Diane, Ben, Ramirez, Daniel, William, and myself."

Jenny rounded the corner and chimed in, "You better have included me in that count."

David nodded. "…And Jenny should be eight and maybe one or two more if we can get them in town on time."

Gator got out of the van and looked around the warehouse. They had plenty of room to park the vehicles so no one would see cars on the lot. "Ok, get ready. I'll call you about 8:00 PM. You said it would take 45-minutes to get to the rally point. I'll have our people in place. You know Billy, he'll handle the underground railway movement."

Gator walked over to the door leading to the building attached to the warehouse. He keyed in the access code, and the door clicked open. "Alright, I've got a lot to do—if you need something, call this number. I'll see you all tonight."

Gator handed his phone to Billy. "Guess you better have someone monitor these phones. We won't get much reception when we get in the pit." Billy nodded and took the phone and waved at the guys in the sound room.

Gator looked around. This was one of the key locations for his network. They had ten people monitoring the internet, news channels and listening to *selected sources* of information as he called them. Billy just called them the spies.

Julie intercepted Gator on his way to the back room. "Is everything ready?" he asked.

Julie carried her clipboard and began running through the status of the room. "We've got three cameras. We set the room up as a courtroom. The cameras will only cover the prosecution, defense, the Tribunal members and any witnesses."

"Everything is draped, so no one will be able to tell where we're located. We have three people on editing so we should be able to edit and release on the fly. We've set up about a hundred internet feeds. About twenty of those are giveaways to distract the Feds. Two of the giveaways internet feeds originate inside of military bases. That should cause a stir when they find those. Three of the newsgroups will look like they are broadcasting the segments live."

Gator looked around the room. It was set up well. "Good. How's the perimeter security? I don't want anyone finding us."

Julie hugged her clipboard. "Amadeus has taken this as a personal challenge. I can't even repeat what he said, but I assume from what he tried to explain to me that the NSA won't see us. But he still claims he designed most of their stuff, so he left places for him to hide."

"Gator, he *still* scares me."

Gator looked back at her as Amadeus headed behind the curtain. "Why do you think he faked his own death?

Julie shrugged. "Maybe he doesn't like people looking for him."

Gator shook his head. "He just likes playing this electronic game of *Hide and Seek*. It's all he has."

"How are we on beds and food?"

Julie returned to looking at her clipboard. "We can sleep almost 40 as long as they don't mind the barracks. We're good on food—lots of stuff on hand."

Julie stopped. "Gator, are you sure about this?"

Gator opened the door to his private office and looked back at Julie. "Why do you ask?" Typically, Julie never questioned Gator.

The clipboard was back to being hugged, but this time Julie's knuckles were turning white from the grip she had on the clipboard. "I don't know. This Tribunal thing is beyond big. I've been watching the news, and everyone is angry, particularly at those mentioned in the Collins Files. Do you think we can pull this off and just disappear like we always do? The Feds are hunting these guys, and if they find us, we could be in real trouble…or worse."

Gator walked over to Julie. He needed to look in her eyes. "Do you want out?"

Julie lifted her head. "No, I think it's right, and I believe it's time for the public to wake up. I just didn't think it would be like this. That kid and the attorney that got killed was like pouring gasoline on a fire. I know we've often talked about what it takes to wake up the sleeping giant of a united American Public. We've had a lot of fun poking at the giant, but this time I think the giant is awake and he's pissed."

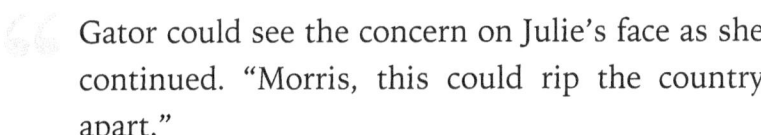 Gator could see the concern on Julie's face as she continued. "Morris, this could rip the country apart."

Gator stopped. Julie never used his real name. He walked over and sat on the couch. "Julie, when I first started as an activist I had all sorts of stars in my eyes about the truth. At least the truth as I saw it. After a while, I saw most of the stuff I thought of as the truth turned out to just be a snow job. I've been blind and willing to stand out there and be moved around like a puppet."

"Once I could see behind the demonstrations, I began to see

the strings of those who were feeding us funds and scripts. They dictated what to say and chant. I watched them, and I learned how to play their game."

"I knew someday a revolution would occur and people would have the chance to see past all of the spin—past the advertising and hype. They would be able to see the truth."

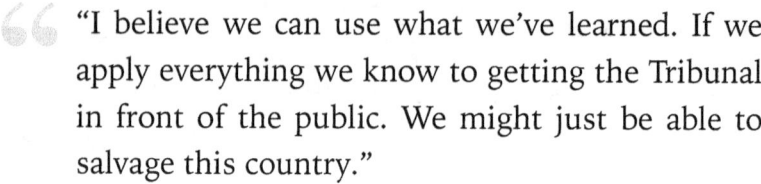

"I believe we can use what we've learned. If we apply everything we know to getting the Tribunal in front of the public. We might just be able to salvage this country."

Morris was dealing with a genuine sense of conviction. He continued, "I like the stuff this country was founded on. I like the Constitution. But everything has been twisted to benefit a very small group who want control. I've played along inside their structure learning. You know how many businesses we've built using their money. Now I think it's time we use everything we have learned and pull back the curtains."

"This Collins kid must feel the same way. He has two paths in front of him. Either he is the hero that exposed the puppet masters, or he's the guy that will be guilty of so many things that they will probably kill him. But Collins information is so far beyond being discredited that either he has to be removed or he is going to rise to the top."

"I just think he is worth helping. I don't believe that this opportunity will ever come again."

Julie turned to leave. "Thanks, I just wanted to be sure. I agree it's time to stand for something. We've played their game long enough. It's time we picked what we do, and this one is a winner. And almost everyone agrees. Everyone wants to get this Collins guy a fair hearing."

Julie walked out and left Morris alone. He pulled out his personal phone and looked at the photos of his wife and kids. Gator hit the speed dial—*better call now* he thought to himself. He might not be able to touch base with them for a while. He hoped when this was over he could stay home and maybe make the real businesses work.

He heard his wife's voice. "Hey babe, how are the kids?" Gator looked across his office. There were no pictures of his wife or kids in his office. Gator kept his family private. He closed his eyes and could see his wife and wondered what it would be like to just be Morris Schwartz.

CHAPTER 37

DANIEL AND WILLIAM SLIPPED OUT OF THE HOUSE and wandered down to the lake. They were sitting under a tree looking out across the water. William was chewing on a piece of grass. "Daniel, I'm sorry. I can't imagine what Mom and Dad are thinking. I didn't believe it would get this crazy. I just planned on dumping the info to the public and then was going to lay low till it settled. I just figured this information might get your Tribunal project a little notoriety and maybe help you get some free press."

Daniel was sitting against a tree. "I almost fell out of my chair when I finally recognized it was you. I couldn't see you at first because of the lighting."

"Then when I saw it was you, I was so angry that you were trying to steal the show."

William stretched out in the grass. He rolled over and leaned on one arm. "I never thought about upstaging you. I guess I just miss read this whole thing. I sure didn't expect the Feds to show up. At least not till it was over. I only planned to be there fifteen minutes. I figured I could dump the information and run. Where else could I find so many electronic savvy people that could help get the files distributed? I didn't think I could pick a better place to get the word out."

Daniel picked up an acorn and tossed it at William. "You should have seen your face when that Fed burst in and said who he was. I can't imagine my brother at the top of the most wanted list. And I didn't plan on joining you on that list."

"Hey *Wild Bill,* when this is over maybe you can help me write my resume? If we ever get out of jail or wherever they send domestic terrorists?"

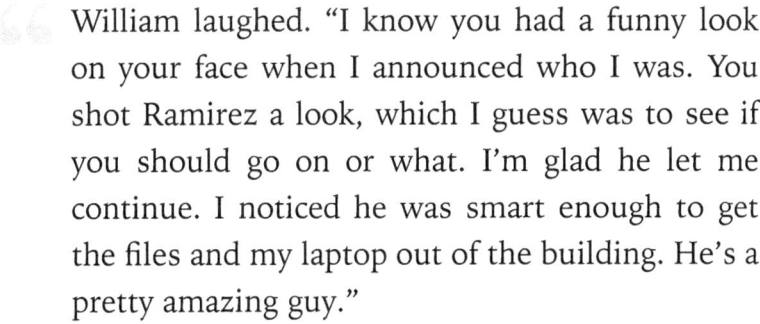

William laughed. "I know you had a funny look on your face when I announced who I was. You shot Ramirez a look, which I guess was to see if you should go on or what. I'm glad he let me continue. I noticed he was smart enough to get the files and my laptop out of the building. He's a pretty amazing guy."

Daniel looked back out at the lake. "Professor Ramirez has been a great teacher. He told us he was going to challenge us to think and learn, not to be programmed. He has put us through some crazy exercises. You should read his articles on *spin*. I never really thought about it, but we all learned so much from him."

"Hey, you missed the look on your face when the fire alarm went off. That was the best thing that could have happened. That guy gator saved our butts."

William laid back. "Yeah, I look forward to meeting him and thank him. I wish I could talk to Shelly, but I told her I was going to expose this mess in D.C. and I would show her I was out of the backroom business. I don't think she had any idea how bad it is up there."

> "William, I've been reading the stuff you are sending out. I didn't believe it when I first started reading it, but the files you've released explained a lot about what we see in the media. And you have pulled back the curtains and wow...now I understand just how corrupt D.C. is!"

"I don't know. Maybe the public will finally wake up. Ramirez talked about how the public is so easily led to believe whatever you want them to believe. In class, Ramirez would pull up stories in the media, and we would analyze the stories behind them or the legislation that resulted. He made us question what we saw. I guess that's why he jumped into this. He wants to see America wake up. He told us a lot about his parents and how both sides of his family were immigrants."

"He doesn't say much outside of class, but in class, it's like a *Vulcan Mind Meld*. I don't think any of us have missed a single class. Everyone knows a good grade from Ramirez carries a lot of weight when we look for jobs."

William sat up. "We should probably head back. Ben said we're going to be moving tonight and they want to start the Tribunal tomorrow. I told him I would give him everything I released and I still have a couple of things I'm holding as bargaining chips for when I turn myself in."

Daniel stopped watching the clouds morph from a dolphin into a strange face. "I hadn't thought about that. I guess we'll all be turning ourselves in if they don't catch us first."

"I guess Ben and Ramirez will coach us on what we should do?"

William sat up. "I heard Ben tell Diane and Walt to contact a couple of other lawyers he knows to have them standing by. He told Ramirez he would represent any or all of us that wanted him to represent them."

Daniel furrowed his brow and got that look he used to get when he was trying to figure out how to tell Mom something that he had done. "I don't think any of us can afford Ben as our attorney."

William got up as he heard Jenny calling from the house. "Daniel, I don't think any of us can afford this, so we better make the Tribunal tell the story. It may be the only chance we get."

He held out his hand to help Daniel up. Daniel took his hand, and they stood for a minute still holding hands as men do when faced with a monumental task. "William, whatever it takes, I'll be there."

"Ramirez asked me to head the Tribunal because he said I was the most likely to judge it fairly. He told me I needed to look at the Constitution and how it has been interpreted. Then I needed to throw out the interpretations and go after the heart of it and what was best for the American people."

"I thought he was just giving me one of those John Wayne speeches on America. But now, I think I get it."

They headed up the path. Jenny was standing on the porch waiting. "You did the right thing—now we go deal with it."

William punched Daniel. "I think you should tell Dad about this when it's over. I think I'll be in the doghouse for a long time."

Jenny called out. "Get in here, David has dinner ready and then we have to get packed. We're moving tonight. So get up here—we have lots to do to get ready."

The boys felt like Mom had just called them in from playing outside. Memories can be good bonds when things get tough, and they were about to get tougher than anything they had experienced.

CHAPTER 38

AGENT PATTERSON AND TILLIS WERE BACK AT THE
same diner trying to figure out what to have for dinner while
hiding from Deputy Director Millington.

Patterson knew the menu already, but he kept looking at it as
if he expected it to change or reveal some overlooked
culinary delight. Interrupting his decision, Tillis asked,
"What are you going to have?"

Tillis was a creature of habit. "Probably the same thing we
had last night. It sure isn't as good as Mattie's cooking. You
know Jack, I think that's the worst part of this job. There is
just so much you can't talk about at home, so you end up
talking about little stuff. Now, I find I miss the little stuff
more than this job."

Patterson put the menu down as the waitress came to take

their orders. She looked at them and rattled off what they had ordered the night before. They both nodded, and she walked off to order the same dinner from last night.

"I think you may be on to something. I took this job to make a difference, but something has changed. We used to hunt people who had killed someone or were running drugs, or guns or doing illegal things. Now we just chase people for not agreeing with whoever is in power this term."

"I was talking to Peg before we started this assignment. She's been encouraging me to find something else. I find being home is more important to me and I am so tired of trying to justify what we're doing."

The waitress dropped off one soft drink and one iced tea. As she left, Tillis looked around and quietly said, "I know what you mean. I think I became concerned when they began to arm the IRS."

"Why in the world do we need to arm the accountants? We now have so many different Federal Law Enforcement agencies that we keep running into each other. We seem to all be investigating the same things. And no one wants to work together."

Patterson sipped at his soda. "I need to give up sugar. You know the new term for *we screwed up this investigation* is *"Joint Taskforce?"*

Tillis fished the lemon out of his tea and put it on a napkin. "You mean like the cluster we're investigating now? So far, we have agents from DEA, ATF, NSA, FBI, Homeland

Security, and a couple of people I don't know who they work for, but my boss said to include them. Oh, and I forgot the *queen* of the DOJ."

"Yep, I think I'm going to look for honest work when this is over if I don't end up in jail for screwing this mess up."

"Brad, this mess is not your fault. We knew this was going to be bad when they told us we were looking for a National security threat and we found out it was some congressional aide leaking details about congressional shenanigans."

"Hell, if the Media were doing what they used to, I think they used to call it *investigative reporting,* then we would be at home right now."

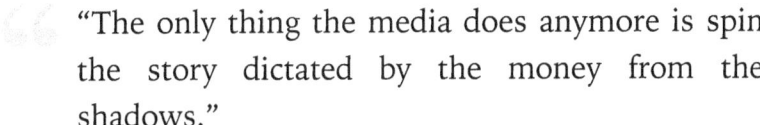

"The only thing the media does anymore is spin the story dictated by the money from the shadows."

"I think we all have been expecting things to blow up. I just didn't plan on being at the front of the line when it started."

The waitress swung by to deliver dinner. "One salad with Italian dressing, one with Ranch, and one chicken fried steak and one meatloaf special. If you guys show up tomorrow night, I'll order for you. You guys need a change!"

The waitress walked away. Patterson and Tillis looked at their plates.

"Jack, if we're still here tomorrow and end up here, I'm going to let her order for me. I think she has an inside track on what to eat."

Jack Patterson looked at his meatloaf special. "I think you're right. Pass me the ketchup. I need to drown this thing."

They had almost finished eating when Bailey Valentine walked over to their table.

He pulled a chair from another table and sat down.

Tillis felt his chicken fried steak advise him that indigestion had just arrived.

Valentine pulled out his phone and muted the ring. "One of your guys said I might find both of you here. I wanted you to hear it from me before you got it from someone else. Millington is calling a press conference to announce that you both have been placed on administrative leave. She's decided to begin deflecting blame on both of you. She can't go after the Campus Police chief. They just announced he had a breakdown and is unable to competently reply to the charges that she was going to file against him."

"The parents of Mason Ballard have filed a lawsuit against the university. The board is calling for all sorts of resignations. The media is howling because they don't know who to blame and they are not getting direction from the *Spin Doctors*."

"Tyler and I have been tasked with picking up the manhunt for Collins and all of the Tribunal members and Professor Ramirez. "

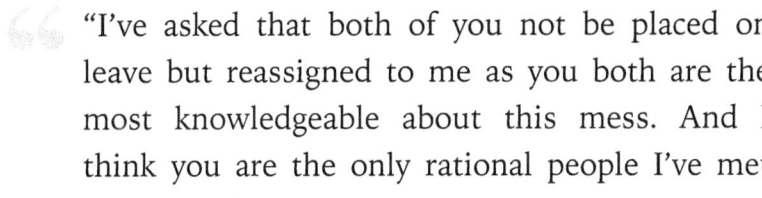 "I've asked that both of you not be placed on leave but reassigned to me as you both are the most knowledgeable about this mess. And I think you are the only rational people I've met since I got here."

Patterson looked at Tillis. "I think I *almost* like this guy."

Tillis was already on high alert. He started off very slow, looking for the land mines, bear traps or whatever was laying out here to hurt him. "I appreciate you stepping in to help us. I think...but what do you want?"

The waitress made her stop to check on the new guest. Before she could take his order, Bailey looked at her, smiled, and ordered a Caesar salad with chicken. "And put everything on one bill and give it to me please..."

The waitress nodded and left without a word.

Tillis sat back. If this was his last meal before the execution, he wished that he had ordered the steak. "Ok, but what do you want? I can't see any advantage for you to stick up for us?"

Bailey nodded. "I agree. From where you sit, I'm just one more jerk from the DOJ meddling in your investigation..."

"Between us little guys, I detest the part-time people. You know the ones that come in each term and are appointed by whoever won the last election. They come in waving the flag of the person who appointed them. Then they make life hell for the career people. My boss is one of those career types like us. He sent me out here to try to help and keep an eye on Millington."

"We know she has an agenda. We just don't know what it is. My boss and I both want to find this Collins guy and get him somewhere safe. It would be better if Collins ends up in FBI custody. If Homeland gets him, he could disappear into the fog of National Security."

Patterson looked at Tillis. "Are we in OZ or Wonderland? I can't tell if this guy is Alice, the White Rabbit or Dorothy?"

Tillis was trying to clear his head. He wondered if the severe lack of sleep over the past couple of days had finally caught up with him. Bailey was making sense and that concerned him. He had been around bureaucrats a long time and never trusted them. "Why are you sticking your neck out for us? Or are you just trying to distract us as we walk to the chopping block?"

The waitress brought Bailey his drink and gave him silverware and napkins. "Your salad will be right out."

Bailey smiled. "Thank you." The waitress continued her route through the tables as she crisscrossed the restaurant.

Bailey squeezed the slice of lemon into the tea. "This will be hard to believe, but there are those of us who still believe in things like truth, the Constitution, Bill of Rights...you get the idea. They used to call us patriots. Now, if I weren't working inside the government, my beliefs would get me reclassified as a homegrown terrorist. But I work inside of the government and keep a low profile. Wow, I hadn't thought about it, but in the old movies, I guess that would make me a spy for the underground. I wonder how Regan would view this subject?"

Bailey leaned back as the waitress made her approach and dropped off his salad. "Anything else I can get you, boys?"

Patterson nodded. "Coffee."

Tillis joined the parade. "Coffee would be good—cream for me please."

Bailey looked at his salad. "Maybe tomorrow night we can find somewhere else to eat?"

"Ok, here is what we need to do now. I have convinced Millington to give us 48 hours to track down Collins. This is a small town. Collins is probably holed up with friends. I want the two of you to get your guys going over everyone who is related to or friends with Ramirez, the Tribunal members and any known associates of Collins. I spoke to his fiancé's parents, and they have assured me that Collins has not contacted them or their daughter since just after the car accident."

Patterson pushed his plate to one side. "I had a couple of agents follow up on her. She isn't going very far after the accident. I understood she still needs several more surgeries to her face. They weren't sure if there was any permanent damage to her eye."

Bailey finished a bite of the salad. "I read the report. We have warrants to wiretap everyone involved, associated or that we just don't like. So, cell phones, hard lines, email, are all fair game. God knows you have to love the coverage of a National Security threat. They just hand us the keys to the park, and we get to go do whatever we want."

Tillis stacked his plate on top of Patterson's. "I take it they haven't been able to stop the Collins files from popping up here and there?"

Bailey sat back and pushed the chair back on two legs. "I want to give this Collins guy a chance to come out. We're going to offer to meet with him or just talk to us. I expect he will have an attorney contacting us any moment. He won't be able to hide much longer. Someone will spill his location."

"As more and more people take the time to read the Collins files, the D.C. crowd is finding themselves in the public's crosshairs. The public is starting to look at this guy as a national hero. D.C. is looking at him in a much less favorable light. Several comments have been *quietly* made about what happens if he dies while resisting arrest?"

"That's why I need both of you to help me find them. We need Collins alive. That won't make the part-timers happy, but we have another election next year so who really cares?"

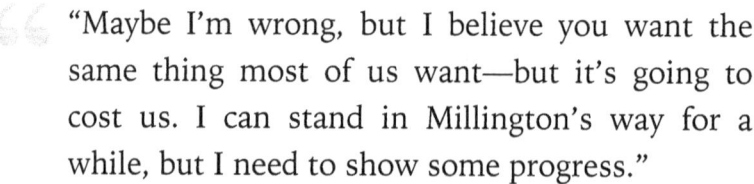

"Maybe I'm wrong, but I believe you want the same thing most of us want—but it's going to cost us. I can stand in Millington's way for a while, but I need to show some progress."

Tillis still didn't trust Bailey. He sounded too good to be true, but with no options in front of him, he asked, "When do we start?"

Bailey waved at the waitress. "Check please...we start tomorrow morning 8:00 AM. We should have all of the warrants, and I have requested some additional agents to back you up. I called your bosses and took the liberty of asking them to send in some agents you could trust."

Bailey handed the waitress a credit card and watched as she left. "D.C. is scared. They have never been this close to a full-fledged civil uprising. A conflict of D.C. against the American people terrifies them."

"We need to do what we can to minimize the bloodshed. This Tribunal group could be the key to getting a lot of information in front of the American people. The American people then need to decide if they want to clean house or ignore the corruption. But there is no reason these kids need to be the scapegoats for a bunch of political thieves that we can't normally touch."

"Call me a conspirator, but I think the public deserves the truth."

Bailey got up. "How is the breakfast here?"

Patterson started getting up. "It's as good as you get this close to the Command Post."

Bailey nodded. "I'll be here for breakfast at 7:00 am if you happen to be in the neighborhood. Otherwise, see you at the command post at 8:00 am."

As Bailey left, Patterson and Tillis followed slowly letting the distance between Bailey and them grow until they could talk privately.

Brad stopped just outside of the door to the restaurant looked around to make sure no one could overhear them. "I don't know if he is legit or not, but I will be here for breakfast. He's the first guy to see this mess for what it is, and I may be wrong, but I think I'll tag along."

Patterson looked up the street, just a typical college town, turning young, eager students into cannon fodder. "I'll try to check him out, but I agree. Breakfast at 7:00 am. Now, take me to the hotel—I need to get some sleep."

CHAPTER 39

DAVID AND JENNY WERE CLEANING UP THE DISHES and putting them away. "We will need to leave as soon as Gator calls. Jenny, is there anything we need to do to help you close the house down?"

Jenny looked around, doing a mental inventory. "No, I'll check in with one of the neighbors in a day or two and have them pick up the mail and keep an eye on things. How long do you think we'll be gone?"

David folded the dish towel and hung it on the back of the pantry door. "I don't know. I can't imagine we have much time before they find us. We need to be very quick in getting the Tribunal rolling, recorded and out to the public."

"Now I need to see if Ben needs any help."

Jenny started going room to room closing everything down. Everyone was gathered in the living room finalizing notes and waiting. Jenny was in her bedroom when she heard David's phone ring. She closed the door and sat on the bed and looked at the photo of Ted and her sitting on the porch.

"Well babe, I wish you were here. I could use your help. I never thought I would see this country in this kind of shape. They're twisting the truth so much that it's hard to tell who the good guys are among all of the bad guys."

> "I'm going to do everything I can to help these kids. I think they deserve a chance."

She got up went to her closet. Jenny stood quietly for a moment, remembering. Even after all these years, she could still feel his presence. She touched one of his favorite shirts, sighed and walked out.

David had gone out to start the SUV. They decided Diane and Walt would drive Cathy's car in case someone was looking for it. Jenny was going to drive her car and take Ben with her. Everyone else was going with David.

David had asked each of them to leave five minutes apart. They all knew the rendezvous point where Gator's people would pick them up and move their cars.

Ben was talking to David as Jenny closed the house down. "David, are you sure this Gator person is reliable?"

David smiled. "Boss, if he isn't, I'll be in the cell next to you."

Ben shook his head. "That's a reassuring thought. Have you got the rest of the staff standing by?"

"Sure, Mindy is staying in town to keep an eye on Anna and help her get through this. And she's available if we need her. The rest are almost sleeping in the office waiting for you to call the press conference."

Jenny had pulled her car out of the garage and was waiting. Ben looked at her and waved. "Alright David, I guess we're ready."

David grinned, as he put the car in drive, Ben heard him say, "Into the valley of death rode the 600…"

Ben turned to David. "You're stealing my line." He walked over and got in Jenny's car.

"While we're waiting, what did you say David was stealing from you?"

Ben chuckled. "He was quoting a line from the Charge of the Light Brigade."

Jenny looked out the window. "Great, couldn't you two find something better to quote? If I remember right, most of the light brigade died in that charge, right?"

Ben had seen the movie dozens of times and leaned back and quoted the last of the poem.

"Cannon to right of them,
Cannon to left of them,
Cannon behind them
Volley'd and thunder'd;
Storm'd at with shot and shell,
While horse & hero fell,
They that had fought so well
Came thro' the jaws of Death,
Back from the mouth of Hell,
All that was left of them,
Left of six hundred.

When can their glory fade?
O the wild charge they made!
All the world wonder'd.
Honor the charge they made!
Honor the Light Brigade,
Noble six hundred!"

Jenny started the car. "Great, couldn't you guys have picked something out of Winnie the Pooh or something a little more encouraging?"

Ben had been in a lot of legal battles. He had defended lots of high-profile clients. But this case was probably going to tear the country apart, or it was going to bury all of them.

Ben looked at Jenny, and in his best "Eeyore voice" he quoted, "We haven't had an earthquake lately."

Jenny turned on the radio. "Great, only you could spoil Winnie the Pooh. Oh, this is going to be a long drive. We need to stop and get gas."

She drove off, and Ben closed his eyes and began preparing his opening statement.

CHAPTER 40

BILLY WAS WAITING IN THE SHOPPING CENTER'S parking lot. He had picked this lot and spot as it was just out of range of the cameras monitoring the parking lot. Anyone seeing him sitting there would think he was just waiting for someone getting off from work. Dale and Tammy sat in the back of the van. They would be driving the other two cars that were coming. David would just follow the van.

Tammy was looking at her phone monitoring several websites. Dale started to get in the front seat opposite Billy. "Just stay back there. It will be easier to move the luggage from there.

Dale sat back in the second row. "Who's going to pick us up when we dump the cars?"

Billy looked at his phone to check the time. "Probably me.

Gator doesn't want any more people running around outside than we need to."

"They should be here in a few minutes."

Tammy looked up. "Wow, this Tribunal thing is getting a lot of attention. Do you guys realize how big this is going to be when we start broadcasting the actual hearings?"

Dale hated being out of his studio. "Gator said this might be the biggest gig we've ever worked. I know he had all of us out shopping to bring in supplies all day."

"How many people are we going to have in the hole?"

Tammy went back to her phone. She was monitoring several Twitter feeds and posting just enough to keep the rumor mill stirred up. "Julie told me to plan for about thirty with our people."

Billy was watching cars come and go. "I think thirty is about right. We picked up seven of the Tribunal members this afternoon. We had to make five trips to get them. They were scattered all over the place and then we had to be sure they weren't followed or bugged."

"Most of them are just watching the news and making notes. Julie told them to prepare to hold the Tribunal just like they'd planned."

Billy saw the SUV pull up across the parking lot. The lights blinked once. Billy responded with a right turn signal. "Ok, you two get ready, the first car is here."

A minute later a red Camry pulled next to the van. The window rolled down, and Walt leaned out of the window. "I guess you're Billy?"

Billy nodded. "Before you get out, how much stuff do we need to move? I want to attract as little attention as possible."

"We're traveling light, one backpack each and one overnight bag."

Billy scanned the parking lot again. "When you get out of the car, the bags come with you." Walt pulled the bags from the back seat and held them on his lap.

Billy called over his shoulder, "Tammy open the side door and trade places with them. Take this car back to The Whales and park it in back where the employee's park."

Tammy opened the side door. No lights came on as Billy had taken out the interior light.

Walt opened his door and got out with both bags. He stepped into the van and Dale moved the bags to the back of the van.

Tammy was already around the car when Diane got out and grabbed her bags. Tammy slid by her into the seat of the Camry and was driving off before Diane got in the van.

Dale took her bags, and Walt helped her in.

Billy looked around to see if anyone was watching. A waitress from one of the fast food places walked over and got in her car. She rolled down her window, and they could hear her radio playing.

Billy watched as she pulled away—never looking at them. Billy let out the breath he was holding ever since he has seen the waitress. "Dale, I thought you had their shifts figured out?"

"Billy, you can't know what these fast food joints will do. Maybe it was slow, so they sent her home early."

A green 4-Runner pulled up next to them. Walt called out from the back, "It's ok, that's our boss."

Billy would be relieved when this night was over. "Ready Dale?"

Dale opened the side door and started around to the driver's side.

Ben was already out of the car and handed his bags to Walt. He turned around just as a police car drove by. He stepped over to the van window and leaned on the door. "Let me know if the patrol car stops. If he does, I'll get back in the car, and you drive away."

Billy nodded. "Good plan." Jenny was still in the driver's seat watching the patrol car.

Dale tapped on her window. "Can you turn off the interior lights before you get out?" Jenny lowered the window. "I don't know how to do that." Everyone in both cars watched the patrol car drive down one of the rows of cars, five aisles over.

Dale was still watching the patrol car. "Lady, is your bag in the back seat or can you get it?"

Jenny watched as the patrol car slowed and a light appeared as they watched the officer shining his light on the license plate of a car. "My bags are in the back."

As Dale watched the patrol car, he slipped to the rear door of the car. "Ok lady, just slide out of the car and I will grab your bags and put them on the ground. Then I'm going to slip into the driver's seat and drive off. Are you ready?"

Jenny was starting to recover her wits. "Call me Jenny, and here I come."

She opened her door as Dale opened the rear door of her car and grabbed her bags. Ben swept around the car scooped up her bags and headed for the back of the van.

Dale quietly slid into the driver's seat of Jenny's car and drove away.

Jenny was still standing there as her car drove off.

Ben called from the van, "Jenny, let's go."

Jenny walked to the van while watching the patrol car. She almost fell when the patrol car turned off his spotlight and turned on his siren. All the lights on top of the car were flashing as he drove to the end of the aisle of cars.

The second siren caused them all to turn expecting a SWAT team to surround them.

An ambulance whisked by them and headed towards the

interrupted him, *"The* Professor Ramirez— I've heard about you for years. I even have a lot of your lectures."

Patrick was caught off guard. "You do?"

Gator and David traded looks. "I like the way you teach. I taped a lot of your classes through some of your students… but we can talk about that later."

The rest of the Tribunal class came in the room. The reunion was noisy and confused as they all tried to talk, ask questions and fill in the blanks since the initial attempt at the Tribunal.

Gator let it go on for a couple of minutes and then he stepped up on the Tribunal platform and tapped the microphone. "I know you all want to get caught up, but we need to get this thing moving. Half of the law enforcement agencies in the country are looking for you guys. Professor, Ben let's get this thing going. My people are ready to start taping as soon as you are."

Ben and Ramirez traded looks and moved to the platform.

Ben deferred to Ramirez. "I know you all have questions, but most of them will have to wait. For those of you that haven't had a chance to meet William Collins, that's him standing next to Daniel."

William raised his hand, looking very uncomfortable.

"William is why we're here. He has provided us with real evidence that we need to present to the American people. I believe we all feel the Tribunal will be a good exercise and let us examine Congress's actions. We must test their actions against the Constitution to determine if those actions have supported the Constitution or violated the Constitution and the trust of the American People."

"Have all of you had a chance to read through the Collins files?"

They all nodded. "Good, then the key change in our process is that we will use the Collins files as evidence and test each one to see how they impact the American people."

Ramirez continued. "I know we're short two members of the Tribunal. Ben is loaning us, two members of his staff, to fill in the holes in our ranks."

"Diane will assist the Prosecution and Walt will assist the Defense." Both Diane and Walt waved at the students.

"Their job is to help you and act as legal counsel. They won't appear on camera but will be whispering in your ear as needed. They are both very familiar with William's files as we have collectively been going over them for the last couple of days."

"Gator has provided us a secure place to work. I urge you to respect he and his staff. They wish to remain as anonymous as possible, so please respect their privacy. We could not do this without their help. As soon as we have completed the Tribunal and it is being sent out to the American people, William, Daniel and I plan on turning ourselves into the authorities. Ben Langley has graciously agreed to act as the Defense Attorney for all of the Tribunal members. Any of you that wish to join us can let us know as we go forward."

"Ok, I know you have questions, but we need to get started. Defense counsel on the left, Prosecution on the right. Judges if you don't know where you are supposed to go, you just failed the class."

"You have one hour to pull it together—we'll start with opening statements."

The class began moving towards their designated assignments, laptops, and backpacks in tow.

Ben and Gator watched as the Tribunal member began pulling out papers, setting up their laptops. Ben turned to Patrick. "Wow, I'm impressed, no questions—just get it done."

Gator shook his head. "You know, I think this might work. In the meantime, I have to go get my troops moving"

Gator walked away. Ben and Ramirez sat down and continued their discussion about how to make the public announcement of the Tribunal and gain the sentiment of the public.

Jenny chased after Gator. "Do you mind if I tag along? As a journalist, I'm curious about your organization."

Gator nodded and led Jenny to a side door. "The first question everyone wants to know is where do we get the money to do this?"

Jenny followed Gator through the door into what looked like a call center or chat room. "Now I am wondering who is the Daddy Warbucks behind all this?"

Gator closed the door. Jenny and Gator were standing on a walkway. Below them were about twenty people all sitting in front of computers. Gator pointed to a couple of big monitors on the opposite wall that were running news feeds. "This is one of our spin rooms. The people down there are working Twitter, Facebook, emails and every kind of electronic input they can think of or invent."

"We get paid by several groups to add spin or hype to various subjects. In some cases, we may have two people working...let's say a Twitter link where one of them is for the subject and the other more or less against."

Jenny was leaning on the railing. "You mean they start a fight but know who is going to win?"

Gator was enjoying this. He seldom got to show off his toy rooms. "Precisely. We more or less fix the fight and then try to influence those watching to join our side. See the guy in the blue T-shirt and the girl sitting next to him with the red ball hat?"

Jenny nodded, and Gator continued. "That's Brian and Wendy. They're married and one of the best spinner teams I've ever seen. They will go at each other like mad dogs, screaming and carrying on like they're going to kill each other. Then when they finish with their act, they go home. It's just a job for them. But boy are they good at it!"

Jenny was still trying to absorb everything that was going on. "So, someone pays you to spin a particular idea or subject?"

Gator bobbed from side to side. "They like to think of it as helping to influence the simple minded that may not have an opinion. We simply help them to justify why they want to agree with whatever we're selling."

"Can I ask who pays you?"

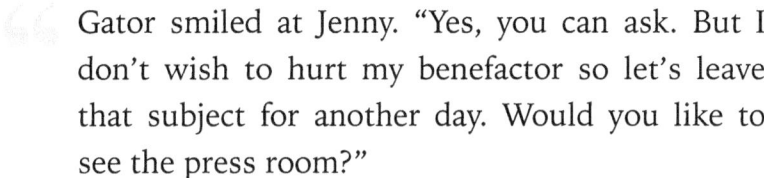

> Gator smiled at Jenny. "Yes, you can ask. But I don't wish to hurt my benefactor so let's leave that subject for another day. Would you like to see the press room?"

Gator started across the catwalk and down the stairs. They crossed the floor of the spin room and entered a door marked *Press*.

Jenny walked in and saw what looked like a smaller version of most of the network newsrooms. "Gator are you hiring? I may need a job shortly if we don't all end up behind bars somewhere."

Julie was talking with a young man sitting in front of one of the monitors. Gator walked over to them. "What's up?"

Julie looked up and saw Jenny behind Gator. She shot a look at Gator. He waved her down. "Julie, its ok. I checked her out. Jenny is more experienced in some of this than we are."

Jenny caught up to Julie and Gator. "I'm flattered, but frankly

I feel outclassed. You guys have a great marketing organization here."

Julie was still looking at Gator. "This is just one of our shops."

Now Jenny was looking at Gator. "How many are there?"

Gator looked out into the nowhere and said, "Fifteen at last count— ten in the U.S. and five scattered around in other places."

Julie was scowling, but not talking. Jenny walked over and pulled out a chair. "I think I need to sit down. Just how big is this? Is this your organization or is there someone else behind it?"

Gator leaned against the cubicle wall. "It's mine. Julie is my production manager and runs most of it. I just provide some oversight and do a little field work to help direct and train the field people."

Having worked in the media and journalism for a long time, Jenny was astounded at the brilliance of what she saw. "So, you influence the opinions by more or less spiking the punch with whatever flavored opinion they want you to add?"

Gator smiled and looked at Julie. "See. I told you she was smart. Yes, we just get directions that may include the buzz words for the various campaigns and then we take the message to the streets. We work talk shows, chat rooms, Twitter feeds, Facebook—it's all part of the campaign to push the opinion, where they want it to go."

"It's brilliant, its marketing 101 updated to include the latest technology." Jenny was excited. "Gator, can I watch them work? We might be able to use this to help the boys get their story out."

Julie looked like she had just taken a bite of a bad lemon. "I don't know if the *powers that be* would like this Gator. We haven't heard which direction to go with this Tribunal thing."

Gator put his hand on Julie's shoulder. "So, this time we move a little before we get told which direction. I've been reading Collins files, and I think maybe we spin it to push the public to support him."

Julie was hugging her clipboard. "If we do this it could mean we lose some funding." She looked at Gator. "Personally, I think you're right, some of the stuff they ask us to spin is very hard to sell. You know I like to influence opinion, it's become a game. But some of what we've pushed out there are just lies. We need to be on the right side of this Tribunal thing."

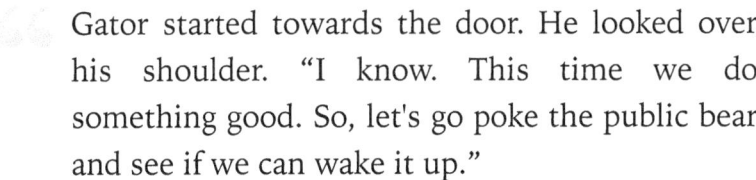

Gator started towards the door. He looked over his shoulder. "I know. This time we do something good. So, let's go poke the public bear and see if we can wake it up."

"Come on Jenny. We'll introduce you to the wild bunch and see if we can get them started spinning for the Collins

Tribunal. Hey, could you help Julie get some buzz words going?"

"Julie, call that guy that did the Tribunal hoodies for us and tell him we will need to get some t-shirts printed and distributed quickly."

"Then, alert the usual campus organizers a big push is coming."

Julie made a couple of notes as they walked. "Oh, I forgot to tell you that the new Campus Security Chief has announced his new policy against cowboy hats and hoodies."

"I understand the nut case running New York was also talking about outlawing hoodies and hats in New York because his face recognition cameras aren't working."

Gator had reached the bottom of the stairs. "So, what's next on the agenda?"

Julie smiled. "Cedric has a great idea. We pushed it out about an hour ago and tipped off that reporter who showed up in the hoodie and then later a cowboy hat. He has promised to do a promo first thing tomorrow morning. Anyway, Cedric said we should follow the English example. He's alerted the organizers in England so that they'll get credit for it. They're in an earlier time zone so it will show up on their news first." Julie stepped into one of the cubicles and then popped back in the aisle. "Tomorrow is Umbrella Day, " and she opened a big umbrella.

Jenny sat down on the steps. "You mean they're

going to encourage everyone to carry an umbrella tomorrow?"

"Not just carry one Jenny, but open it every time they go outside. We passed the word to the campus crew a little while ago. I've heard the stores have sold out of umbrellas already."

Jenny clapped her hands. "I can't wait to see the news tomorrow. Well done Julie! I hadn't thought about the demonstration against the face recognition, but it's a stroke of genius. The face recognition guys are going to go nuts."

Gator took the umbrella opened it and danced down the aisle singing the Gene Kelly song *Singing in the Rain*.

Julie held her hand out to help Jenny up. "Come on. We need to introduce you and start working on the spin. It looks like you just joined the ranks."

CHAPTER 41

BEN HAD BEEN WALKING FROM GROUP TO GROUP listening to the defense, the prosecution, and the tribunal judges. He walked back and sat down with Professor Ramirez. "Patrick, you've done a great job working with these kids. I can't find anything wrong with any of their law or their tactics. I think this could be the best defense Collins could ever have."

Ramirez was scanning his laptop. "I'm glad you approve of their training. This may be my last class, but it is certainly one of the best. When I first started, I hoped it would spur each of them into embracing the Constitution and teaching them to think. I had no idea that it could make or break their futures."

Ben sat across from Patrick and opened his laptop. "I'm hopeful that the public will fully embrace the efforts of these young people. It also may be the best way for Mr. Collins to get a fair hearing. If we can get this Tribunal recorded and distributed before they shut it down, he stands a fair chance of becoming a public hero. My team and I've been going over the files Collins has released to the public. I've never seen so much damaging evidence on elected officials in one collection."

Ramirez looked at the three groups. "If the public reacts to this evidence the same way the students are, I don't doubt that this will trigger a major house cleaning across the country. Some of the evidence Collins is presenting goes much deeper than even I had imagined. It doesn't appear that any level of government was not involved in some form of corruption or illegal activities. I'm sorry that this Tribunal does not have the authority to indict or convict based on the evidence we've seen so far."

He turned his laptop to display an e-mail sent from a mutual friend. As Patrick read the e-mail, he leaned forward so no one could overhear him. "Judge Scarborough seems to agree with you. He's offering to help. He's listed some other judges and leading attorneys who are volunteering their services to defend Collins and the Tribunal. I'm thinking of having them join me in a joint press conference to announce that we will be collectively defending the Collins Tribunal members and William Collins."

Patrick looked up, visibly overwhelmed with emotion. "I can't tell you how much I appreciate you jumping in here. For a while, I was afraid to reach out to anyone. I didn't want anyone else drug into this cesspool. It's bad enough that I had stumbled into it. It seems I have already drug to many others into this mess;...Michael, Cathy, Anna, Professor Tanager, his wife, you, and Jenny. And now it looks like Gator and his troops."

Ben looked around. "I'm impressed with this kid Gator. I still haven't figured out where he gets his funding, but I have a feeling that I know who's supporting him. I just don't believe it. I don't think anyone has any idea how well-funded Gator's marketing efforts are or how effective they are."

Patrick nodded as he looked around. "Gator was showing me around earlier, and I asked him if a particular individual we both know was the financier behind his operation. He didn't confirm or deny the identity of his financing, but he did indicate that he runs several marketing firms that use his services behind the scenes. Apparently, our friend Gator is working both sides of the fence. He operates as a capitalist making money hand over fist. He is actually doing legitimate marketing and then uses the same tactics and backside operations to peddle the spin for whichever political direction given to them."

Jenny walked in and sat down with Ben and Patrick. "Boys, I think I've found my calling. I just spent the last hour working with Julie. I believe we have a great story that they're going to help us spread."

Patrick shifted and stood up to stretch as he'd been sitting a lot the last two days. "Ben, I think you may need to include Gator and his crew in your defense plans."

"Patrick, I somehow feel that Gator will land on the positive side of this exercise and probably make a profit. But right now, we need to get this show on the road."

Ben stood up and clapped his hands to get the attention of the Tribunal members.

CHAPTER 42

TILLIS AND PATTERSON WALKED INTO THE CAFÉ AT 6:58 am. Bailey was sitting in the same corner booth as last night. There were place settings for three, and he was reading from his iPad.

"I guess you expected us?" said Patterson as he slipped into the same seat he had last night.

Bailey waved at the waitress, and she headed toward the table with a coffee pot and two menus. "I was hoping you would join me for breakfast. We're going to need to work closely. The Collins files are tearing D.C. apart. Apparently, there have been several fights between some of our elected officials in the very halls of Congress."

Bailey pushed his iPad in front of Tillis and Patterson and pressed the play button on the YouTube clip. The clip showed what looked like a bad wrestling match with two of the senior members of Congress, apparently brawling in the hallway. "This showed up last night after our meeting. It was captured by two of the security guards who just watched them fight until they got tired."

Patterson replayed the clip. "Brad, isn't that the senator that gave us so much grief at the last hearing we attended?"

> Tillis reached for his coffee cup. "Yep, that's him. He's the one that lectured us on ethics. It looks like he should've taken a couple of courses in self-defense."

"I thought you guys would enjoy seeing this. The phone calls to Director Millington have continued all night. I know because she has called me every hour on the hour asking for an update. I have assured her that we are doing all we can. But I feel she is going to begin tearing this campus and town apart until she finds the Tribunal members and Mr. Collins. I need both of you to work every angle and see what you can find. We must be missing something. Go back over all of their family and friends."

The waitress stopped by the table to take their order. As she was leaving, Patterson's phone beeped. He read the text and handed it to Bailey.

"You should enjoy this." Bailey read the text and then gave the phone to Tillis. "Would either of you want to alert the campus security staff as to what to expect this morning?"

Bailey tapped the link in the text, and a news clip started to play from England with a reporter covering the English protest in support of the Collins Tribunal as they showed thousands of pedestrians carrying open umbrellas as they walked to work. "I think we should finish breakfast before I go tell the Queen what's happening."

Tillis chuckled. "If I get a choice, I'll let Patterson alert the campus security."

Tillis reached for his phone and texted his wife to check the news when she got up. "My wife will enjoy that clip." The waitress brought their breakfast orders, and for a while, they lapsed into the chatter of previous investigations.

CHAPTER 43

DAVID WALKED INTO THE TRIBUNAL ROOM. BEN and Patrick sat at a table in the back.

"Boss, got a minute?"

"Sure, David what is it?"

David handed his iPad to Ben. "Mindy's been talking to the office, and we thought you should see this. We've had fifty calls asking us to represent various people in D.C."

Ben looked at the iPad and read through the names of people asking his firm to represent them. "So, fifty different people from D.C. are asking for representation? My God, these are all congressional staffers and a couple of House members. I think you know some of these Patrick..."

Ben handed the iPad to Patrick, and he began to scan the

names. As Patrick read the names, David continued. "Mindy said she did some checking with some of her friends in D.C. It seems every law firm in D.C. is overwhelmed with people asking for legal representation."

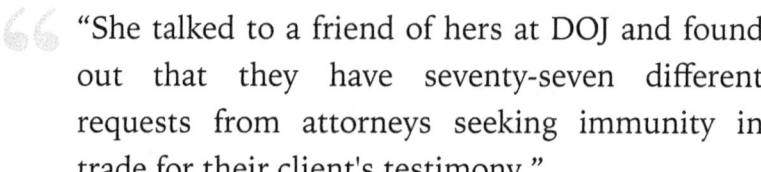

"She talked to a friend of hers at DOJ and found out that they have seventy-seven different requests from attorneys seeking immunity in trade for their client's testimony."

Patrick looked up from the list. "I recognize several of these names—they were students of mine. Can we find out who is asking the DOJ for immunity?"

Ben nodded and turned to David. "Knowing you David, I guess you and Mindy already have the list or will have it shortly?"

Jenny had just walked in with Gator. As they walked over to join the small group meeting, Patrick handed her the iPad as they read through the list. Gator pulled out his phone and pressed a speed dial number.

Jenny was still reading as she heard Gator say, "Julie, check with our sources at the DOJ and see what's going on there. I think they are going to get some requests to play *"Let's Make a Deal."* When you find out, come find me in the Tribunal room."

David reached out and took his iPad from Jenny. She smiled shaking her head. "I would bet I already know the answer to this question, but I still have to ask it. Do you have a list of those who are talking to the DOJ?"

David gave Jenny a hurt look. "We should have the list in an hour. Mindy's friend at DOJ said the joke inside DOJ is they're going to have to change the name from Department of Justice to the Department of Selective Justice."

"Her friend said the powers to be inside of DOJ are being told which cases to consider. And yes, we should know who they are, shortly."

Jenny held out her hand to David. "If I can't adopt you, would you consider marriage?"

Ben stepped in front of David and took Jenny's hand. "He's too young for you Grandma, but I am sure we can find you a suitable husband if we survive this."

Julie walked into the room and handed Gator a packet of paper. He started reading it while everyone waited. "Julie, can you get copies for the rest of us?"

Julie opened her notebook and handed one to Ben, Jenny, and Patrick. "I only made three other copies...I'll get one for you, David."

Ben started to look at the briefing package from Julie. It was a detailed list of each person who had contacted DOJ for immunity and a paragraph on what their attorneys were asking. "David, as soon as you get anything from Mindy's friend, be sure to share it with Gator and Julie."

"Julie. If you ever want to change jobs let me know. I would be proud to work with you."

Patrick was already making notes by each name. "Can we get backgrounds on these people and cross-reference them with the Collins files?"

David and Julie answered at the same time. "Already working on it."

David bowed slightly to Julie. "My apologies, ladies first."

Julie wasn't sure how to respond. She had never worked with someone like David. "We figured you would want to start looking for the weak points on each person. We're digging into everything we can find."

She turned to Gator. Her manner let the others know she was talking to her boss and politely excluding them. "I figured you would want to start spinning the information as soon as possible. We're working on setting up a priority list and looking at how we can best use the information. Are you sure we support William Collins and the tribunal in our spin?"

Gator hesitated for a moment, "Yes, this is something we have to do."

He looked at the students in their three groups working to prepare for the toughest class of their lives. He watched as William Collins spoke to the Tribunal prosecution group. He was very animated and waving his arms as he made a point.

Gator glanced at Daniel Collins and the Tribunal Judges. And then his heart flashed to an image of his wife and children at their last birthday party.

And just like that, he turned to Ramirez and said, "Professor, I think we need to place all of our efforts into defending William Collins and his efforts to expose the corruption in D.C. I believe that we will make William Collins a national hero."

Julie was visibly surprised. She almost swallowed the ever-present gum she chewed. "Morris, are you sure? I can't believe I just heard that from you. So, we're going for the truth? The straight up truth and then push to make Collins a hero and plead for immunity?"

> The small group was quiet, waiting to see what Gator would say. "Julie, I hope you're with me on this. This time we do what's right, I know this may not sit well with the troops, but it's my call."

Julie hugged her clipboard as her whole body moved back and forth. "Thanks boss, but I think nearly everyone is on board. I haven't been able to tell you because it's been crazy trying to keep up. But the other offices wanted to know where we're going on this one. All of the offices are ready to take it on. They've been reading the Collins files and are angry. A couple of our offices overseas said that the temperature outside of the U.S. is pro-Collins and they're ready to push it."

Gator nodded. "Go for it. Jenny, will you help us? We're going to need to build a full-fledged marketing campaign on the fly."

Jenny picked up her notebook computer and shoved it in her messenger bag. "I'm in. Who do I work with and where?"

Julie turned and spoke to Jenny. "Do you want a private area or in the middle of the bullpen?"

As Jenny and Julie headed for the door, Julie stopped to look at Patrick. "You'd better prepare the Collins boys and the rest of your class. They're about to be put in the spotlight."

Patrick felt the weight of this decision begin to weigh on his shoulders. "I wish I could talk to Anna about this. She's still my best counsel."

Ben looked at David. He didn't need to say anything else. David pulled out his phone to call Mindy.

Ben stood up. "I guess it's time for a quick health break and then we need to make some decisions about when to take this show public. Gator would you sit down with Patrick and I so we can finalize a plan? I would appreciate your input."

Patrick stood up with Ben. "I agree. Your input would be a great help. You have your finger on the pulse of the public, and we need to know what will catch their hearts on this."

Gator wasn't sure what he was feeling. It scared him. He'd been manipulating stories a long time. Spinning them one direction or another was easy—the truth hadn't mattered. Gator had learned telling lies was easy, and in most cases, you just kept repeating the lie until people begin believing it as the truth. Then the lie became their truth.

Gator had never been around men like Ben and Patrick. The men he knew were out for themselves. Now, he found himself with two of the most stand-up people he had ever met asking for his help and asking him to stand with them. *No one* had ever asked him to stand with them. Most of the people Gator worked for just wanted a story spun to help their agenda. They didn't care about the truth—just making the sale.

But Professor Patrick Ramirez was someone he had secretly admired. Everything the guy wrote or taught pushed you to think. Weeding out the spin and seeing the truth. Ramirez taught his students to seek the truth. Question it and then use it.

Ben Langley had made a career of standing up for truth. His career showed over and over that the cases he took on focused on an honest defense of the truth. He wasn't afraid to stand up to anyone.

Morris Schwartz, alias Gator, and dozens of other identities had always worked the shadows. Could he come out of the shadows and stand the light of telling the truth?

Gator chewed on his lower lip as he looked at these two men. Gator clapped his hands together drawing way more attention from the other three groups than he'd expected. "I would be proud to join you. Let's take that health break and grab some food. I have a couple of ideas that might be helpful."

Ben put his hand on Gator's shoulder as they headed out the door. Ben was already laying out a plan to make a run at the DOJ to see if they would accept his request for immunity for Mr. Collins and the Tribunal class.

As the three of them stepped out of the Tribunal room, David handed Patrick a phone. "Your wife is on hold."

Patrick took the phone in both hands. His eyes clouded with tears.

"Thank-you David."

CHAPTER 44

JENNY AND JULIE WERE IN A SMALL ROOM WITH several TVs running the latest news shows. Jenny was reaching out to her friends in the media to see what they knew. At this point, no one knew of Jenny's involvement with Ramirez or the Collins Tribunal.

Julie was sitting across from her, working her back-door contacts to see what they would share. Julie looked up at the TVs and reached for a remote. She turned up the volume as the local reporter who had covered the Hoodie and Cowboy hat protests on the local campus was now being highlighted on the national news.

Jenny looked up as the volume grew louder. The reporter was back in the same spot he had introduced the Tribunal hoodie protest movement. The reporter was talking with a national anchor. "Yes, the school has stated that hats and hoodies should not be worn anywhere on campus. But we understand that the Collins Tribunal protest is continuing." He held out his hand and looked up at the sky. "Hmm, it looks like rain..." and with that, he opened an umbrella.

The national anchor began showing videos of people carrying umbrellas open even though there was no rain.

The anchorman began, "It seems the support for the Collins Tribunal is growing and people all over the world are protesting the facial recognition cameras and raising their umbrellas in protest. Even one congresswoman was shown stepping out of a building and opening her umbrella."

They then did interviews with people in London, Toronto, New York, Miami and San Diego. Each person hiding behind their umbrella said that they were supporting William Collins and it was time to clean out the corruption in D.C.

Julie turned down the volume and typed a couple of quick emails. She looked up at Jenny as she felt the question even though Jenny had said nothing. "This is something we can use. We will push this on every campus, finding as many special interest groups as we can to support us. You know, get a couple of Unions to throw their support behind it."

Jenny just nodded. "I never really thought about it, but you've mastered media manipulation beyond anything I ever thought possible."

Julie sat back in her chair, pulled out a fresh stick of gum and offered one to Jenny.

"Most of my generation's parents seem to fall into two groups. First, those that had roots in the protest movement somewhere back to the 60's. The seeds they planted took root and sides were chosen. Drugs, Sex, Rock n Roll, anti-war, anti-church—you name it. That was the time they stopped listening to authority figures and began to question the decisions of anyone in authority. No matter the answer, it was just cool to disagree and burn your bra, dodge the draft, become a hippie, you know, whatever…"

> "Lots of the kids from that generation are now deeply seated in jobs throughout the government and business community. They thought their new thinking would change everything. They never thought the next generation would laugh at them."

"The second group is the TV sound bite crew. They're not attached to anything. They barely remember the last TV commercial—which is why we had to build in so much repetition to our messages."

"If you look at how we market an idea. It's simple. We don't care if it's true or not, we just have to say it a lot and in a way that will stick in their heads."

"We found out while we were building the *Spin-Net* as Gator calls it, that most people will voice the last opinion they heard and treat it as truth. They really don't know much about any subject—they just repeat the last sound bite they heard."

Jenny was still holding the piece of gum. It was hard to believe that these small groups of protesters that Gator employed as a front-line were part of the most sophisticated marketing organization she had ever seen. "Ok, let me catch up. I know the Sunday morning talk shows have their talking points because you can hear the exact same catch phrases on every show. But are you telling me you use those same tactics?"

Julie shook her head. "No, we don't use *their* tactics—*they* use ours. We taught them."

Jenny's email notification chimed. She looked at the email notice and clicked on it.

She read it twice then turned her laptop around and pushed it toward Julie. "I think we better go tell the boys."

Julie read the email and got up. She headed for the door as Jenny was grabbing her laptop and hurrying to catch up.

Gator, Ben, and Patrick were drawing on a piece of paper, taking turns adding to the scribbles when Jenny and Julie walked in.

Julie looked at Gator. "You guys better see this." Jenny put the laptop in front of Ben. As he read it, Jenny began the condensed version of the email.

"One of my sources has confirmed that ten new people have come forward turning in corroborative information to support the Collins files. They are all accompanied by requests for immunity. It looks like D.C. is on fire with fear. No one is safe. Everyone in D.C. is hiding something."

Ben slid the laptop to Gator, Patrick moved so they could both read the email. Ben reached for his phone and called David. "Grab Walt and Diane and bring them into the kitchen area. I also want you to get Mindy on the line—we're going to need help."

Ben put the phone down. Gator looked at Julie. "See if you can confirm this."

Julie nodded and pulled out her phone and began making calls as she left. Jenny walked over to the coffee pot, trying to analyze the new data from her media perspective.

She put too much cream in the coffee and mumbled, "Have a little coffee with your cream," and as she turned around, she realized the boys were listening. "Sorry guys, I dumped too much cream in my coffee and was talking to myself. It's a bad habit of someone who lives alone."

Gator pushed the laptop over to her seat as Jenny headed back to the table. Gator grinned at her. "I talk to myself all the time. I even answer myself. It's just part of our DNA as geniuses."

Patrick chuckled and shifted the conversation back to the email. "Ben if this is true then we have corroborating evidence to prove the Collins files are true. Do you think we can use this information?"

David, Walt, and Diane walked in and lined up across from Ben. "Jenny, read the email for them please."

Jenny pulled the laptop in front of her and read. "This is from one of my friends at the DOJ."

"Just wanted you to know that we have ten new cases. Each one is submitting files that look like they back up the Collins files. Each one is asking for immunity, but they've taken a lesson from Collins. The files are being posted to the internet before they ever contact us. Check the web. The files are everywhere. We're drowning in information."

"I'll let you know what I can, but you were right, the truth is finally coming out. It will be interesting to see if it makes the front page or just page ten."

"My friend attached several links. I can forward these to you if you want"

David, Walt, and Diane nodded in unison. Ben took over. "I think you know what we need to do—David, please alert the rest of the staff. I'm going to make a couple of calls to see who is representing these people. Maybe we can share information."

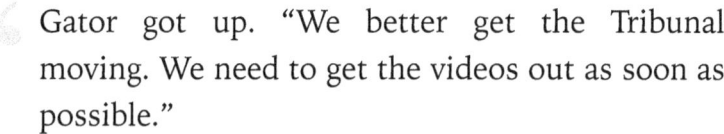

Gator got up. "We better get the Tribunal moving. We need to get the videos out as soon as possible."

Ben and Patrick got up and followed Gator to the Tribunal room. The Tribunal was about to place the Collins files in front of the American people and call for their support.

Patrick touched Ben's arm. Ben stopped and turned. "Ben, I never thought this could happen. I'm scared for the country. Are you sure we should do this?"

Ben put his hand on Patrick's shoulder. "I have never been more certain of anything. It's time to wake the giant and let the politicians and bureaucrats stand or fall by what the Tribunal reveals. If the public goes back to sleep after this, then we should flee the country. Now let's go help these young people."

CHAPTER 45

Liz Tyler had been living in her office for the last three days. Her staff had brought her clothes, food and more bad news than good. Two of her staff members had resigned and disappeared without talking to her. One of her staff was reportedly at the DOJ trading *more* evidence for immunity.

She pressed the intercom and called Janice. The voice that answered was not Janice. "Yes mam, this is Justin. Janice stepped out."

Liz looked at her watch. It was the middle of the afternoon, Janice never left before 6:00 pm. "I have something I want you to do, grab whoever else is available and come in here." Liz hung up without waiting for his answer.

Justin was young and eager to make his name. His Dad had

gotten him this job through several large contributions. It was certainly exciting to be here. He was in the nation's capital working with all of the most important people. Justin was ready to change the world by any means and doing whatever was needed. He called to one of the other interns, picked up the envelope Janice had asked him to give to Liz and headed for the inner sanctum.

As Justin entered the door with another junior intern trailing behind him, Liz looked up. She tried to hide the shocked look on her face as she thought, *Is this all that's left of my staff, just a couple of new interns?*

Justin walked over to her desk and handed her the envelope. "Janice said to give you this, but I've been answering the phone—it's kind of busy out there."

Liz took the envelope. It was handwritten and addressed to her. She recognized the handwriting—it was Janice's. She grabbed her letter opener and slit the envelope open. The two interns lined up in front of her desk eagerly waiting for their new orders. Liz opened the one page inside the envelope and read.

Liz, I just spoke to my husband, and I have decided it is time for me to retire. I have turned in my papers to payroll and given my credentials to the security desk. I know this is a shock, but it is time for me to retire.

Thanks,

Janice

Liz was still holding the letter opener. Her grip was becoming so tight her hand began to shake. Her face was turning red with rage, and both interns took a step back.

The knock at the door was a relief to the interns, but it simply refocused Liz's anger. The door opened, and four FBI agents stepped in with several security officers.

> The lead agent announced. "Liz Tyler, we have been instructed to take you into custody and bring you to our offices for questioning."

Liz threw the letter opener at the lead agent and missed. The letter opener hit the security officer behind him and harmlessly fell to the ground. Liz was on her feet screaming, "Do you know who I am?"

The lead agent nodded. "Yes, ma'am I do. Our orders are to take you in for questioning. The White House and the DOJ have authorized this, would you please come with us?"

The other agents spread out and began boxing up files computers, and anything that wasn't nailed down. As agents escorted the interns from the office, they advised them they also would be required for questioning. Justin felt his new career was not heading in the direction his father had told him it would go. Justin turned to the agent escorting him and sheepishly asked, "Can I call my dad?"

The agent shook his head. "When we get you to our office you can make your call."

Liz was following behind them screaming as they dragged her down the halls of the Congressional offices. She was educating the agents in the most colorful language about her importance and the fanciful things she was planning for their future careers.

The press was as always, faithfully waiting for a sound bite and today they got the mother lode. Liz's parting comments were immortalized on the news and the internet. Liz Tyler's career and those of the *Back Nine* were ending.

The lead agent paused outside of Liz Tyler's office to direct the other agents to seal the office. He took out his phone and dialed a number, stepping off to one side. "Yes Ma'am we have her in custody. Yes Ma'am, she is naming names. No, she has not mentioned you. She has made several references to the President. We should have her at the office in ten minutes. Do you still want us to invoke the National Security rules for her?"

The agent stopped to listen, knowing his job depended on this call. "Yes Ma'am, I understand. The NSA will take over as soon as we have her in our office. Yes Ma'am, we will turn everything over to NSA when we bring over the files. No one else will see them. I understand."

The agent put the phone in his pocket and wondered if they still needed a sheriff in Wyoming. Getting away from this mess would be good. This job certainly was not what they told him it would be when he was at the academy.

CHAPTER 46

THE TRIBUNAL HAD BEGUN. EVERYONE WAS nervous and it showed. There were no retakes as they had all agreed to run the Tribunal live with no edits.

Ben and Patrick sat on a platform in the rear watching as William Collins testified to several documents. Both the defense and the prosecution questioned William. Ben leaned over to Patrick and whispered, "I see why this guy is so effective. He should have been a lawyer."

Patrick whispered back, "I think he's done enough as a deal maker to shame most lawyers. Even you couldn't broker the deals this kid has made."

Ben nodded. "You're right. Now we'll see if he can broker a deal to get out of this mess alive."

The Tribunal was relaxing, and everyone was starting to settle into their roles. The process was flowing.

After the first hour, they broke for recess. Gator had been watching from his office. He found Ben and Patrick picking over a tray of sandwiches. "I just saw the preview of the video. Are you ready to release it? I have it queued up, and we can dump it to the internet whenever you're ready."

Ben looked at Patrick. He nodded. "I think it's time, let's send it and see if the public is ready."

Ben picked up a ham on rye and tried to find the mustard. "How long do you think it will be before the Tribunal is discovered on the internet?"

Gator smiled handed him a bottle of sauce. "Try this. I make it myself. It's Chipotle and a little of this and that...it's just the thing to spice up your day." Ben took the bottle and squeezed some on the sandwich.

Gator looked at his iPad. "We should have all of the key media people receiving the first part of the Tribunal upload in five minutes. It should make *YouTube* in about ten minutes. We have it setup to download from about twenty fictitious sources. The campus networks should be getting it now. I expect the media will take about ten minutes to preview it. Then they'll want to scoop each other. They will all be interrupting whatever programming is on with their *BREAKING NEWS*. So, I expect it will be worldwide in about 15 minutes. I would suggest we get the Tribunal members back to it as we don't want them watching it for now."

"I agree we should keep them cloistered until they finish the Tribunal. Gator you're right. This is a great sauce." Ben and Patrick began herding the Tribunal members back to work.

As they left the room, the media monitors began to interrupt the regularly scheduled programming for a news update. The Tribunal was now public. The Pandora's Box of secrets was open and on display. Jenny and Julie watched the coverage and began making notes for the next wave of information.

CHAPTER 47

BAILEY VALENTINE WAS TALKING ON HIS CELL phone constantly. It was impossible to keep the phone charged. Finally, he sent one of the agents to get him a couple of burner phones. He just couldn't get off the phone. He was in the middle of a call when his phone buzzed. He looked at the caller ID. "I will call you back, my boss is calling..." He hung up the first call and answered the second call. He looked around to see who was listening. "Yes, Sir."

Brent Underwood had put his head on his desk. He felt like a scene from the Poseidon movie where the ship turns over, and everything is upside down. "Bailey, I wanted to get an update from you and give you a heads up. We have started taking people into custody, starting with the *Back Nine*."

Bailey found a bench and sat down. "I didn't think we were ready to move on them yet?"

Brent looked at the files on his desk marked secret, top secret, etc. The piles were growing by the minute. "I know this was your case, and we were hoping to be much further along in the investigation before we even thought about arrests. But a lot has happened. We have at least one suicide. Four of the *Back Nine* are missing and presumed in hiding or trying to leave the country. Two of them are trying to bargain for immunity and The President is attempting to distance himself from everyone."

Bailey thought about the months of work on this case as he had discovered the *Back Nine* and their dealings long before Collins had released his files. The *Back Nine* had been good at hiding. They were hard to track and even harder to find anything that they would not be able to deny. But he had been close to making a breakthrough when the Collins files arrived. The first round of Collins' files had named all the players *in* the *Back Nine* but had not mentioned the *Back Nine* as a *group*. The second series of files identified the *Back Nine* and outlined their structure, members and their achievements to date. That part would be the critical information Bailey needed. Now the *Back Nine* were just public knowledge and denials.

"What do you want me to do?" Brent looked around his office and thought about the price he had paid to get here and keep his conscience clean. Getting here wasn't hard, but keeping his record clean had been unbelievably hard. "I want you to think about offering Collins immunity. I believe that we can cover him as a whistleblower, but it will be tough. I just got a call that the White House is thinking about siding with Collins. They seem to want to deflect attention from themselves by going after the corruption in the Congress and other government offices. They believe that they can deflect the attacks on the President by just throwing everybody under the bus and claiming he had no knowledge of the corruption."

Bailey was good under pressure, he rarely showed any emotion, but this was bringing him to the boiling point. "Brent, we both know how deep this goes. We know who is really behind it. Does the White House think they can use *plausible deniability* as a defense and come out clean?"

Brent opened a file on his desk and looked at it. "Bailey, they think they can slip right through the crack on this. One of the drafts sent to me even suggested that the President may come out and suggest that William Collins represents the new breed needed to clean up Washington."

> "The line that caught my attention is where it says, *William Collins may be the best person to replace me when my term is up, and I would be proud to help him clean up D.C.*"

Bailey was trying to decide if he was walking in Wonderland, OZ or some other fantasy world. "You are kidding! They are going to try and suggest Collins should run for President?"

Brent closed the file. "Yep, it looks like this is one of *her* strategies. They grant him immunity, pin a medal on him and put him in the front to deflect. One of the analysts sent me information that someone is already selling Collins for President t-shirts. Welcome to Never, Neverland for adults, otherwise known as Washington D.C.

"Anyway, I need you to be the one who takes Collins into custody."

Bailey felt the stress of the last several days multiplied by this new twist. D.C. was always a surprise. Here he was in the middle of one of the largest manhunts on record. And now the President was talking about granting this guy immunity and then nominating him to be the next President of the United States. "Boss I will do everything I can. Um, does Lisa know any of this?"

Brent reached for a glass of water. "I haven't told her yet. She has her own sources. I wouldn't be surprised if she already knows. You need to be careful. I'll let you know what happens here. Right now, we're trying to take the *Back Nine* into custody. We are also wading through all of those that have suddenly had a change in conscience and swear they want to help us by coming clean in return for immunity and cash deals. I am sorry you aren't here to watch this. If we weren't in the middle of it, it would almost be funny."

Brent's secretary knocked on the door. They had worked out this signal years ago. She had a special knock no one would notice. It was her way of signaling someone important was coming in. The door opened, and his secretary shot him a look of warning.

Brent stood up. "I have to go, I'll call you later."

Bailey heard Brent say, "Yes Ma'am, what can I do for the White House?" and then Brent disconnected the phone. Brent had stayed on the phone long enough to let Bailey know "she" had left the White House.

For now, Bailey needed to find Collins.

Agent Patterson came out of the auditorium and waved at Bailey. He trotted over to meet Bailey as he headed back to the command post.

As soon as Patterson was close enough to talk and not be overheard, he started. "The Tribunal kids are going ahead with the Tribunal. They just released the first hour of the trial. The Collins kid is front and center dumping one incriminating fact after another. The word is they are going to keep dumping it out in one-hour segments until the Tribunal is finished. Then they will ask the American people to vote on a verdict. Guilty or Not Guilty?"

Bailey stopped and looked at Patterson "Do you want to bet on the verdict?"

Patterson laughed "No. You should have seen Millington when the news announced the first hour of the Tribunal was on *YouTube*. She looked like a missile revving its engines and getting ready to launch. I left to find you and get out of her path. We don't want to be close when she does go off."

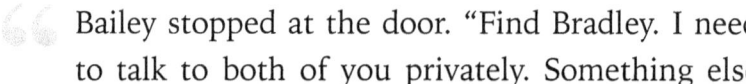

Bailey stopped at the door. "Find Bradley. I need to talk to both of you privately. Something else has come up. Has there been any progress in finding Collins?"

Patterson reached for his phone. "I'll call him, and no we haven't found them. But everyone is looking."

Bailey let the door close. "Tell Brad to meet us at Professor Ramirez's home. I want to personally talk to his wife. Let's take my car."

Patterson called Brad to tell him to meet them at the Ramirez's home. Bailey decided there was no need in stepping into Lisa Millington's line of fire. She would be looking for someone to punish, and he didn't have time to play her game.

Agent Bradley was sitting in front of Professor Ramirez's home when Bailey and Patterson arrived. As they got out of their cars, Bailey turned to Patterson. "Can you go over to The Whales and talk to the manager, Michael O'Brien? Tell him what we talked about and give him my cell number. Try not to draw too much attention. I understand the place is always packed with students. We all know how well they can hear when they want to." Patterson nodded. "I'll be discreet, do you think I should wear my FBI windbreaker or just my usual I'm a fed suit?"

Bailey tossed Patterson the keys. "The windbreaker should do it." Patterson caught the keys and grinned "Fill it up and wash it, sir?"

Patterson got in and drove off.

Bradley and Bailey knew half the neighborhood were watching them. Bailey smiled and looked around, spotting the car and the agents assigned to watch the Ramirez house. He waved at them. "Bradley, I want to talk to Ramirez's wife. We need to get a message to Collins, and company. I think the best path is through Ramirez wife or Michael O'Brien. So, hang in there with me and try not to fall off the couch when I unfold this one."

Bradley followed Bailey to the door feeling like he had just walked into the middle of a play where he didn't know any of the lines.

Anna Ramirez answered the door. Bailey introduced himself and Agent Tillis. "I would like to talk to you—may we come in?"

Anna looked around and saw several of their neighbors trying to hide behind bushes or look like they were tending their yards. "You might as well—at least we shouldn't be overheard in here."

Anna led them to the living room and sat down. Bailey looked around. "You have a lovely home."

> Anna cut him off. "I have not seen my husband in days, and I do not know where he is. What do you want?"

Bailey leaned forward. "If you happen to talk to your husband or anyone who might run into him, I would like you to ask him if we could talk."

Anna looked at Bailey as only a protective wife could. "And what is it that you wish to tell my husband if I should talk with him?"

Bailey had read the background on Anna Ramirez, and the profile was dead on. She was professional, a loving wife and not afraid of much. Invading her home put Bailey on unfamiliar ground, but that was what he wanted. He needed Anna to be as comfortable as possible. He needed to find a way to get her to trust him if this was going to work. And Anna had no reason to trust him.

"Mrs. Ramirez, I would like to talk to your husband and Mr. Collins. The DOJ would like to offer a deal for your husband, his students, and Mr. Collins if they turn themselves into me. In return, I believe we can obtain immunity for Professor Ramirez and his students. We should also be able to grant immunity for Mr. Collins as well."

Anna looked at Bailey as if she was trying to decide to step on a bug or ignore it. She studied him and then looked at Agent Tillis. Tillis unconsciously put his hand to his cheek, remembering his first encounter with Anna. The silence was awkward, but Bailey knew the ball was in Anna's court, and he had to wait.

"Mr. Valentine, my husband nor his students have done anything wrong. But they have been pursued as criminals. I have had twenty-four-hour surveillance on our home and myself. Our name has been drug through every media channel imaginable. I have had to call the police six times in the last two days to have reporters removed from our front yard and the backyard. I even had to have them remove one of the news stations trucks from my driveway that blocked the garage door."

"Why should I believe you now?"

Bailey liked Anna Ramirez. "There is no reason to trust me. This whole thing has been poorly handled. I am sorry for that. Agent Tillis here was originally sent to find Mr. Collins and arrest him. Since then a lot has come to light. The public and many of the officials in D.C. are shocked at the information Mr. Collins released. I don't think there is any good way for this type of information to come out. I am sorry for you and your husband. You should have never been put in this position."

"I work directly for the Deputy Attorney General, and he has asked me to open negotiations with Mr. Collins and your husband. We would like to offer him immunity. I will be glad to do that in whatever manner you are most comfortable with."

Bailey took out his card. "You or your husband can reach me at this number twenty-hour hours a day."

"Please check out my credentials. I checked yours, and I know you know how to do a background check. I think you will find I do what I say I will. I want to help your husband and his students. I hope we can help Mr. Collins, but I need to talk to him first."

Bailey got up. "Thank you for listening, if you would like, I will have the watchers out front removed."

Anna got up and led the way to the door. "No, leave them there. They at least keep the neighbors in check. As long as they sit there most of the neighbors are afraid to talk to me."

"If I hear from Patrick, I will give him your message."

Bailey was standing on the porch with Agent Tillis. "Anna, I am trying to help. So you know, I have sent another agent to The Whales to give the same message to Michael O'Brien. I know he is a good friend of Professor Ramirez, and I thought he might also be able to get a message to the Professor. But I wanted to tell you personally."

Bailey turned and walked away with Tillis trailing behind, trying to figure out what had just happened.

Anna watched as they got in their car and drove away. She waved at the watchers and closed the door.

She went in the kitchen trying to think what she should cook for dinner. What would Patrick want? She opened the fridge, looked, did a quick inventory and closed the door. She pulled out the phone that Mindy had given her and dialed the number Mindy had pre-programmed for her.

The phone rang once, and Mindy answered. "Hello?"

Anna started into her act. "Hey, I need to pick up some groceries at the store. Do you want to meet and grab a bite? I hate to cook for just one."

Mindy looked around the hotel room. "Sure, can you give me 20 minutes and I'll meet you there. I have to get the kids off to practice first."

Anna started a grocery list. "Great see you there," She hung up the phone, and went to her office and made a copy of Bailey's card. It would be easier to give to Mindy, and she wanted to keep the card. She still had some research to do on Mr. Bailey Valentine.

Anna grabbed her car keys, pulled out of the garage and waved at the watchers. They, in turn, alerted another watcher who followed Anna.

Mindy called David to let him know something was up and she was meeting Anna at the grocery store. They would probably get something to eat to keep her cover.

Mindy drove to the grocery store and began walking through the produce section. She picked over the lettuce and finally bought a bunch of red leaf lettuce and was sorting through the peppers when she saw Anna grab a cart and head for the fruit. Anna picked a couple of apples and then headed straight for Mindy waving and talking to her as if she were an old friend.

Mindy picked up the guy coming through the door about thirty seconds behind Anna. He was in such a hurry to keep Anna insight that he forgot to get a cart and had to go back and get one. Mindy smiled and started walking up and down the aisles with Anna. "I see your tails are still with you."

Anna stopped in front of the Tortilla chips. She picked up a bag of hot chips and left a folded paper on the shelf. "Patrick likes these. You should try them. They're delicious."

Mindy picked up a bag and the note. "What salsa do you suggest?"

Anna continued down the aisle and stopped at the salsas. She picked up a jar and put it in the cart. Then she picked up another one and handed it to Mindy. "Try this one. The note I gave you is a copy of a card from a DOJ guy. He wants to get word to Patrick that he wants to talk about a deal for Collins, Patrick, and the students. I don't know if he is serious or just trying to find them. So I figured you and I should have lunch and see what we can do."

Anna and Mindy spent twenty minutes wandering the aisles. They then went to the deli counter and picked up lunch. They sat in the eating area in the corner so no one could get behind them. Mindy sat so she could watch the watcher and was also able to pick out his partner in the parking lot.

As they ate lunch, Mindy pulled out a deck of cards. "Do you play Gin Rummy?"

Anna smiled, reached over and took the cards. As she shuffled the deck and dealt, she smiled. "This should drive them nuts— two girls meeting for lunch and a friendly game of cards."

Mindy took the folded piece of paper out of her pocket, opened it and then refolded it to use as a score pad. "I will text our office and see what they know about Bailey Valentine. Then I'll contact Ben and Patrick when I leave."

Anna drew a card. "I caught the news on the way over and it sounds like everyone in D.C. is playing *Let's Make a Deal*."

Mindy drew a card and looked at her hand. "The word we get is that the public opinion is all for Collins and about half the country is ready to tar and feather their elected officials."

Anna picked up her fork to take a bite of her salad. "Do you think they have a chance of getting out of this?"

Mindy drew a card and smiled as the watcher was trying not to look at her and eat his pizza. "I don't know what else Ben and Patrick are planning, but making videos of the Tribunal and putting it on the internet is priceless. The public is eating it up. One of the English news channels said the Collins leaks have so rattled the President that he didn't know whether to go play golf or go on vacation."

> "...The world is laughing at our government with all of the resignations and plea bargaining going on in D.C. The public is starting to call for mass resignations and talking about starting over."

Anna drew a card, smiled and laid her hand down. "I believe that is what you call *Gin*. I haven't spoken to hardly anyone since this started but I hope they flush them all out of office. I know I am mostly mad at what they are doing to Patrick and these kids. I don't know this Collins kid, but I have met his brother Daniel. Based on what I've read of the files William has released, I don't think this can be swept under any rug."

Mindy finished her sandwich and gathered up the cards. "Well, I have to run. It will be interesting to see if they follow you or me. If they choose me, we are going to go shopping— probably women's lingerie—that usually separates the men from the boys."

Mindy and Anna stood up. Mindy hugged Anna and whispered in her ear. "Don't give up. I'll call you later and tell you if I bought anything on my shopping spree. Here's a fresh phone. Pull the battery out of the other one and toss it."

Mindy and Anna picked up their purses and Mindy dropped the new phone in Anna's grocery bag. Anna headed for the parking lot, waving as Mindy went off to find her car. Anna loaded her groceries and saw the watcher get in his car with his partner. They were waiting for her. She closed the trunk and smiled. Maybe she should shop for something just to help the boys pass the time?

Anna headed for a department store that was close by. She glanced in the rearview mirror as the agents followed. "Let's see how you guys do in the makeup department." Anna grinned at the rearview mirror and thought what a bad influence Mindy was, and she hoped that when this was over, they could get to know each other for real.

David's phone rang. It was one of the burner phones. "Hello?"

The voice on the other end was Mindy. "Hi *Hon*, just thought I would check and see if you're going to be late again?"

David got up and went looking for Ben. "It looks that way, but you knew when I took this job I wouldn't be home early. Where are you?"

Mindy was looking at bras. She was using the mirror in the corner to enjoy the obvious discomfort of her tail. Nothing was funnier than a man trying to keep her in sight and not attract attention while stumbling around the women's lingerie department. He was trying to look like he belonged here and failed. "It looks like I picked up a *tail* after lunch with Anna, so I am trying on lingerie."

David had just entered the Tribunal room and stopped. He had to lower his voice. "You're doing what?"

Ben heard the door and turned to see David waving at him. As Ben got up, David stepped back out of the door. The Tribunal was in full swing, and David was having a hard time not laughing. "I wish I could be there to help you decide what to buy."

Mindy had moved over and was now rummaging through the Women's panties section. She kept picking up panties and looking at them while she watched her *tail* in the mirror. He was having a terrible time not staring, and Mindy was enjoying herself. "I need to get a message to Ben. Bailey Valentine from the DOJ visited Anna at home. He wants to talk to you guys about a deal."

Ben stepped out, of the Tribunal, and David handed him the phone as he heard Mindy's voice say, "I wish you could see

wrapping up this argument in a few minutes. Do you think the DOJ is serious?"

Ben nodded. "They have less to lose if they offer a deal rather than try to fight this. It's getting way too much public attention. Let's get Collins and Gator at the break so we can talk strategy."

CHAPTER 48

BAILEY STOOD ON ONE SIDE OF THE COMMAND post, listening to Lisa Millington as she poked and prodded those under her command. Lisa had a reputation. On her last several assignments she had left the same fear and bad taste with everyone who worked with her. She was known to sacrifice friend and foe, with no regard for anyone.

In the last half-an-hour, she had widened the gap between the Federal agents and the local police and the entire campus administration and security. No one was exempt from her style of management which had been compared numerous times to the Spanish Inquisition.

Patterson and Tillis were currently in the hot seat. Lisa berated them for their lack of progress, professionalism, and methods. The beatings would continue until she'd finished.

Thankfully Bailey's phone vibrated. He pulled it out, looked at the caller ID. He turned to head out the door. He could feel the daggers in his back as Lisa shot him a look of disbelief that he would dare walk out without being granted permission to leave her presence.

Bailey pressed the answer button on his earpiece. "Yes, sir."

Brent Underwood was watching the various news stations. "Have you seen the news coverage in the last half an hour?"

"No sir, we've been in a staff meeting with Lisa." Bailey remembered what the other agents had told him about the wonderful acoustics of the auditorium foyer, and he quickly moved outside.

Brent leaned back in his chair. "Meeting or Inquisition? I don't think she knows the difference. Anyway, you better get caught up on the media coverage."

"It seems that one of the members of the House of Representatives who was mentioned in the Collins files and subsequently in another set of documents released by one of her aides is applying for immunity. She decided to go home and hide out. We assume she thought her hometown would be friendly territory."

"From the news coverage, the small northern California town did not seem to appreciate the information in the Collins files. Apparently, she tried to hold a small-town meeting to calm the locals."

"But it backfired. A number of the residents decided to

follow the example of the Collins Tribunal and turned her town hall meeting into a Tribunal."

Bailey had moved to what he thought was the safest spot to talk, without being overheard. He stepped just inside the foyer doors so that he had a wall on each side of him and hopefully a semi-secure spot where he could talk. "What happened?"

Brent reached for a file on his desk that contained the current status report on the California incident. "It seems the town hall meeting did not appreciate the creative accounting and other actions of their hometown girl. The police chief is quoted as saying: *There was little they could do to contain the situation and he was sure the Congresswoman would recover.*"

Bailey knew Brent was baiting him. "Ok, you have my attention, what happened?"

Brent smiled. "If this wasn't fueling every fire in D.C. and across the country, it would almost be funny."

"After a very short trial, they pronounced her and her not-so-bright husband guilty. It seems they didn't have any tar handy. But someone provided some sort of industrial strength glue and feathers. Once they were both covered in glue and feathers, the locals physically chased them to the town limits with shouts about never coming back."

"The event is now immortalized by dozens of mobile videos and one local news crew. It's all over the internet, and the media coverage is almost non-stop."

Bailey wished there was a place to sit, so he pushed open the door and moved to the bench outside the auditorium. He was exhausted and had a feeling this was going to take time. "So, what are we going to do?"

Brent picked up another file. "It gets better. Another one of our elected officials in the spotlight of corruption decided to go to a church in his district."

Bailey interrupted, "Let me guess, they baptized him, and he's now born again?"

Brent laughed. "No, but that would have been interesting. It seems that our elected official tried to hide on the front row of the church. Unfortunately, the pastor had been mentioned in the papers filed by the Congressman's aide. It seems the pastor is accused of aiding the Congressman in some land scheme that was supposed to get the pastor a new church. But get this, *the pastor* has agreed to testify about the whole mess if he gets immunity. So, the aide and the Pastor are both less than friends of the Congressman. Anyway, the pastor zeroed in and began to direct a hellfire and brimstone sermon at the Representative."

"Apparently, the church got behind the pastor, and the service is reported to have become very spirit-filled. Unfortunately for the Congressman, he got up to leave, and the women of the church lined up on both sides of the aisle forming a gauntlet of sorts."

"As the Congressman tried to head for the back door, the women beat him with everything from purses, Bibles, canes, umbrellas and you name it. The video shows he fell several times and when I first watched it I was surprised he survived the stiletto heel stomping he got."

Bailey wished he had brought his iPad—these were videos he couldn't wait to see. "How bad was he injured?"

Brent tossed the folder back on his desk. "Someone called the police and an ambulance. When the police got there, the church was still in session, and the Congressman was lying on the street. The hospital says he will recover, but he has multiple puncture wounds, bruises, and several broken bones."

Brent was enjoying bringing Bailey up to speed on current events—it was the first time he had laughed in days. "Bailey, you will have to read the report and watch the news. The police said there was nothing they could do, it seems, the mothers of several of the responding officers attend this church, and the mommas were very clear to their sons as they came out of the church."

"One reporter interviewed one of the ladies—and she was great—she had on a big red hat, and she told the reporter that the *mommas* of this church were not going to put up with this anymore. She said she and what's now being called the *Momma Brigade* are going to be sure no other crooks are elected or take advantage of their families."

"Brent the media is going wild. The *Momma Brigade* is growing as we speak, it seems every church across the country is sprouting a version of their own. The mothers are organizing, and we all know that old saying: *"When Momma ain't happy ain't nobody happy."*

 "They already have Momma brigade T-shirts in some areas."

"Enough fun. The reason I called you was to bring you up to speed on the next step. We're authorizing you to grant Mr. Collins and the Tribunal participant's full immunity. We need to bring them in and show the Department of Justice is on their side. We're going to go after those who represent the people and have broken the law."

Bailey watched as a group of students with umbrellas began gesturing at the security camera. It was interesting how fast the protests had developed across the country. Every attempt by the authorities to control the situation had been met with a counter move by the public. The public was voicing their disapproval of being watched by a government that was now seen as a controlling interference to their lives.

"Brent we have never seen the public outraged like this before. Do you think the powers to be really believe that the usual delay tactic of cover-up and delay until things die down, will work?"

Brent sat up and pulled out the latest paper placed on his desk. "Normally, I would agree, but I will send you the two latest announcements I just got."

 "The first is a Presidential Executive Order

stating that the President, with the full support of Congress, excluding all those under investigation, will be investigated and brought to justice. They even named a Special Prosecutor to head this action."

Bailey leaned forward. "You said two announcements, we've seen a lot of Presidential Orders, but they lose a lot of their meaning if Congress is not behind them."

"Brent, you get to go to the head of the class! The second announcement is a letter jointly signed by what's left of the Senate and the House members who are currently not named in the Collins files...which by the way is a much smaller number of people than even I had expected."

"It seems Congress has agreed for once."

Bailey still didn't believe it. He had been in D.C. long enough to know the trauma and drama tactics of politicians. "So, who got the short straw to head this investigation?"

Brent pressed the email-send button on his PC. "You should be receiving an email any moment now, and you can offer me your condolences later. I've accepted the role as Special Prosecutor, and by the way, you may want to give Lisa a few minutes. I named you as my Deputy and Special Investigator."

The door to the auditorium burst open, and a dozen people headed out of doors. Patterson and Tillis were in the middle of the escaping crowd. "I think she knows. So, do I get to pick a team of investigators?"

Brent watched his email as D.C. insiders began to bomb his email with questions. "Yep, we have no budget constraints and as much autonomy as we want. Everyone wants this cleaned up, and if we find someone with their hand in the Peoples cookie jar, we don't just slap it, we cuff them and haul them off for prosecution."

"Bailey just make sure you can trust the top guys. We need some people we can really trust. This is going to be the dirtiest fight this country has ever seen."

Bailey waved at Patterson and Tillis. "I think I can find a few guys to help. Is Lisa being relieved or removed or what?"

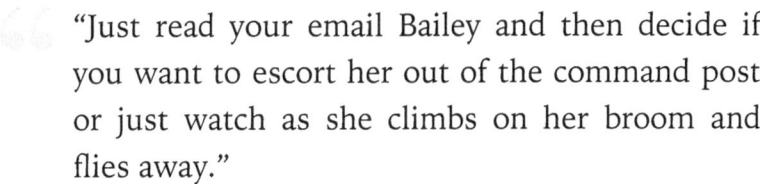

"Just read your email Bailey and then decide if you want to escort her out of the command post or just watch as she climbs on her broom and flies away."

Patterson and Tillis stood in front of Bailey waiting for him to finish his call. Bailey held up a finger to let them know he wanted them to wait.

The door to the auditorium burst open, and Lisa Millington flew out with Tyler Winston trailing behind. They could all hear the tirade of threats as Lisa, told Tyler to get her car, and then she listed the people who were going to pay for this.

Brent stood up. "Boss, I don't have to wait, she knows and is climbing on her broom to leave. By the way, she did just mention your name, and it sounded like she was questioning your family history."

Brent laughed again. "It's ok, what was it the old man said about amateurs?"

Bailey thought about their mutual friend and mentor when he used to say, "I've been threatened by professionals. Amateurs no longer bother me."

"Yep, and we know how to spot an amateur don't we? Now go find Collins and let's make a deal. I have to make a statement to the press."

Bailey watched as Lisa stood waiting for Tyler to open the door of the car so she could get in. "Thanks, boss, we will do our best. Good luck and blessings—you are going to need them."

Bailey put the phone in his pocket and turned to Patterson and Tillis. "How would you guys like to be part of a new task force?"

As Special Investigator, Bailey Valentine assumed his new job and walked into the command post to pass along what he knew to Patterson and Tillis. As he did, his phone rang. Though he didn't recognize the number, he pressed the receive button. A voice on the other side of the call began.

"Bailey Valentine, this is Ben Langley. I represent William Collins, Professor Ramirez, and the Tribunal Students. I understand you wish to talk to us about a deal?"

Bailey grabbed a piece of paper and wrote: "Check out Ben Langley. He's representing Collins and Company." He handed the note to Patterson and sat down in Lisa's chair. "Yes Mr. Langley, I would very much like to talk to you, and I'm sure we can reach an agreement. When can we meet?"

CHAPTER 49

G OVERNOR C ORTEZ AND S ENATOR D ELANO WERE counting heads. They needed two-thirds of the States represented to hold a Constitutional Convention. But they would need three-fourths to approve it.

No one was sure if there were enough of the Senate or the House left in D.C. to make up two-thirds of anything, let alone to amend the Constitution.

Both Delano and Cortez knew they had set themselves up for the fight of their political careers. Everyone they talked to said getting support to amend the Constitution would be near impossible. Especially with all the turmoil of the Collins Tribunal.

Cortez and Delano had told several reporters this was the perfect time to draw a line in the sand and show the public who was serious about cleaning up D.C. and who wasn't.

The media was trying to work all sides of the debate, some pointed at the Constitutional Convention as a noble effort, some called it a way to hide the truth...everyone had an opinion. The only thing no one could refute: the public was looking for someone to hold accountable.

Delano looked at the pad in front of him. "I figure we have almost forty states represented, so if they all agree, we should be able to start."

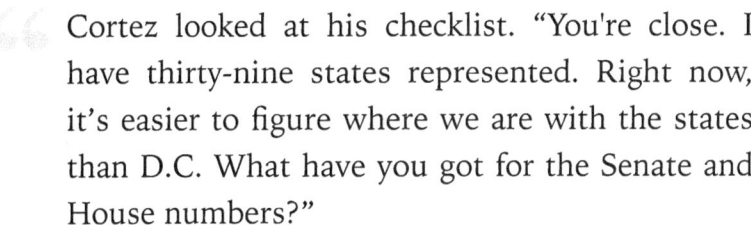

Cortez looked at his checklist. "You're close. I have thirty-nine states represented. Right now, it's easier to figure where we are with the states than D.C. What have you got for the Senate and House numbers?"

Delano flipped the page on his notebook. "I understand we have 300 of the House committed to supporting us. But my staff tells me the Collins files have incriminated 215 members of the House. Out of 435 members, almost half are facing investigation. Fifty-two members have announced their intentions to return to private life. Thirty-seven are currently missing."

The Senate is equally impacted, forty-two senators have agreed to openly support a Constitutional Amendment. It's not enough, but my staff reports we have about twenty more saying they will support us. We just don't know how to count the fifty-eight or so that may be under investigation. About twenty-five of them are being sought for questioning or have already resigned. I understand another fifteen or more are being picked up for questioning.

Cortez looked at the crowd of Governors and Congress members trying to jockey for seats. "Maybe this won't work. But we have to do something. The country is in chaos. The public needs something to believe in. Yesterday, they had to call out the National Guard to protect some of the companies named in the Collins files. The people expect someone to pay for the alleged crimes that Collins has exposed."

Delano looked at the clock on the back wall. "I hear you. The media is running from one incident to another. One of the unions in the car industry had their membership walk out, and they say they won't come back to work until the President of the company resigns and returns the money he got from the bailout. The Union officials protested, and they were locked out of the union hall."

"Two of the other labor unions held elections and ousted their leadership and are taking steps to prosecute them for embezzlement."

"What we don't know is what the President will do. Every time the White House Press Secretary talks, he contradicts the last position they had. The rest of the world is watching. They're waiting to see if we recover, have a civil war or just disintegrate. I understand the military is on high alert as they are worried about someone taking advantage of the chaos in the country."

"Well, it's time for us to do our part."

Cortez stood up and tapped the glass on the table. The audience quickly quieted.

"Security, can you please make sure the doors are closed? No one from the press is allowed in the room for now."

Several reporters had slipped into the room and had to be escorted out while protesting the rights of the media all the way through the door and twenty feet beyond.

The head of the Oklahoma State Police waved at the Governor that it was ok to proceed. Cortez waved at Jack Torrance. Jack was a full-blooded Choctaw and one of the most honorable men Governor Cortez had ever worked with. He knew Jack would do his best to protect the meeting. "Thank you, Jack. Now, if you will all give us your attention, Senator Delano and I would like to outline the plans to hold a Constitutional Convention. We have spoken with all of you, and by your presence here, we believe we have your support."

"We're going to break down into work groups to get this moving as quickly as possible. There will be no breaks, and none of us plan on leaving until we reach a consensus."

 "As soon as we have agreed, we will hold a group press announcement and let the American people know what we're proposing."

Cortez turned to Delano. "Senator Delano has broken down

the assignments, so I will let him fill you in, and we can get going. Please remember we want this written in plain English so everyone can understand it."

Delano stood up. "What my friend Governor Cortez is saying is the same thing one of my constituents told me last week. Please make it clear so the people, not politicians can understand it. I think what he meant to say is, '"No weasel-wording."'

Most of the group laughed, but a few were offended. Delano continued, "We have an obligation to the American citizens. We have failed them. Career politicians and their staffs have placed themselves above the people that elected them. It's time to correct that. We will be focusing on a few key areas. The first is drafting a Constitutional amendment that Congress and the President must obey the laws that they pass. No one is exempt from the laws of the United States especially those of us making the laws. Similar legislation will be proposed in each state that wishes to comply."

"Included in this amendment will be a restriction that the President nor any congressional, administrative or judicial body can grant exemptions from the law to any person or group of persons."

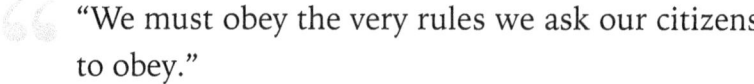

"We must obey the very rules we ask our citizens to obey."

"Some of you will also be developing legislation to assure the

American people that elected officials are accountable to those that elected them."

"The draft legislation is being handed out to each of you."

"We are proposing that those elected to represent a state will be paid by the State and not the Federal Government. Those of us elected to represent the State, and our staff will be compensated by our State. This includes health care and benefits. The legislation proposes that the public will vote each year on the salary and budgets of the elected officials of the state and those that go to Washington. Those elected will no longer be able to legislate their own salaries and benefits."

"We are also proposing that each state will develop their own State Tribunal that has the authority to review the conduct of any elected official. Any elected officials found to have violated the law, the Tribunal will have the power to recall that official and determine if the elected official is innocent or guilty. If an elected official is found guilty, a special election will be held to replace them, and they will forfeit all benefits of that position.

 "We can no longer count on Congress to self-evaluate misconduct. Our past conduct shows that we have not represented the American people, but ourselves."

"This will be a revolutionary approach, and many career politicians will balk at any change to their comfort. But the last week has shown us the need to make a change. We have a choice. We in this room can lead the charge and try to restore the faith of the American people, or we can wait until the American people take action."

A voice from the middle of the room called out. "Either we change or expect more tar and feathers when we go home!"

Cortez looked at Delano. Delano stood up next to Cortez. "Ladies and Gentlemen, we have all seen the actions of the American people this last week. Senator Delano and I have drawn our line in the sand, and we are going to stand with the American people. If we have to run a few crooked politicians out of town on a rail, then I will be glad to help carry that rail."

The press would eventually hear these comments as half of the people in the room were using their cell phones to video the speech or were calling one of their staffers to listen. But something unusual happened, and the duly elected stood up and cheered. Oh sure, a few were still not convinced, but every movement has its doubters. These doubters just wanted to be seen as on the side of the people. They had already seen how the public had reacted to those that had failed them.

Delano and Cortez shook hands, and another round of applause and cheers went up. As they quieted down, Delano began to read the assignments. The audience broke up into their various working groups. The hard work was just beginning. Now they had to agree and get this done. For now, in this room, there were no party lines.

Cortez's phone beeped. He looked at the text message: "Collins group willing to talk deal for immunity."

Delano picked up his notebook. He and Cortez agreed that they would float around the room trying to break deadlocks and keep the groups moving. Cortez showed him the text message. "Maybe we should include these guys. It might boost the public support?"

Delano crossed his arms and chewed on the tip of his thumb. It was one of those things the press had picked up about Delano. It was the only "tell" Delano had shown to the public, and half the time he didn't even realize he was doing it. "I think you're right but how do we include them?"

Cortez sat down. "Let me make a call and see what we can do."

Delano stepped off the platform and headed for one group where he knew the honorable representative from Massachusetts was already working to block progress. Delano also knew that one of the new whistleblowers was on the representative from Massachusetts staff. He was sure the honorable representative from Massachusetts would become very helpful after Delano let him know his number-two staffer was seeking immunity for testimony.

CHAPTER 50

GATOR, RAMIREZ, BEN AND WILLIAM COLLINS WERE sitting in Gator's private office. The rest of the Tribunal were eating and resting before the next round.

Ben was recapping the brief conversation he had with DOJ's Bailey Valentine. "Mr. Valentine has assured me that the newly appointed Special Investigator wants to bring you in as a friendly witness. He indicated they would grant you full immunity for your testimony."

Ramirez interrupted. "What about the students?"

Ben knew Ramirez was worried about his flock—he didn't even mention himself, just the students. "Yes, Patrick, the students, you and even Gator and his organization will be granted immunity. I did suggest that Gator, you and yours would probably like to remain out of the public eye."

Gator bowed his head. "We appreciate that. It would be bad for business if we were seen standing too close to you guys."

"Gator when this is over we need to talk." Ben looked at Collins. "How do you feel about this William? You're the key witness to the largest Government corruption investigation in history."

William had bowed his head. He was contemplating his feet and the mess he had been tracking through the lives of these people. "I appreciate everything you all have done. I just want to be sure no one else pays for my mistakes. If I have to go to jail, I will as long as they leave all of you alone."

Ben was holding a folder which he handed to William. "I think you need to read this and let me know. I've read it as your attorney and advise you that you and everyone associated with the Tribunal project are safe from prosecution."

William took the folder and then one of those dawning questions he had forgotten about came to the surface. "I don't have any money—they froze everything—I can't pay you."

Ben leaned back. Here was a young man who a day ago was about to face charges of treason. He was accused of breaking several National Security agreements and his big concern today was for everyone else and that he couldn't afford an attorney. "William, you don't need to worry about it. I understand several groups have come forward and agreed to pay your legal fees. And I am absolutely certain you will make a fortune in royalties and public appearances."

Gator pulled out his laptop and began to type while he talked. "Don't worry about it, William. I know someone who can represent you to the media vultures and guarantee you will make a profit. I'll set it up, and you can talk to her when we get to that point. I work with this woman and she's the best."

"Professor, do you want her to represent you too? I know there have to be several book deals in this and a lot of public appearances."

Ramirez was caught totally off guard. He looked at Gator and tried to make the quantum leap from being worried about being arrested as a co-conspirator in a National Security investigation to talking about book deals. "Umm, I hadn't thought about it…"

Ben took out a pen. "Let me note this as the first time I have ever heard Patrick Ramirez start a sentence with *umm*."

Ramirez relaxed and sat back. "Ok Gator count me in, this is your field I'll follow your lead."

Gator was typing and moving around in his chair. He was excited and was busy laying out an entire campaign for the *Collins Tribunal Triumph Tour*.

Ben's phone beeped, he took it out and read the text message from David. He read it twice to himself. "Gentlemen I think the tide has turned in our favor. David just told me that

Senator Delano and Governor Cortez from Oklahoma are at this minute drafting legislation for a Constitutional Convention. They believe they have enough Governors, House and Senate members to pull it off. They're also proposing several new laws that are being referred to as part of the *Collins Reform Act.*

> "Congratulations William…and it's even more interesting that they are asking if you and the Tribunal class would help."

Gator's phone rang and his email began beeping on his computer and his phone. He picked up the phone and heard Julie shouting, "Erase everything! Go to plan black! Gator, the cops are banging on the doors. They're calling for Collins to surrender or they're going to storm the place. Look at the cameras. They have SWAT teams and everything."

Gator grabbed the remote for the TV and turned on the outside security cameras. Everyone in the room turned to see a half dozen local police and campus security cars pulled up outside the fence, and a dozen or more police pointing guns at the building. A massive SWAT vehicle was still emptying officers in full assault gear out of the back door of their van. They began taking up positions across the front of the building.

Gator pressed another button, and they could hear a voice on a bullhorn demanding that they open the doors and send out William Collins and the rest of his conspirators.

Ben was reaching for his phone when it rang. David was on the other end and asked, "What do you want us to do boss?"

Ben was grateful that David never seemed excited about anything. He just remained cool and handled what was in front of him. "See if you can talk to the crazy one with the megaphone while I call our friend at the DOJ and find out what happened."

"Ok boss, but if I get shot, I want a big funeral, and you get to tell my momma." David hung up the phone and headed for the door. Julie was already on her way to join him.

Ben pulled up his recent calls and redialed Mr. Bailey Valentine.

Bailey was in the command post at the school with Patterson and Tillis working on how to provide enough protection for the Collins crew. He looked at his phone just as the local news station broke for an instant update. As Bailey pressed the talk button, the TV news station was running the trailer at the bottom of the screen that the local police had cornered William Collins and group. "Hello?"

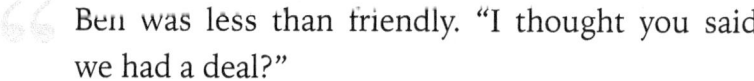Ben was less than friendly. "I thought you said we had a deal?"

Bailey was already up and waving for Patterson and Tillis to join him as he started for the door. He hollered as he began running. "Find out where they are and get all of our people over there before those idiots start shooting! Ben, I just saw it on the news. I had no idea the locals were still looking for you, let alone setting up a raid. Tell me where you are and see if you can stall them till we get there."

Ben could hear David over the speaker system. He was standing in plain sight with his hands raised trying to talk to the officer with the bullhorn.

Ben was scared. "Valentine if you're serious, you better call off the police and get over here right now, or we're going to be facing a full-armed assault on a bunch of unarmed students."

Valentine was already in the car. He was starting to pull out of the school when he stopped and looked at Tillis. "Where the hell am I going? Tillis shrugged his shoulders." Ben, I need an address, hang on I'm putting you on speaker so I can drive while we talk. We don't even know where you are."

Tillis was on the phone yelling at whoever answered the phone at the local police station.

Ben looked at Gator "Where are we? I need an address."

Gator put his hand over the phone he was holding and said, "4670 Central Industrial Drive.

Valentine heard the address and started to punch it into the GPS.

Patterson pulled his car up next to Valentine's car. He signaled for Valentine to roll down his window.

Valentine rolled down his window. Patterson yelled, "Follow

me I have the address." And he drove off lights flashing and siren screaming.

Valentine rolled up the window, while Tillis finished punching the address into the GPS. Valentine was trying to follow Patterson and wishing he had taken a course or two in pursuit driving. "Ben we're coming, just try to stall till we get there. Tell them the FBI is on their way."

Tillis hung up his phone. They can't get the Police chief to answer his radio or his phone. Apparently, the Chief is on TV and telling the press about his investigative skills and how he was able to track down these fugitives before the Feds did. His assistant kept telling me the Chief is busy with a press interview.

The GPS finished plotting in the address and the route. Valentine glanced at the display. "Ben, we're about 5 minutes out, you should be able to start hearing our sirens."

Ben tried taking a deep breath. But his chest hurt. He was used to tension, but not like this.

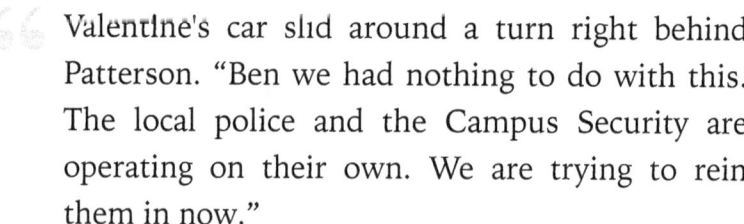 Valentine's car slid around a turn right behind Patterson. "Ben we had nothing to do with this. The local police and the Campus Security are operating on their own. We are trying to rein them in now."

Ben and everyone watched the showdown outside the building on Gator's security cameras. Gator was talking to

Julie as she was going through the building executing their plans to dump and destroy all files.

Ben couldn't wait any longer and headed for the door. "Valentine, if you don't get here immediately, these cops are going to start shooting. You told me we had a deal. This sure as hell doesn't look like a deal. The media is outside filming this. How is it going to look when SWAT starts shooting? I have one of my people out there trying to talk to the Police, and they aren't listening to him."

Valentine was weaving through traffic trying to keep up with Patterson in the lead car. Patterson was dodging traffic, honking his horn and screaming at people as they ignored his siren and lights.

Valentine slid around another corner. In his rearview mirror, he saw four unmarked SUVs with their emergency lights flashing red and blue. He prayed they were his guys. He was going to need them.

Valentine's phone calls were stacking up one after another. He could barely understand Ben as the phone kept beeping with new calls. Everyone calling him had discovered the local news coverage and the siege at the Collins compound. At least, that was what the media was calling it. *A full-fledged hostile siege.*

Tillis' phone was also starting to ring nonstop. He answered his phone and found Bailey's boss screaming at him and asking what was going on. Tillis didn't know Bailey's boss (which was probably for the best).

So he screamed back, "We just found out, we are on our way to try and stop the local idiots from killing anyone!"

"No, he can't pick up the phone. He's talking to Collin's attorney."

"Yes, he is in the building with Collins…"

"No, he can't pick up the phone he's driving. He'll call you when we get a handle on this!"

Tillis disconnected the call and turned the phone off. Valentine was still talking to Ben, trying to assure him they would be there in two minutes. He looked at Tillis. "If that was my boss, you know we're going to hear about that later."

Tillis was being tossed back and forth in the seat as Valentine played *dodge cars* with the oncoming traffic. "If we live through this, he can holler all he wants. I think I may retire when we're done. Let's just pray you can get us there alive."

David was still holding his hands up and trying to talk to the officer with the bullhorn, "Officer, I assure you no one has any weapons. Could you please lower your guns? My boss will be here in a couple of minutes he represents Mr. Collins and those in the building. I am sure we can clear this up. Please lower your guns."

Officer Bullhorn was not impressed. He and his detectives had tracked down the Collins group, and they were going to make the arrest. He pressed the button on the bullhorn. "I told you. I want everyone to come out with their hands up. You have five minutes to get everyone out of the building."

The media already had a camera vehicle in place, and the cameraman was on the roof of his van broadcasting live to the world.

Ben had reached the door leading out to where David was trying to talk to Officer Bullhorn. Two of Gator's staff headed for the far end of the building. Ben watched as they jumped in a green hatchback at the far end of the garage. One of the garage doors began to open.

Julie dropped her clipboard and started running towards them—yelling at them to stop.

David turned and saw the garage door opening, and then the car burst out onto the parking lot. Several tense SWAT team members took the car leaving the building to be an act of aggression and they opened fire. David, heard the gunfire and dove off the porch, taking cover behind a dumpster. Ben, hearing the gunfire started to run to the door yelling, "David!" Ben reached for the door leading outside as the gunfire continued and bullets began coming through the windows, garage doors and were knocking on the door in Ben's hand.

Gator showed up from nowhere and pinned Ben to the wall.

"Just wait. David jumped behind the dumpster. He should be ok. Let them finish then we can try and surrender without getting shot."

Ben and Gator both heard Julie's cry as she was struck by a bullet coming through the third garage door. As she collapsed to the ground, both Gator and Ben ran down the stairs two at a time towards Julie.

> As they started to run, praying the bullets would stop or not hit them, they heard several sirens approaching and someone on another bullhorn screaming, "FBI! Stop shooting!"

Patterson's car was first to arrive. There were now two local news trucks on site and pandering for that special shot that would make them famous for a night. Patterson saw a gate to the left of them and swung his car towards it. As he crashed through the gate, he swerved to miss the green hatchback and tried to get his car between the Police and the building. He never thought about the local police firing at him. Patterson heard Valentine's voice in the car behind him shouting over the PA system in the car, "Stop Shooting! I repeat, stop shooting! We're the FBI!"

Unfortunately, the local police continued to shoot as six bullets hit Patterson's car, two in the front tire, and three in the engine. The last shot came through the window which caught Patterson in the arm as he held up his FBI credentials. The gunfire stopped, as Patterson's car came to a halt next to the dumpster where David was hiding.

Bailey and Tillis's car screeched to a halt just missing Patterson's car. Tillis jumped out of the car and ran to Patterson's car still screaming, "Don't shoot we're FBI!"

Patterson was angry, bleeding and operating on pure adrenaline as he pushed the car door open and stood up still waving his FBI credentials.

Tillis saw the blood running down Patterson's arm and began yelling for a medic. He was holding his Homeland Security Credentials in one hand and screaming, "You shot an FBI agent!"

Finally, the local police began to lower their guns, and several officers ran forward to help.

Valentine was standing between the local police and the building. He was still on the phone with Ben. He continued to yell at the local police. "Who is in charge? I want whoever is in charge! I am Bailey Valentine of the DOJ. You will cease fire and stand down. This is a Federal investigation. I want whoever is in charge now!"

Several of Tillis and Patterson's agents had arrived and were trying to move the press back and keep the local police away from the building. Two of the FBI agents were calling for medics as they ran towards the green hatchback that had tried to exit the building. Valentine looked over as the medics pulled one person out of the passenger side and put them on a gurney. The second medic stood up after examining the driver and called for another ambulance. The agent standing by the driver's door looked at Valentine and shook his head to the obvious question.

Valentine knew this would be a media disaster, another death for no reason. He knew the media would second guess this death from every angle. The local police would most likely end up in a very costly lawsuit.

Right now, Valentine had to shift into disaster cleanup mode. "Ben, is anyone in there hurt?"

Ben and Gator were trying to stop the bleeding in Julie's leg. "Yes. We have at least one wounded. We're close to the open door."

Bailey turned and hollered at the medics. "We have an injured person just inside the open doors. Charlie—go with them! No one leaves the building, and no one goes in but us."

Charlie was still standing by the door of the car that had tried to leave. He headed toward the open garage door with the medic close behind him.

David peeked out from behind the dumpster. He saw Agent Tillis kneeling next to Patterson who was sitting on the ground while the medic tried to stop the bleeding in his arm.

Tillis saw David and turned towards him. His hand instinctively landed on his gun. David stood up and raised his hands. "Don't shoot! I work for Ben Langley who's representing William Collins."

Tillis relaxed and took his hand from his gun. He waved for David to come toward him. "You better come over here before one of those trigger-happy cops takes another shot at you."

David walked over to where agent Tillis stood. They both

looked at the dumpster where David had been hiding. Tillis looked at the dumpster and started counting. "You are a lucky young man. I count eighteen bullet holes in the front of that dumpster."

David felt a cold shiver as he thought about how close death had passed by him. "My Momma always said I had an over-worked guardian angel."

Patterson was trying to get to his feet. "Maybe you can put my name in the hat for one of those guardian angels?"

David and Tillis went to help him up. The medic asked them to keep him still while he got a gurney. David looked back at the dumpster. His phone rang. "Yes sir, I will be right there. Yep, I'm ok." He turned and headed back into the building.

Bailey was heading for the door and waved at Tillis to come.

As Bailey and Tillis stopped at the stairs, Bailey looked at the growing crowd behind them. "I think we'd be better off not trying to move anyone out of the building for a while. See if you can round up enough of our people to surround and secure this building. I don't want anyone in here except you and me. Is Patterson ok?"

Tillis was tired. He looked at Patterson as the medics were putting him on the gurney and wheeling him to the ambulance. "He got a bullet in the arm—it's too early to say if it hit any bones. I guess we had better send some of our people to the hospital. How many others are injured?"

Bailey looked at the ground and kicked a rock out of his way.

"So far the driver of that car is dead, the passenger was hit twice, another wounded in the building and Patterson. I don't know about anyone else yet."

Tillis surveyed the area, looking at the local police as they put their guns up and tried to blend into the surroundings. *Officer Bullhorn* was trying to deal with the media, another job for which he was ill-suited. His actions today would later prove to be the final chapter in his law enforcement career. His new career would be acting as a witness in numerous lawsuits where he would try to defend his actions.

Tillis looked at Valentine. He heard the whispers of doubts calling him. This was the second round of shootings and death since he arrived on this investigation. Second guessing what he could have done differently would follow him for a long time. "Bailey, what did I miss? We should have been able to prevent this one. I felt bad for the Ballard kid and that attorney Carlson. And now this…"

Valentine looked around sharing a similar line of regret. "Brad, this was out of our control. The best we can do is act as the political janitors and try to clean up this mess. When this is done, we can go have a good cry and help each other to bury the second guesses. For now, I need you to help me protect these people. Can you do that?"

"I'm with you," replied Tillis. "You can count on me."

Bailey turned and climbed the steps. David was waiting at the top of the stairs. "My boss asked me to bring you in. He would like to meet with you privately."

Bailey nodded and followed David. He could see the medics were loading another person on a gurney and pushing her out through the open door. A man watched her go and then turned and headed towards the stairs.

Gator followed behind Bailey. As soon as he knew everything was ok, he would need to make some calls to next of kin. His prayer was that he only needed to call one family.

David led Bailey to Gator's office where Ben, Patrick and William Collins waited.

Bailey knew everyone in the room except David and Gator from looking at the photos in the command post.

> "I want all of you to know that we had no idea the local police and Campus Security planned this raid. We didn't even know they had any idea where you were."

Ben sat down. "David, are you ok?" Ben was still looking at Bailey, trying to decide if he could be trusted.

"I'm ok, but I'll be sending you a bill for a new change of clothes. If you're going to keep working on this case, then I'm buying a bulletproof vest."

Ben watched as Gator moved behind his desk. Valentine was still standing. Ben had played a lot of positioning games in his years as an attorney. Bailey obviously had played some as well. He was waiting to be invited to sit down. "David if you're ok, could you find some fresh coffee and whatever else these gentlemen want. I also would like Walt and Diane to join us—we have a lot to discuss."

David looked at the bullet hole in his jacket sticking his finger through it and waving it at Valentine. "That was close."

David left to find coffee, Walt, and Diane.

Ben gestured at a chair. Bailey nodded, and the negotiations began.

Gator looked at Ben. "Perhaps a little larger room would be better?"

Ben looked around and mentally calculated space. "I believe you're correct. Gator, is there one close by?"

Gator dialed his phone calling Julie's number out of habit. Jenny answered as he remembered Julie was on her way to the hospital. "I'm sorry Jenny, I was calling Julie."

Jenny was in full mother hen mode. "I figured it was you. Julie gave me her phone when they took her to the hospital. I'm just trying to keep a lid on things and keep everyone calm. What can I do to help?"

Gator stepped over to a door that led to his private conference room. "I was going to let Julie know we would be in my conference room and we may need someone to get stuff."

Jenny got up from Julie's desk and waved at a couple of the staff she had gotten to know. "I'll see if I can round up some stuff for you. One of your staff, I believe she calls herself Yellow, is on the phone with the hospital checking on Julie. As soon as it's safe, she wants to go to the hospital."

Gator moved to the head of the table and gestured to Ben. Gator knew how to read a room; he also knew when to sit on the sidelines. "I'll check on when we can get someone to the Hospital and let you know. Thanks."

Ben had moved to the head of the table, and Bailey sat at the foot opposite Ben. Ben turned to Gator. "I can have one of my staff head over to the hospital to check on Julie if you would like?"

Valentine cleared his throat. "Let me make a call and have one of our agents clear the way for you. If you want to send someone to the hospital from here, I can have one of my agents drive them. I understand you have several wounded people."

Ben looked at Gator, and he nodded. "I would appreciate that."

Bailey took out his phone. "I would like to call one of my agents so he can get someone to drive you to the hospital if that's ok?"

Ben nodded. "...And you might let them know one of my staff members Mindy Matthews will be showing up to represent them."

Bailey called Tillis and asked him to get a car and driver to escort Yellow to the hospital and to have him advise the security detail at the hospital about Mindy."

A knock at the door and Yellow stuck her head in followed by Jenny. Gator got up and walked around the table. Yellow was crying and hugged Gator and started asking, "Why did they shoot them? Billy and Dale were trying to get out and distract them. And Julie didn't do anything…"

Gator hugged her. "I need you to go to the back door and look for Agent Tillis." He turned and looked at Bailey.

"Agent Tillis will be waiting for you with a driver to take you to the hospital. And let me assure you we will get to the bottom of this."

Yellow turned to leave, and Jenny started to back out when Ben called to her, "I would like you to sit in on this Jenny. We need your input."

Jenny looked at Patrick and Gator. Both nodded agreement. Gator pulled out a chair next to him, and Jenny moved over and sat down.

Ben looked at Bailey, "Now how do we proceed from here?"

CHAPTER 51

BILL HAD DONE EVERYTHING LIZ TYLER HAD ASKED. He had come in the back and was trying to keep George away from the windows, off the phone and away from email. Babysitting George was pushing Bill to the edge.

The media coverage just kept getting worse. His phone had not quit ringing as other staffers were calling him with their stories. None of them were good. Most of his colleagues were looking for immunity deals.

Bill heard Juanita come in the back door. She was carrying groceries. She put down the bags and began putting the groceries away. Bill had moved into the dining room to talk to an attorney friend when they heard George yelling. Bill hung up the phone and ran into the study. George was on his knees behind the desk trying to open a safe and talking as only someone who had been drinking for days could talk.

Bill looked at the TV and caught the tail end of the media bulletin showing them hauling Liz away in handcuffs. Juanita came in the room carrying fresh glasses for the bar. She almost dropped them as she saw her boss being hauled away.

Juanita put the glasses on the bar and turned to leave, as she passed Bill she whispered, "I'm leaving. I suggest you get out of here—they will be coming here next."

George finally got the safe open and was pulling out files and portable hard drives. He looked at Bill and held up the files. George was so drunk he was hard to understand. "She thought I was stupid, but I kept copies of everything. Call my attorney. I want to make a deal, and I want a divorce."

Bill looked back at the TV, and his phone rang. He looked at the screen and saw it was his attorney friend at DOJ. Bill answered. "Marty, they just arrested Liz, what can I do?"

George handed Bill a handful of files. "Call my attorney. I want to make a deal."

Marty was looking at a growing list of bureaucrats trying to turn whistleblower. "Bill you need a lawyer, and I can't help you. I was calling to tell you I can't talk to you anymore. Your name just came up on a list of those people they are looking for as part of the Liz Tyler investigation. This one is going to the NSA. What did you do?"

Bill was skimming through the files George had handed him while George was trying to find a phone number for his attorney. Bill stopped as he read one sentence on the fourth page. "Marty, I don't have a lawyer, but I want to turn myself in, can you handle that for me?"

Marty was watching his door. He shouldn't be talking to Bill, but they had been roommates at college and joined the same fraternity. "Bill, you need a lawyer. Why don't you call Stephanie from school, she's an attorney, maybe she can help you?"

Bill looked outside. The crowd of reporters was growing. "Marty, I'm at Liz's house trying to watch her husband, and he is drunk and crazy. He just opened a safe and is pulling out all sorts of files. And they have details of stuff I don't want to know about."

Marty sat up, he had just slipped off the edge of helping a friend and was about to slip into the river of aiding and abetting. "What files are you looking at?"

 Bill flipped back to page four and read to Marty. "The *Back Nine* met privately with the President to discuss the deal with..."

Marty was shouting, "Don't tell me anymore! I'm going to tell my boss you are an old friend and you're asking for immunity. Stay there! We will be sending someone to pick you up. Get everything you can and pray you can find a good attorney. Stay put and don't talk to anyone else."

The phone went dead. Marty heard the door slam and assumed Juanita was leaving. George was still trying to find his cell phone and was crawling on the floor looking under the couch.

Bill slipped behind the desk, looked at the open safe it was packed with files, money and a couple of laptops. Bill grabbed the pile of files and a laptop. The money was tempting, but he wasn't a thief. Right now, he was just scared. Bill grabbed his backpack and began filling it with files from the safe.

The noise outside grew as a siren grew closer and then quit. George and Bill went to look out the window. Several men in suits got out of the car, and two police cars pulled up and started trying to push the media back. George turned and staggered to his desk. He picked up a pile of the remaining files from the safe.

He held them to his chest and started for the front door. "I'll show her."

Bill watched as George opened the door and staggered off the porch and shouted, "It was all her idea!" And George tossed the files in the air. The media rushed George as the files floated through the air. The two agents started to try and stop the rush, but watching the media fighting over the files and papers was safer than trying to take them away. Instead, they tried to get to George.

Bill stepped out on the porch, closed the front door and walked over to the agent who was trying to get George back on his feet.

"My name is Bill Clayton—I want to turn myself in."

The one agent let George stay on the ground. "We were instructed to pick you up."

 Bill handed him his backpack. "You will want this, and there is a safe full of stuff in the house."

The agent waved at the police and told them to secure the house and not let anyone in. Several more police cars arrived, and a dark SUV pulled up.

Four people got out of the SUV and headed for Bill. They flashed their credentials at the agent holding the backpack. "We'll take that."

The team of four surrounded George and Bill. The lead agent turned to Bill. "Bill Clayton, we would like you to come with us."

Bill looked at George and kicked him. "I never did like you or your wife."

Two of the NSA agents hauled George off.

Bill turned to the NSA agent. "I just told these guys I am turning myself in and there are a lot more files in the house. They're all about the *Back Nine* and the President. Look at the safe in the study." The other agent headed for the house. The agent took Bill by the arm, and they headed for the SUV.

The media were already on their phones back to their stations. George and Bill would be featured over and over as the media tore apart Bills comments about secret files, the *Back Nine* and the President.

Several more unmarked SUVs showed up, and the local police were instructed to clear the area. A half-dozen people with no badges showing began going through the house. Boxes of files were carried out, and few would ever see or read their contents.

George had passed out in the back seat of one of the SUVs. Bill looked at the agent sitting next to him. He could hear his mother asking him, "Why do you want to work in politics, you could get a good job with your Dad's company…"

The SUV pulled off and disappeared with George and Bill.

The lead agent was standing on the porch. His phone rang. He stepped off to one side. "No Ma'am we were too late. Yes Ma'am, they are both in custody, but I think the press has some of her files."

The phone went dead. The agent went in to be sure the files were boxed, and no one read them. He went into the study. "Take it all, just box it and get it out of here."

When the TV began replaying George's file throwing, everyone stopped and watched. Then a reporter stuck a microphone in front of George and George in his drunken glory said way too much. The agent turned off the TV. He smiled as he thought about the pending divorce of George and Liz, and how it would make a great TV reality show.

CHAPTER 52

CORTEZ LOOKED AROUND THE ROOM. THE GROUPS were exhausted. They had been hammering out the amendment and the various pieces of legislature needed for the states. This had to be a unified package for it to work. There were still those in D.C. and lots of lobbyists trying to derail this effort. Fortunately, one after another of those objecting seemed to be falling under the growing number of whistleblowing documents surfacing.

Delano came in from outside. He was looking at emails on his phone. His staff and those supporting the amendment in D.C. were keeping an eye on developments in the Collins investigations. They were constantly checking to be sure they had the support needed to pass the amendment.

 Delano sat down across from Cortez. "We lost

two supporters. Their aides turned whistleblowers and were waving all sorts of interesting facts in front of the media. On the bright side, we've had five very late entries swearing their support and sending letters endorsing a Constitutional Amendment."

Cortez sniffed, "Conscience or trying to buy cover?"

Delano rubbed his forehead "Probably a little of both. The five Johnny-come-latelys are known for their ability to waver in the wind of opinion. None of them have shown up deeply implicated in any of the Collin's files. So, all in all, we're good to go."

Delano looked at his laptop. "The DOJ is swamped. They can't handle the incoming calls or those that are just walking into DOJ and giving themselves up. The whistleblowers are hiring attorneys and having them hold press conferences. Their attorneys are stating their clients are seeking immunity and offering selected files in return. The media is on the worst feeding frenzy I've ever seen. They just run from one event to the next. The news is almost non-stop interviews with people trying to duck prosecution. We even have several dozen lobbyists making statements that they were being extorted by elected officials and their staffs."

Cortez was exhausted. They had been at this for twenty- four hours with just a four-hour break so some of them could sleep. "I just got several emails from my staff saying the DOJ is asking for help. They want us to use our state law enforcement people to help handle any of those from our states that are seeking immunity. They want us to take statements, seize evidence and hold them until the DOJ can get to them. We had better handle this carefully. We won't be able to guarantee any deals, but they want us to help gather the evidence. If you have a short list of people we can trust, let me know."

Delano looked across the room. Three people were lying on the floor trying to get a nap. Only one group had someone standing and waving his arms. The others were passed that. "How close are we?"

Cortez looked at a sheet in front of him. "It looks like everyone, but our friend from New York is ready to sign. I see he's still on his feet. I understand he's trying to exclude New York from the state version of the amendment. I expect his name will show up in the indictments shortly."

Delano leaned back in his chair. "I hope it's soon, everyone is exhausted, and the press is surrounding the building waiting to hear something."

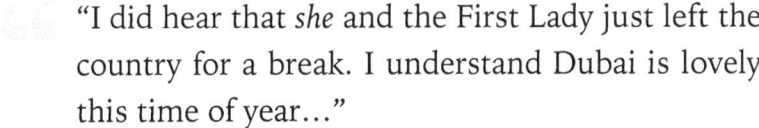 "I did hear that *she* and the First Lady just left the country for a break. I understand Dubai is lovely this time of year…"

Cortez looked up as the room got quieter. "Our friend from New York just walked out."

Representative Martin from Georgia left the group and walked over to Cortez and Delano. "I think we can call for a vote. New York just got an urgent call and had to leave. My staff just sent me an email that one of his staffers just called for a press conference in Times Square. Apparently, several of his staffers are going to join the whistleblowers union and have already been sending out documents."

"It also appears we have six new supporters. The Governors of Vermont and Oregon have announced their support for the amendment. Also, one senator and three more House members have announced their support, so I think we're good to go."

Cortez looked at his phone and read an email from his staff. He looked at Cortez. "The DOJ has just taken Collins and the Tribunal group into protective custody. It seems the local police found Collins and company before the Feds got there. The local Police opened fire on the unarmed Collins group. Which has resulted in one dead, two or three wounded."

> "The DOJ representative is Bailey Valentine. He has just announced they have secured the compound and are holding everyone on-premise."

Delano got out his phone and started texting his staff. "I know him. He's one of the straight arrows over there. He works for Brent Underwood."

Representative Martin started to head back to his group. He stopped and turned back to Cortez and Delano. "You know what we should do? We should go down there and sign the amendment where they're holding them. And let them finish their Tribunal. We could use it to put all of this under public scrutiny."

"I'll bet we could get some judges and attorneys to make the whole Tribunal a legal process for accepting the files as evidence. We might even be able to sell the idea of establishing State Tribunals for all elected officials from within their own states."

"I wonder how you two are going stand up to the kind of scrutiny you're proposing?" The rep from Georgia laughed and walked back to his group.

Cortez and Delano just looked at each other for a very long minute. Cortez broke the silence. "We could call this the Collins Amendment. We go there and sign it. Maybe we have Collins sign it?"

Delano nodded. "I was thinking the same thing. I'll call Brent at DOJ and see how he feels about it. See if you can get this group to vote and we can catch some sleep before we go meet Mr. Collins."

Delano walked over to a quiet corner of the room. Cortez headed off to check with each group and see if they were ready to vote. The media would have one more thing to add to the nightly coverage—a new Constitutional Amendment.

CHAPTER 53

BRENT UNDERWOOD HADN'T LEFT HIS OFFICE IN forty-eight hours. He was working his assistants and secretaries in shifts trying to keep them on their feet. His wife had brought him clothes, soup and a hug. He had promised her a week away as soon as the fires burned down to a manageable level. His third shift secretary stuck her head in the door. "Senator Delano is on the line."

Brent nodded, looked at his wife's photo and picked up the phone. "What can I do for you, Senator?"

Delano watched as the vote continued. "Well right now you might get ready for the Constitution to be amended."

Brent sat back. "Are you sure? I didn't think you guys could pull it off."

Delano watched as Cortez took the last vote. He looked at Delano and gave him a thumb's up and announced, "The 28th Constitutional Amendment has passed unanimously." The room filled with cheers and shouts.

Delano held one hand to his other ear. "Did you hear that Brent?"

Brent typed out an email to his wife to let her know. "I pray you guys can make it stick. We need to get some order back in this country."

Delano stepped into a side room so he could hear. "So, fill me in. We've been cloistered here and just get bits of news as people duck out to hit the bathrooms."

Brent pulled a file from the left pile on his desk. "Where do I start? Ok...let's start with this: There have been forty-seven Public Tribunals held across the country trying various elected officials and others. Here are a couple of the more creative ones. A Latino gang in LA tried their Representative to the House and found her and her husband guilty. The Tribunal had the word "THIEF" tattooed on their foreheads."

"Another group in Florida tried one of the local politicians. Then one retired member of the Tribunal drove a bulldozer through the elected official's home."

"In Chicago, another group tried their Representative and found him guilty. It was a local gang that held the Tribunal.

They felt it fitting to hang the rep from a street light in front of the guy's home."

"We hoped that law enforcement could help, but this stuff is breaking out all over the country. The idea of local Tribunals has caught on, and I don't think anyone knows how to turn it off."

Delano smiled. "Maybe we can help refocus the nation's attention. Is Bailey Valentine still cloistered with the Collins group on that compound?"

Brent felt the favor coming. "Yes. Why?"

Delano could see Brent sprawled out in his chair. "We want to move the official signing of the amendment to the Collins compound. Then we want to sit in and let them finish the Tribunal. We want you to line up all the high-level legal names you can to observe both the signing of the amendment and the Tribunal."

> "We want to take the last part of the Collins Tribunal and open it to public viewing, C-SPAN, the internet...the works. Let them finish presenting their case to the public *live*."

Brent leaned forward and picked up a pencil. He started writing down names. "I need to call Bailey and see if the Collins people would be agreeable. You know this is going to finish tearing the roof off of D.C. I'm sure we'll have hundreds of nuisance lawsuit from this."

Delano lay down on the table in the conference room. He was alone in the room and the temptation to lie down for a minute was too much to resist. "I think it'll be more like thousands of nuisance cases. I would bet this will finally push the public to stand up and clean the house. Will you do it?"

Brent looked at the picture of the President that hung in almost every office in the DOJ. "I should tell you that I have to check with my boss. But I have lost two bosses in the last twenty-four hours. According to the White House Staffer that just called me, in the interim, I am in charge. So, let's get it started and see if I can stay employed until you get it done."

"Oh, I forgot to tell you. It looks like we might have two openings on the Supreme Court. It seems many of the files being released have caused enough questions that two of the newer justices have announced they are resigning for health reasons."

Delano looked at the frescos on the ceiling and wondered who painted them. "Brent, I guess I should congratulate you? Any idea how the President is taking all of this?"

Brent looked at the clock. "He should be just about finished with the back nine if he holds to his usual schedule. All we hear is the staff is keeping the President updated, but he's not saying anything."

"How long do you think it will take to pull all of this off?"

Cortez opened the door, Delano didn't even sit up. "Cortez just walked in, let me ask him."

> Delano turned his head towards Cortez, "Brent wants to know how much lead time do we need if we move to the Collins compound. Then we can sign the Amendment and sit in on the last of the Tribunal."

Cortez had already been building a timeline with his staff. "Two days. We want this to start on Friday. That way the people can watch it all weekend. I already have the media getting behind it."

Brent looked at his calendar. He had heard Cortez faintly, but loud enough. "Ok, let me get on the phone, I want to give Bailey a heads up and be sure they're on board. And I know a couple of Supreme Court Judges that will be eager to attend this party. I'll call you back."

Brent hung up the phone and looked at his wife's photo. "It's going to be a little longer, but we are going to go away—I promise."

Delano grinned at Cortez. "He needs two days to clear it with the Collins group and work out the details with them. But I'll bet Collins and his attorneys will want the public audience."

Cortez was already back on his phone making arrangements. He walked out, closing the door behind him.

Delano lay there on the table. It was quiet and lying flat felt so good. He closed his eyes for a minute and lost twenty minutes to a wonderful nap, which ended when his phone rang. He answered from an interrupted deep sleep. "Yes?"

"It's Brent. We're on board. I've lined up two Supreme Court justices and about a dozen Federal Judges and Prosecutors who said they would pay to attend this—they'll be there."

"Were you sleeping?"

Delano sat up. "No, I just closed my eyes for a minute."

Brent laughed. "And that is what I'm going to do when I hang up this phone. My couch is calling me, and I have told everyone to leave me alone for an hour. So, let me know if you need anything, but don't need anything for the next hour."

Delano was still trying to return to the land of the living. He stood up, shook his head to get the blood flowing. Now after that refreshing nap, he just needed coffee and his staff. It was time to wake up the rest of America. A new day was coming.

CHAPTER 54

SENATOR SHERATON WAS TIRED OF WATCHING THE news in his self-sequestered cabin. He had started a list of those who were trying to make a deal and who they worked for—it wasn't good. The members of the *Back Nine* were not faring well. One suicide. Three had been caught at the airport trying to flee the country. Three more had been arrested at their homes. One was still unaccounted for, and Sheraton was still free for the moment.

Almost everyone the *Back Nine* worked with was showing up on the news. One secret file after another was being exposed and used to try and negotiate immunity from prosecution.

The news had reported the First Lady was taking a break and the photo showed *she* had left with *her*. The President was still living in a world of his own. Even the media was starting to whisper about how he might have to resign, or maybe impeachment…or *worse*. Enough names were coming out of the Collins files surrounding him that someone would be looking to make a deal.

Sheraton was trying to figure out how to work a deal, but it wasn't working. His name was linked with way too many deals that he should never have made. If it hadn't been for that Collins kid, he could have skated out in another year and spent the rest of his life retired on a quiet beachfront out of this country.

The TV flashed another of the endless special bulletins. This time they were announcing the new 28th Amendment that would require the President and Congress to obey the laws they passed. No more special deals or exemptions.

Sheraton read the ticker at the bottom of the screen ignoring the media's talking head. Great, thought Sheraton this is going to upset a lot of profitable deals. Only the American people who know more about TV and sports than their own laws could make this big a mess. What a joke.

The newscaster announced the new Constitutional Amendment would be signed just outside the building where the last part of the Tribunal would be broadcasted live.

The Collins Tribunal was going to have public and governmental support. Sheraton got up and poured his last drink down the sink.

It was time he did something. He closed the cabin door, got in Marty's pickup and drove off. He needed to make a couple of calls, and pick up some extra phones. He pulled out his phone and used the GPS to plan his trip.

He looked at the distance and the drive time. That would work. He could nap in the truck if he got tired. He turned on an oldies station began his trip.

CHAPTER 55

GATOR HAD GATHERED EVERYONE IN THE PARKING area inside the building. It was the biggest area. Ben wanted to talk to everyone and let them know what was going on in the negotiations with the authorities.

Bailey stood off to one side. He felt like he had become part of this group and his fate seemed to be attached to theirs.

Ben looked at Bailey and nodded. He turned to the Tribunal group. He had come to know most of them. There were still a few of Gator's people that he had not met, but the rest he knew and respected their abilities.

"The DOJ has agreed to grant immunity to all of us. We, in turn, will be turning over all of the files and information William brought to us."

"Patrick, your Tribunal idea has gained national support, and Tribunals have sprung up across the country. Many of those Tribunals ignored due process and have taken action in many independent ways. Some have become vigilante groups and need to be stopped."

"But one thing for sure. The country is in agreement that the public has the right to recall any elected official and question their ethics and actions."

"What you've started has birthed the 28th Amendment. Enough Governors, Senators, and Representative of the House joined forces and were able to hold a Constitutional Convention and unanimously passed the new amendment."

"Governor Cortez and Senator Delano spearheaded this effort. They have asked to sign this amendment here with all of you acting as witnesses to the signing of what is now being called the Collins' Amendment."

"They would also like you to finish the Tribunal and present to the American people the rest of the Collins files. The process is being supported by the DOJ who will let the information presented at the Tribunal be accepted as evidence."

"The Tribunal will be broadcast through the internet and via C-SPAN. No media coverage will be allowed inside the building."

"We have two days to get ready. Gator has assured me that

this area will be able to hold all of those joining us from the Constitutional Convention. This will be the stage for the Tribunal. The signing will take place outside on the parking lot."

"Mr. Bailey from the DOJ has assured us this facility is under the protection of the DOJ, Homeland Security, and the FBI. No one will be permitted in the building without clearance."

"We need to hang in there for a couple of more days, and then we can all return to our homes."

> "I want you to know that I have never been prouder of a group of people than I am of this group. History will reflect your efforts. Now, we have a lot to do, so let's get to it. The nation and the world are going to be watching."

The groups began to head off to their tasks. Bailey, Gator, Ramirez, and William stayed with Ben.

Ramirez shook his head. "I think I'm going to retire. I don't think I could take on another class. This one has been a career-changer."

William hadn't smiled much in the last ten days. "I think I'll join you, Professor. My political days are finished."

Gator looked at Bailey waiting to see if he was going to respond. Bailey nodded at Gator. "William, you need a break, but I think you may find you have just started your political career. The polls are showing that if you ran for

President, you would be the favorite candidate hands down."

Gator stepped forward holding out his hand to William. "Congratulations Mr. President, can I be your campaign manager?"

William shook Gator's hand. "You guys are crazy. I figured I was going to jail or just disappear. Who in the world would want me to run for any office?"

Gator let Williams' hand drop. "Talk to Jenny. The idea of you running for President is all over the media. We just released a whole line of shirts and hats with Collins for President on them. Jenny said we sold out instantly. And that was 10,000 shirts and eight thousand hats. Dude, you have to run. Don't worry about the details. Jenny and I have already started setting up your campaign."

Ben stepped in. "For now, we need to get ready. Patrick and I need to brief William so he can take the stand."

> Ben and Willian headed for the room they would use to prep William. Ben stopped and turned back to William. "After you Mr. President."

William shook his head and headed for the door with Patrick and Ben close behind.

Bailey watched them go. "Gator we need to be there for him. This is going to change his life in ways he never thought of."

Gator smiled. "Jenny and I already decided we're going to

take care of him. Besides, it should be more fun than this rodeo has been. But now, I have to go salt public opinion with the right attitude."

Bailey stood on the platform looking across the room. He could see the Public Tribunal filling this area and opening the eyes of millions as they heard the testimony of William Collins. Bailey had been around D.C. a long time but even he was stunned by what was happening behind closed doors in D.C. He wondered if he would ever be able to trust another elected official.

Maybe he should talk to Jenny. There had to be a couple of book deals in this experience.

Ben's phone rang, and Tillis came in from outside looking for him.

CHAPTER 56

THE MORNING WAS CLEAR AND SUNNY, THE temperature was perfect, with just a slight breeze with a few clouds drifting by. Tillis and Patterson were going over last-minute details preparing for the arrival of the Constitutional Convention constituents. It was lucky that Gator had picked an area with a lot of abandoned property surrounding it. Patterson and Tillis had been through every building and designated holding areas for the Governors, Senators, and Representatives. The addition of so many Judges and prosecutors made this one of the most influential gatherings in history.

Every building had security people on top of the roofs. Observers and snipers were located strategically covering the path to the main area. A parking lot on the edge of the secure area had been designated for press vehicles. Most of them were still complaining about the long walk to the signing area. Their complaints warmed the hearts of every agent like Patterson and Tillis who could not stand the arrogance of the media. Most of their agents had learned to say nothing and never to trust the media. Most of Patterson's agents felt the media would sell their children and parents for a few seconds of prime-time coverage. Two dozen golf carts had been brought in to ferry the dignitaries from the waiting areas. It was fun watching the press try to commandeer them. But Tillis had assigned a U.S. Marshall to each cart with strict rules. Only people on the list were allowed to ride.

A few creative media types had tried to bring in their own carts, which started a battle. The additional carts and the protesting media were banned from the area, which just caused more complaining from the media.

Tillis had just returned from the first entry checkpoint to be sure they had the proper list of attendees. The road into the Tribunal was to be kept clear at all costs. Patterson was going over the seating plan and last-minute changes when Tillis got out of his golf cart. "How does it look?"

Patterson scanned his clipboard again. "No cancellations. But about a dozen not on the list are throwing their political weight around trying to get in. It seems that there were a number of last-minute conversions trying to be sure they would be seen on camera."

Tillis walked up the steps and stood next to Patterson. "How's the arm?"

Patterson lifted his arm and replied, "It's ok—the pain meds help."

Tillis continued, "You know you don't have to be here. You could be at home. Somewhere sane."

Patterson grinned. "I came this far with you, I'm going to finish this. Besides Gator promised me a T-Shirt when it's over."

Tillis shook his head. "I think you hit your head somewhere along the way."

> "I understand Delano and Cortez have drawn a line in the sand on this one. If you weren't at the Constitutional Convention, you have to wait until they present it in D.C. tomorrow. And then they must publicly declare *for* or *against* it."

Patterson sat down in one of the chairs on the side of the platform. "Do you know Charlie Stanton?"

Tillis scanned the area again, just praying all went well. "No, his name doesn't ring any bells."

"He's on assignment in D.C. He said he drew the wrong straw and got assigned to the floor of the House today. They're holding a protest and making all sorts of proposals, but they don't have enough people to do anything. He said the place is like attending a funeral for a guy no one liked."

"Most everyone left in D.C. is trying to make sure their names don't show up in any of the immunity files. Charlie said two of the House Reps tried to turn in their staffs, saying they didn't know what their staffs were doing and they had no knowledge of any wrongdoing."

Tillis finally sat down. It was the last chance to rest before the circus started. "I talked to my wife last night, and she said the rumors are that the President is gearing up to grant pardons by the dozens and issue a half dozen new Executive orders. She knows a couple of the low-level office staff at the White House. One of them told her that they are down to the third string of staffers. Almost everyone else has run for cover. The ones that are left are in total denial about what's happening."

Tillis stretched out in the chair watching a sweep team with a dog going through the seats again. "I heard the President is still running his schedule like nothing is happening. It should be interesting when this crew shows up in D.C. tomorrow."

Bailey Valentine came out of the building and walked over to them. "How are you guys holding up?"

Patterson lifted his wounded arm. "It's ok. It throbs a lot, but that keeps me awake. But as soon as this over, I'm taking a couple of weeks and going home to sleep."

Bailey looked at his phone and continued checking emails and texts. "I understand Cortez and Delano will be here in twenty minutes. They want to spend some time with the Tribunal crowd. So, keep an eye out, they are the only ones allowed in the building."

Tillis saluted. "Aye Aye Captain. Any word on how the public is reacting to all of this?"

Bailey looked up from his phone. "The American public is funny. No matter what our elected officials have done they just changed the channel, grumbled and moved on. I guess Congress thought the people just didn't care and they could get away with anything. But this Collins thing has woke up the giant. Every city is having marches and demonstrations calling for a house cleaning in D.C. The most common outcry is for state-level Tribunals to be put in place to be able to hold the D.C. elect responsible to the people who elected them. If Collins did nothing else, he has united the public. They have rallied around the idea of Tribunals. The people want whoever is elected to be accountable to them. They want term limits, no more career politicians, and backroom deals."

Bailey looked over the area where they would sign the amendment. "You know this whole thing couldn't have gotten this far without that guy Gator. He has quite the operation. Which he says is simply a marketing company. But his staff says they're *opinion mercenaries*. You tell them what you want to sell and they spin it up and make it popular."

"I like the guy. I hope he stays on the side of the Collins kid."

Tillis looked up at the building behind them checking to see if the security team was in place. Patterson got up. "It's time to get in place before Cortez and Delano arrive."

The radio on Patterson's belt beeped. They all heard the

same message on the command frequency. "The guests have arrived and are on their way down."

Valentine headed for the steps. "Guess we'd better get ready. Tillis, can you let Ben know they're here, he'll want to be here to greet our guests."

Tillis nodded and went into the building to find Ben.

Patterson headed down the steps to direct traffic. Bailey waited at the top of the steps. He looked up. "Ok, we need all of the favor we can get if any angels are listening send help," he whispered. While he believed in God, he didn't advertise it. Believing in God had become very politically incorrect, so he kept his faith quiet and prayed for a new day.

From the top of the steps, Bailey closed his eyes and could see the photos of the area surrounding the building that housed the Tribunal. He traced the roads that lead into the warehouse area and down to the Tribunal compound. He prayed they had blocked all of the roads so no one could sneak into the compound.

The radio said the Constitutional Convention attendees would be gathering at 10:00am. The signing would take place around 10:15am. Delano and Cortez had promised no speeches, just a few introductions then they would all sign the amendment. Once that was done, some would stay and attend the finale of the Collins Tribunal.

He watched and waited...this would be a long day.

CHAPTER 57

At 9:50AM PATTERSON REGRETTED HIS LAST CUP OF coffee. He should have listened when Tillis told him to eat breakfast. But Patterson was a bit stubborn and his order of *just coffee* was burning his stomach. Most of those on the attendee's list were in place. The last few were being shuttled from the three parking areas to their seats. The golf carts were racing back and forth, each driven by a U.S. Marshall. No one else was allowed past the checkpoints.

Two spotter drones had been deployed which no one claimed. All Valentine would disclose was that drones were being deployed for surveillance purposes. Patterson looked up but didn't see anything. The media had been told no aerial reporting. The airspace was declared a no-fly zone for the rest of the day.

Patterson stood on the roof of the warehouse that housed the Tribunal. From a security viewpoint, this place was a nightmare. Abandoned warehouses surrounded them. Several tall buildings were within a half mile as well as several hilltops looking right into the parking lot where the signing was to take place.

His radio crackled in his ear, and he heard Tillis calling him. "I'm on the roof. I just wanted to check again. I'll be down in a minute."

Bailey and Tillis were looking over the crowd of gathered dignitaries as Patterson walked up. Bailey took a deep breath and let it out slowly. "I just spoke to Johnson with the U.S. Marshalls. They're set up and ready. Patterson, that was a good idea to have them handle the entry point. They've taken over parking lot three. According to Johnson, it's the most private and should help them as the dignitaries leave."

Tillis put his foot on the railing and leaned forward. "So how many of our dignitaries are they planning to take into custody."

Bailey snorted. "The last I heard, 37 of our honored guests have warrants pending."

Patterson was stretching his arm trying to work out the throbbing, "I guess Cortez is just happy they didn't take them into custody until after they signed the Constitutional Amendment."

Nodding, Bailey found himself trying to spot the guilty as

they left. "Yeah, well that took a little negotiating. The Marshalls wanted to take them into custody when they arrived. But if they did that Cortez wasn't going to have the numbers he needed to sign the amendment. Once you two went over the security plans and the Marshalls figured out that they could have one whole parking lot just for those with warrants, they agreed.

Tillis waved at one of the security team, "Yeah and it didn't hurt that you reminded them who was on the committee that oversees their budget."

Bailey turned to Tillis. "Negotiation is a fine art of knowing who holds what chips and what they are willing to bet. Besides, this way there is no one from the media making a fuss. It's all done quietly, and those with outstanding warrants just disappear."

The signing ceremony went without a hitch. Just introductions, lots of applause and shouts about a new America.

Introducing William Collins got a standing ovation and shouts of "Collins for President." Bailey was sure Gators staff started those, but a lot of people joined in with the chant.

If everything stayed on schedule, they would have most of the dignitaries on their way home, in the building to attend the Tribunal or in federal custody. The only thing for certain was Bailey, Tillis, and Patterson would feel a lot better once they got these political targets out of the open. The reports were the streets around them were filled with crowds calling for a new America.

Inside the compound, they just prayed it would end without a hitch.

CHAPTER 58

SHERATON WAS RUNNING LATE. THE OLD PICKUP truck just wasn't ready for the long drive he had just put it through. He had to stop and add oil twice. The radio was covering the Constitutional Amendment signing, and it was just about over. He stopped and looked at the GPS on his phone. He was about three minutes out.

There was only one road to the Tribunal. And from the looks of things, he would not be able to get very close. He looked at the boxes in the front seat and wondered how close he could get to the building.

Sheraton started to pull away from the curb and felt something thump the passenger's side of the truck.

Instantly alarmed, he looked at the side view mirror and saw a girl falling off a bicycle but she quickly disappeared out of his view..

Sheraton immediately put the truck in park. He got out and hurried around to check on the girl. She was laying on her back, partially under the truck.

Sheraton knelt down to check on her. The girl rolled clear of the truck and sat up. "Sorry, I wasn't paying attention. I was talking on my phone."

Sheraton helped her to her feet. "Are you ok?"

 She picked up her bike, looked at it and swung a leg over the seat. "Yeah, I'm all right. Sorry I scared you, I've got to go. I'm late."

Sheraton took a couple of steps after her, but she was already gone turning and heading down a cross street.

He looked at the truck but couldn't see any damage. As he walked back around to the driver's side, he heard cheering coming from the signing.

He slammed the truck door and headed down the road to the signing. At the top of the hill leading to the Tribunal, a U.S. Marshall stopped him and told him he had to go back. Sheraton smiled and turned on the charm that had gotten him elected to four consecutive terms. "Call your boss and tell him Senator Sheraton is here and would like to talk to whoever is in charge."

The Marshall backed away from the truck and pulled the

microphone from his radio and started calling through the chain of command. The word *Senator* carried a lot of weight today, even if his name wasn't on the guest list. But his name was on the Marshall's list.

No one in the security detail today wanted to offend anyone that might remember their name tomorrow. Finally, Bailey heard the call requesting someone to clear Senator Sheraton or come get him.

> Bailey stepped to one side to be able to hear over the noise as the signing was ending. He keyed his microphone. "Did you say, Senator Robert Sheraton?"

The answer confirmed it was him and he wanted to talk to whoever was in charge. Bailey looked around but he didn't see Patterson or Tillis. He pressed the transmit on the microphone in his hand. "Tillis, Patterson, I need you right now."

Both Patterson and Tillis tried to respond at the same time. Which if you know anything about radios, it didn't work. Patterson stopped and listened.

Tillis was on the west side of the crowd and began heading for the stage. "This is Tillis; I should be at the stage in a minute."

Patterson was at the gate to the parking lot and headed back in the golf cart. "I'm right behind you."

Bailey waited for Patterson and Tillis. He didn't want to broadcast Sheraton's name again. Too many people were listening. Patterson pulled up just as Bailey and Tillis left the crowd to join him. Bailey looked around. "Senator Robert Sheraton is at the entry point. He wants to come in. I need both of you to go and get him. Check him out carefully. Then take him over to the command post in the north building. I don't know what he wants. But Delano and Cortez won't want him walking in here. Just hold him at the command post in the north building. I'm sure he's up to something. Take one of the cars. I don't want people to see him. Half of the law enforcement agencies in this country have been looking for him. And the Marshalls are aware he is here. We need to move quickly or they'll grab him."

"I'll be there as soon as I can. Make sure you keep this quiet."

Patterson and Tillis drove the golf cart up to the parking lot where their cars were. Tillis was barking orders into his radio to be sure things were covered while he was away. As soon as Tillis took a breath, Patterson continued ordering backups to cover him as well. They left the golf cart and picked up one of the cars.

They pulled up to the checkpoint. The Marshall was standing in front of an old blue pickup that had seen better days. Patterson and Tillis got out of the car. Instinctively, their hands went to their guns. The Marshall saw the reaction from Tillis and Patterson and started to reach for his gun. Tillis called out, "Stand down—we have this."

Patterson moved to the passenger side while Tillis walked to the driver side.

> Sheraton had the window down and held up both hands. "No need for you to be worried agents."

Tillis approached the window cautiously, knowing Patterson was in position if anything didn't look right. "Senator Sheraton, what can we do for you, sir?"

Sheraton smiled. "This is where the Collins Tribunal is being held?"

Tillis nodded and moved closer to the window. "Yes sir, now what can we do for you?"

> Sheraton gestured towards the boxes on the floor and in the front seat. "I want to offer these files as evidence...and I am seeking immunity." He handed Tillis a file. "This should give you something to tell your boss."

Tillis took the file, read a few lines and looked at Patterson. "Senator can you turn off the vehicle and wait right here?"

The Senator nodded and turned off the truck, smiling at Patterson as he kept both hands on the steering wheel.

Tillis took out his phone and called Bailey.

Bailey was smiling at everyone and trying to appear calm as the guests were still shaking hands and trying to be sure they were seen. He tapped the earpiece for his phone and answered, "Yes?"

Tillis turned his back on the Senator. "Bailey, I have Senator Sheraton here, and he wants to turn himself in. He says he has several boxes of files that he wants to turn in, in exchange for immunity. He handed me one which I have in my hand, and if the rest are like this one, Collin's information won't even be remembered. Listen to this…"

Bailey walked away from the crowd listening as Tillis read a couple of lines from the file. "Get him and whatever he is driving off the street. I need to call D.C. No one talks to him. No one. Is that clear?"

Tillis turned back to Senator Sheraton. "Senator, can you follow me please? We want to move to a more secure spot." Tillis looked in the truck again. He wanted to be sure they were just files.

Sheraton smiled. "It's ok son, I don't have a gun or anything, but I tell you what, if they think the Collins kid's files were something, wait till you see these. The Collin's stuff will move to the back page of the newspaper where it belongs."

Tillis waved at the Marshall to move the car blocking the street. "Please follow us, Senator."

Patterson and Tillis got into their car and drove down the street to the parking lot of the command post. Tillis got out of the car and stood in the road directing the Senator to follow Patterson.

Patterson pulled off to the far side of the building, and the Senator pulled in next to him. Tillis looked around. He didn't see any media people, so that was good. Tillis stopped to tell the agent at the gate not to let anyone on this lot. He dialed his phone to call Bailey.

> 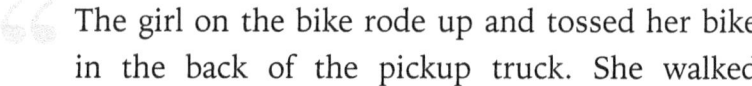 Patterson got out of his car and Sheraton opened the door of the truck. He handed Patterson one of the file boxes. "I kept records on everything. When I get done telling you what I know, D.C. will be empty."

Patterson took the box and waited while Sheraton pulled another box from the back seat of the truck.

Bailey had just answered the call from Tillis when the explosion echoed in his phone and rolled across the parking lot.

He heard Tillis say, "Oh my God..." and Tillis ran towards the inferno where the truck and Patterson's car had merged consuming Senator Sheraton, Patterson and the files.

———

On the hill overlooking the Tribunal, the cloud of smoke assumed the traditional mushroom shape.

> The girl on the bike rode up and tossed her bike in the back of the pickup truck. She walked

around and opened the door on the passenger's side and climbed in. "Time to go."

Michael O'Brien started the truck. He looked at the smoke and could hear the fire trucks responding. "Guess we'd better get back. We need to get The Whales ready for the dinner crowd. I've a feeling we're going to be busy."

Cathy nodded and texted, "Done."

CHAPTER 59

BAILEY WATCHED AS THE CONSTITUTIONAL signing members were moved into the Tribunal building through the garage doors. He was trying to regain some sense of control while barking orders and trying to answer questions on his phone and radio.

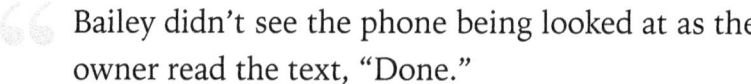 Bailey didn't see the phone being looked at as the owner read the text, "Done."

The owner nodded and moved in with the rest. Now the secrets were gone with Sheraton, and no one would be looking in his direction.

It took twenty minutes to calm everyone after the explosion. But everyone agreed the best thing to do was continue with the Tribunal.

Daniel raised the gavel and called the Tribunal to order.

Daniel Collins was back in charge of the Tribunal hearing even though the cast of characters had changed dramatically. They were missing two of the original members. They had gained thirty-two Governors, forty-four Senators and 127 members of the House. Two Supreme Court judges were observing. Three federal court judges were acting as counsel to the Tribunal. One sat with the prosecution. One sat with the defense. One sitting directly behind Daniel so he could privately consult him if needed.

C-SPAN was covering the event as well as several internet blogs. The event was being fed live over numerous internet feeds—thanks to Gator.

Daniel looked around the room. Ben Langley sat next to Professor Ramirez. Daniel tilted his head towards Ramirez, and he nodded.

The Tribunal had become a form of therapy for the American People. Most people had already decided that those exposed in the various Collins files and the follow-up whistleblowers were guilty. The American people were united. That was something that hadn't happened since World War II. The American Public had a common enemy, and it was D.C.

Legislation was being finalized to overhaul the things that had become twisted over the last two hundred years. Congress was going to be required to live by the laws they passed—no more exemptions. If it was a law, *everyone* had to obey it.

Part of the changes in legislation made the States financially responsible for those elected to the United States House and Senate including their respective staffs. They would no longer be able to vote on their own benefits and salaries. They would be accountable to their States. No more free rides. Retirement, medical plans, and other benefits were all to be determined by the individual states. There would be real checks and balances to keep them honest.

Thirty-seven states were proposing legislation that would allow the states to recall any elected official accused of misconduct. They would then be tried by the State's Public Tribunal. No more code of conduct sessions in D.C., where they look the other way when one of their own is accused of misconduct.

If an elected official or one of their staff were accused of misconduct, they would now be responsible to the people who elected them and not their peers.

The media was having a field day with the new proposals. They were attacking anyone objecting to the proposals. Public opinion was so strong in favor of bringing control back to the states and the people that no one wanted to stand in the way. Petitions for change were so numerous no one could keep track. But the number of people signing them was staggering.

The President and the White House remained quiet. They continued issuing watered down statements about what was best for the American People. The remaining eleven months of the President's term would be recorded as the quietest term of office in Presidential history.

At the conclusion of the Tribunal, the custody of all the records submitted to the Tribunal were taken over by the DOJ. Bailey supervised the actions and had the records duplicated before transferring them to D.C.

The members of the Tribunal were being celebrated as heroes. All of them were receiving job offers, even though they still had to finish out their year of school.

The Tribunal took eighteen hours to conclude with one six-hour recess. The crowd in the second session was much smaller and even more committed to exposing the corruption and the public support for the Tribunal was overwhelming.

The internet viewing was worldwide and was reported as the single largest viewed event in recorded history. The verdict was as expected. The D.C. Congress was found guilty. They didn't even try to list the number of counts, and there were still the thousands of files that had not yet been viewed.

As the Tribunal broke up, one reporter was allowed an interview. Jenny was seated with Governor Cortez and Senator Delano. They were talking about what changes were needed.

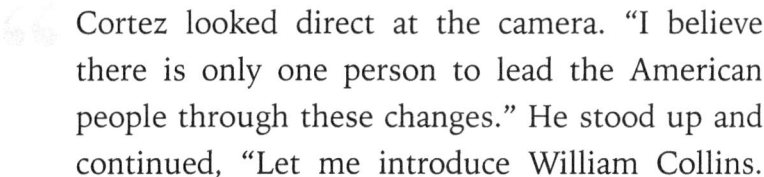

Cortez looked direct at the camera. "I believe there is only one person to lead the American people through these changes." He stood up and continued, "Let me introduce William Collins.

William stepped forward and shook hands with Governor Cortez and Senator Delano. Once they were seated, William quickly outlined a plan to make the changes necessary."

When Jenny asked if William would consider running for President, William looked at the camera. "I am here to serve the American People, and I will do what they want."

Reporters were already writing that this day would change the face of American politics.

The interview ended. William walked onto the floor of the Tribunal. The gathered dignitaries stood in line to have their photo taken with William Collins.

Gator and his machine were hard at the spin. T-shirts with Collins for President, bumper stickers, hats and more were selling out as fast as they could print them. Twitter, Facebook, and every social media were working at promoting the People's choice – William Collins.

Tillis and Bailey stood on the walkway overlooking the scene. Tillis felt the growing weight of the few pages Sheraton had given him. "Why don't you take Sheraton's file—I don't want anything to do with it."

Bailey put one foot on the railing and leaned on his knee. "It's better if you hold it for now. We will need to make copies and find some safe places to keep them. With Sheraton gone, all we have is that file with no one to corroborate it."

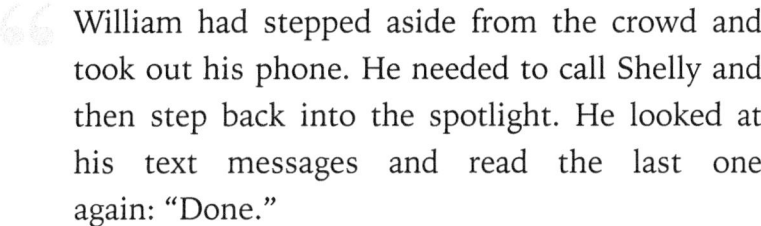 William had stepped aside from the crowd and took out his phone. He needed to call Shelly and then step back into the spotlight. He looked at his text messages and read the last one again: "Done."

William looked up and saw Tillis and Bailey standing on the balcony. He smiled and gave them a thumbs up. Then he called Shelly...the next First Lady of the United States of America.

EPILOGUE

BRAD TILLIS WALKED INTO THE DELI. BAILEY Valentine stood up and waved from a table near the back.

Brad walked back and shook Bailey's hand. Bailey was worried about Brad. "So, how are you doing?"

Brad sat down and looked around. "It's been tiring—just one testimony after another and a constant flood of reports. How are you?"

Bailey waved at the waitress. "I'm about the same. The new guys are trying to hold what's left of the government together while we evaluate who they want to prosecute or grant immunity to."

Brad looked around the room. He wanted to be sure no one was close enough to overhear them. "I don't think we will be done with this mess for years."

Bailey smiled. "It's ok Brad, I have this place swept for bugs every couple of weeks. The owner and I are old friends. No one can overhear us from back here. If you like pastrami, this is the best place in D.C. Be sure to save room for the chocolate upside down cupcake."

The waitress took their order and disappeared.

Bailey looked at Brad and cocked his head. "Well, are you staying or retiring?"

Brad shifted in his chair and looked around the room. "I want to take a couple of weeks off and spend some time with my wife. I may go see my brother and take some time to rest."

"I've got several offers, but there are still a couple of things I can't put in place."

Bailey took a folded paper from his jacket. "You mean like this?"

Brad felt his stomach tighten. He recognized the papers. "If that's the file Sheraton gave me before the explosion...yeah, that bugs me."

Bailey unfolded the paper and read the first paragraph for the hundredth time. He shook his head and leaned forward. "Brad after the explosion and you showed this to me; I couldn't quit reading it. We were so busy with the Collins files and wrapping up the Tribunal, all I could do was tell myself *not now*."

The waitress slipped up to their table and delivered two

pastramis on rye with mustard, two Kosher potato salad sides, ice tea and two upside-down chocolate cupcakes.

Bailey thanked the waitress. "Wait till you try this, you'll never want pastrami from anywhere else."

Brad took a bite and nodded. "Sold."

Folding the paper back up and putting it in his pocket, Bailey took a sip of iced tea. "I think we need to look into this. I share your concern. I know there's something we've missed. I keep waking up at night and find myself questioning how we got here. It just seems…"

"Like we were being led to a conclusion?" Brad put his sandwich down and leaned back to watch Bailey.

"Brad, we're in the business of investigating, and we see a lot that makes us question things…but I think we missed something."

"If you're interested, I pulled some strings and arranged for you to work directly for me as a special investigator. I can get you a couple of folks to work with, but we need to take this document and quietly find the truth."

Brad liked Bailey. They had worked well together, and Brad felt he could trust Bailey. Not just the kind of trust people talk about over drinks—but the trust that tells you this guy will be there when the bullets start flying. "I need a couple of weeks to get my head clear, but if my wife agrees, I'm in."

Bailey nodded "Take your time. I may take a few days off

myself. I need to try and get back to normal—whatever that is."

Once they were down to the cupcakes, Bailey smiled. "I talked to Gator yesterday. I told him we were going to have lunch. He said to tell you hello. He's agreed if we need anything that he will be glad to help us with our research… *privately of course*."

"Gator said something funny. He said he was reviewing everything that had happened. He thought he might find some new clients and connections he could use. But in the process, he kept feeling that we had missed something as well, even though he wasn't able to put his finger on it."

Brad took a bite of the cupcake and closed his eyes. "Ok, you win. This is the best place to eat. I'm taking some of these cupcakes home. Do I get an expense account for this place?"

Bailey laughed. "No, but they do deliver."

Brad sat the cupcake down and wiped his fingers on a napkin. "You know I had them pull all of the phone and text records from that day?"

"Yeah, I saw the request. I was the one that authorized it. And I think I know where you're heading. The Collins thing isn't *done*."

They finished lunch and Brad left for vacation. Bailey began to lay the groundwork for Brad's return. He pulled the paper out of his pocket and reread the first paragraph. Muttering under his breath, "You bet we're not done."

ALSO BY CLIFF BLAKE

I've created an entire universe of stories very much like the one you just finished in **Public Tribunal**. And that place is called **Alternate America.**

It's a place very much like the one you are sitting in today, but it's a slightly skewed alternative. The stories are slightly different and so are the people in it. The stories from **Alternate America** focus on one or two people who stand up and do something different from this reality.

Initially, you might think, "They can't do that! Can they?" But as you continue to read, continue to understand what drives each person to do what they do, you might find yourself moving more and more into the **Alternate America** camp. And maybe it inspires you to act a little different on this side of reality.

I encourage you to visit alternateamerica.com and learn a little more about the stories and maybe bring some of it back with you. Either way, it's going to be an adventure and it's my personal invitation for you to join and jump in.

There are so many more stories to share and characters to meet…

www.ingramcontent.com/pod-product-compliance
Lightning Source LLC
Chambersburg PA
CBHW060343260626
47160CB00006B/2190